Follow the author on social media for all upcoming projects and news.

TikTok: @RhaeAeden

Instagram: @RhaeAeden

HAMMER TIME

This is a work of fiction. Names of characters, places and incidents are products of the author's imagination or are used fictitiously. Any resemblance to actual people, living or dead, or actual events or locales is entirely coincidental.

This book in its entirety and in portions is the sole property of Rhae Aeden.

Authored by: Rhae Aeden

Cover Design: Rhae Aeden

Second Cover: @wantedroyalty

Edited by: Bridget L. Rose Books Inc.

RHAE AEDEN

To my favorite Doctor,

Edi <3

HAMMER
time

Rhae Aeden

RHAE AEDEN

To the dreamers, visionaries, and the ones who believe in the impossible.

Never stop reaching for the stars.

PROLOGUE

Selene
Twenty years ago 2003

The day is immortalized in my memories. It was one of the hottest days of the year, the kind that made the asphalt sizzle. The sun hung in the sky like a fiery ball, and the sand beneath my feet felt like hot coals. I didn't know it back then, but what seemed like another family day, a Sunday spent at the beach with my parents, would change my life forever.

Around noon, my dad put my tiny hand in his, and hand in hand, we walked towards the only bar on that beach. The closer we got, the more I noticed the crowd of men standing in every single corner. Lucky for us my dad was able to spot a barrel that was set up as a table, three stools surrounding it. Lifting me into the air, he sat me on one of them and then asked the nearest bartender for some burgers that we could bring back to the beach later.

I wasn't sure what was going on, but I even at my young age, I knew it had to be something huge. Every single man in the room – and there were only men here – had their eyes fixated on the tv screen hanging in the middle of the place. I looked at it too and saw fast cars blurring in a row, the loud noise of what I would later recognize as engines piercing my ears and making my heart race a little bit faster. That was the first Formula One race I can remember.

Everyone's eyes were fixated on the cars speeding at their limits on the screen. The air was buzzing with excitement, and even if back then I wasn't too sure of what exactly was going on, I could still feel the tension in the room.

I remember the exact words I said to my father.

"Daddy, why Is everyone so nervous?"

He smiled at me like he always did, always the patient man he was and would remain to be. It didn't matter that I was interrupting his race, he would still take the time to explain everything to me.

"Well, amor," he began, "it's a special day for these men. You see the TV? Those cars are racing in Formula One, and the man leading the race is Philipp Burton. He's from Spain, like us, and he might win his first championship today."

I remember the scene as if I was watching it instead of living it myself. I remember how I nodded, not fully understanding the details, but sensing the passion in my dad's voice.

At some point the chatter from the bar tuned down into a whisper, while I watched with fascination. The world had pretty much narrowed down to those cars racing at breakneck speed.

Time stretched on, the tension in the room growing palpable. People's faces wore expressions of anticipation, anxiety, and desperation. Fingers drummed on the bar top; I could swear that some people were holding their breaths.

Then through the speakers, a voice pierced the silence. "Philipp, it's hammer time!" the masculine voice said. "Push, push, push!"

The room vibrated with collective tension, everyone's eyes on the Spanish driver, watching how he was driving his car through the twists and turns of the circuit.

There was only one more lap to go.

Philip Burton was on the verge of making history.

And then, it happened.

The roar of everyone's screams filled the place once more, as Philip Burton's car shot across the finish line. Everyone was cheering with happiness. Even I was.

"Daddy," I said, tugging on his hand. "I like this."

CHAPTER ONE

Selene
Present 2023

I stand in front of the bathroom mirror, my reflection staring back at me when I hear my roommate's voice echoing through the thin door.

"Selene!" I hear her say. "You got an e-mail."

A rush of nervous energy courses through me. Is this it? Could this be the moment I have been waiting for? I don't respond right way, lost in my feelings. But my roommate's voice calls out my name again, and I know I can't keep her waiting much longer. Hell, I can't wait much longer.

"Give me a second!" I call back, my voice slightly shaky.

I take a deep breath, willing myself to calm down and before stepping through the door, I cast one last glance in the mirror, seeing the woman I have become. I still have trouble embracing womanhood, even as I study my appearance.

Nobody ever guesses that I'm from Spain. People always assume I'm Scottish or Irish when they see my bright copper hair and the way it cascades in waves over my shoulders. The bright color is a stark contrast against my dark eyebrows, which only help my green eyes shine more.

Sometimes, I still think about myself as a teenager, a girl.

The same girl watching her first F1 race twenty years ago.

I was a little girl back then, but the sound of roaring engines, the speed of the cars, and the thrill of the competition did a number on me. From that moment on, Formula One became a part of my life. I have watched every single race ever since, read every article, and followed every driver's career.

My fascination turned into passion, and my dream took shape – working in Formula One was the objective. I have been making countless life choices to make it there. From excelling in my studies, to pursuing internships in the motorsport world and networking tirelessly, I did it all in pursuit of my dream.

I step away from the mirror, leaving my reflection and my memories behind. Miriam sits perched on the edge of the sofa, her hazel eyes filled with curiosity and excitement. She's strikingly beautiful, with her dark skin glowing in the afternoon light. I notice instantly that her hair is newly braided, almost at her waist's length.

RHAE AEDEN

"I already checked. It's from Cavaglio," she tells me with a guilty expression, while I walk towards the couch "Here's your phone. Call your parents," she practically orders, handing me the device.

She knows that I have specific instructions to call them as soon as I get news from Cavaglio Nero. We have all been waiting for this moment for a long time. Dad thinks this is my first time applying to work for an F1 team. What he doesn't know is that I have already applied to other teams in the past. All of them rejected me, saying I am too young, too inexperienced… The typical. But this is the first time I feel like I can get the job.

Cavaglio Nero Racing has two headquarters, one in Milan and one in London. The latter is the one that I was applying for, as Milan has become more of a museum, while the business and marketing departments have transferred to the London offices.

"Okay, let's do this." My fingers are shaking while I facetime Dad. My phone beeps as I wait anxiously for an answer. The seconds feel like an eternity until finally he picks up. "Hola, Papa, do you have some time to talk?" I rush before Dad can say anything.

"Hey, honey, is everything okay?" he says and then Mum pops onto the screen with a face that says she can see my anxiety even when she's two countries away.

"Hola, cariño," Mum says with a calming voice.

HAMMER TIME

"I got an e-mail from Cavaglio. I wanted to open it with you guys."

"Oh my god! Go ahead, open it," Mum instructs while Dad smiles at her, his eyes full of love for her.

"Here we go." I take a deep breath and look at Miriam who gives me an encouraging smile. I open the e-mail and read aloud:

```
Dear Miss. Soldado,
We appreciate your interest in
Cavaglio Nero Racing and the time you've
invested in applying for our marketing
strategy team.
Unfortunately, we won't be moving
forward with your application, as we
cannot offer visa support at the moment.
We wish you all the best in your job
search and future professional
endeavours.
Sarah Parker
```

A heavy silence falls upon the room, broken only by Mum's voice.

"NO!"

My heart sinks, and sadness washes over me. It's a crushing blow, knowing that my dream job has just slipped through my fingers because of a visa. Ever since Brexit, it has become so much harder to make it into the industry. It's ridiculous.

My original plan was to move to London after I finished my degree, but then Brexit happened, and everything changed. I had to adapt, so I ended up packing my bags and moving to Monaco. Sure, I could get a lawyer to help me somehow get a working visa, but the truth is, in my early twenties I am still looking for a level entry or junior position job, and in the current job market, nobody in the UK is willing to hire someone from the outside unless you are bringing in experience and contacts. So, what would be the point?

"All the budget in the world, and they still don't offer visa sponsorships," my dad starts, but I am barely paying attention to his words. I am more focused on not crying in front of them.

"It's fine," I lie. "It will work out eventually," I add and smile, like a great actress.

It pains me to have been rejected, but I know my time to shine will come. I have worked my ass off to land in that industry and I am determined to make it there, no matter how much it costs me.

"We miss you," Dad says, noticing that I am in need of a subject change. "You should come over the weekend for a visit."

"Dad, Miriam and I are going to Silverstone this weekend." I might not have gotten a job yet, but at least I will be going to the legendary British Grand Prix over the weekend and enjoy an amazing Sunday listening to the engines roar to life. "But I promise to come home soon," I assure him.

"You girls have fun and take care of each other. I hear they are going to make an announcement. Have you seen anything on the news?" Dad asks.

I exchange looks with Miriam, "Don't look at me. You are the expert; I am just here for the sweaty hot guys and the boss ladies. Did you see the article about Di Lauris on LinkedIn? She has made the team more efficient without even coming near the budget cap…" Miriam starts ranting.

"So, I'm the expert, huh?" I chuckle. "No, I haven't seen anything besides the ongoing negotiations of the new teams trying to join. Maybe they finally signed something."

"Mmh…" Dad sighs. "Let us know if anything exciting happens. We'll let you go now, and don't be sad, love, keep working hard. You will get there eventually." His smile is so reassuring and warm that it makes me feel as if he was here, hugging me.

"Cuidense mucho!" Mum screams a Spanish *'take care.'*

"Love you!" I blow a couple of kisses to the screen and then hang up.

I feel like a deflated balloon. My body slumps onto the sofa, the cushions absorbing the weight of my disappointment while the built-up tension starts to wash over me, leaving me drained.

"Are you okay?" Miriam asks.

I force a weak smile and repeat the words that I know are far away from the truth.

"I'm fine." I can't help but hope that if I repeat it enough times, it will somehow become the truth. "Have you started packing yet?"

"There are two types of people," Miriam says, raising two fingers in the air. "The ones who pack with enough time and the ones who do it an hour before leaving the house. You know damn well I am the latter."

I laugh at her statement. I do know her damn well. After all, she is my best friend for a reason. We have spent our adult life together, since we met in a college class and hit it off instantly. When we graduated, Miriam started her own consulting company, specializing in helping black women build their new businesses and giving them financial advice. Meanwhile, I worked for a couple of sports broadcasters and some football teams, specializing in marketing. Eventually I moved to Monaco to work for its local football team, and Miriam followed.

"Got it, stay chaotic! I will make sure I bring extra clothes just in case," I joke.

CHAPTER TWO

We arrive in Silverstone just before the afternoon sun starts to cast long shadows across the track. It has been a hectic day, with Miriam packing her luggage last minute and then racing to the airport so we wouldn't miss our flight, but finally we are here. I am equal parts exhausted and excited. I feel invincible right now.

"Let's go out for a hot meal," Miriam suggests after we checked in at the hotel – which is conveniently right next to the track - and are settled in.

"Have you checked out any places yet?" I ask, while I check my luggage for a comfortable pair of jeans and a crisp white shirt. I am used to packing light for Grand Prix weekends. It's usually raining and muddy. But this time, I felt like I needed some extra outfits. One of the members of the

Cavaglio Nero team, involved in my interviewing process connected with me through LinkedIn, and I am secretly hoping that I get to meet her this weekend.

"There's a Vietnamese place. It is a twenty-minute car ride from here," Miriam informs me.

"I am driving!" I howl in excitement.

"Ugh, okay," Miriam hisses at the same time she rolls her eyes. "Alright, but I'm in charge of the music."

"Deal."

The commotion outside the hotel hits us as soon as we make it through the crystal doors. Paparazzi and fans are camped out everywhere, their cameras flashing like storms of lightning. Through the corner of my eye, I see some people taking pictures of us, and I can't help but feel uncomfortable.

"Enjoy your two seconds of fame," Miriam jokes, noticing how tense I have become.

"Just give me the directions," I grunt, and then drive away.

After dinner, we stroll through the small city, wandering around the narrow streets and taking in the sights and sounds. It's clear that most of the people are only here to watch the race over the weekend. They are all wearing colorful shirts and caps, representing their teams.

"I don't want to go back to the hotel." I yawn.

"Me neither," Miriam agrees, echoing my yawn.

My phone suddenly starts ringing, and I quickly fish it out of my bag to check it. My eyes go wide at the name displayed on the screen, and I can feel my heart racing.

"It's Sarah," I explain.

"Pick it up!" Miriam encourages me, waving her hands at me, urging me to pick up the damn phone.

I snap out of my trance and answer. "Hello?"

"Selene? Hi! This is Sarah from Cavaglio Nero," she says, her familiar voice filling my ears.

"Hi, Sarah. How are you?" Somehow, I manage to compose myself and control my voice, not showing how nervous I am.

"I'm fine. Listen, I'm in the city with some coworkers. I was wondering if you might want to join us?"

Oh. My. God.

This is it!

"Now? Sure," I rush, noticing Miriam's hazel eyes watching me, expecting more answers and information. "I came with a friend, is it okay if she joins me?"

"The more the merrier, darling. I'll text you the details"

"Sounds great, I'll see you in a bit."

"Sounds good." The line goes dead and for a second, I wonder if I just made that whole thing up in my head. I blink a couple of times, look at the phone in my hand, and try to process the conversation.

"What just happened?" Miriam asks, confused.

"She just invited us for drinks," I blurt out.

"When?"

"Now."

My phone vibrates again, a notification from Sarah lighting up the screen with the address of the pub she is at. We're only seven minutes away.

"I guess we better get going." Miriam grabs my elbow, and we start heading to the pub. "We are going out with the Cavaglio team members!" she sings, and I jump with her in a happy daze.

A few minutes later, Miriam and I step into the pub, and the buzzing of chatter and laughter immediately surrounds us. The place is full of locals and motorsport enthusiasts alike. I scan the crowded room, taking in the diverse faces, and it doesn't take too long until my eyes find the person I'm looking for. There, sitting at a table, surrounded by men, is Sarah. I walk towards her, never losing sight of her curly blonde hair.

"Good evening, Sarah," I greet her once I make it to the table.

"Selene!" She welcomes me, standing up from where she is sitting, allowing me a glimpse of her blue eyes, framed by beautiful wrinkles.

"It is so good to meet you in person." She smiles at me, then turns to Miriam. "You must be the friend," she says.

"Pleasure to meet you, even if you destroyed my friend's heart when you rejected her. Your loss, not hers." My face goes pale at Miriam's harsh words. "The name is Miriam." And in Miriam fashion, she dares to wink at Sarah.

"Miriam," I hiss at her.

"I like this one, she's honest," Sarah says with a smile on her face. "I fought the team on this one. They hired someone with less experience. Another man... Nothing against them, but it would be nice to have more women for a change. Jessica here is our current intern." She nods with her head towards the other woman at the table. "She is assisting me with some tasks, but besides her there are not many of us around." I look at Jessica. Her hair is in a tight ponytail, and her eyes are a deep shade of brown. She seems younger than me, which makes me wonder, how did she get this job?

"It's fine. Miriam is just being dramatic. How was your day?" I ask, trying to change the subject because being reminded of my rejection still stings.

"Hectic, we are struggling," Sarah says before taking a sip of her bubbly drink while Miriam orders something for us.

"How come?" I ask, intrigued.

RHAE AEDEN

"We are facing a possible revenue loss," the blonde woman answers without much interest, as if she was discussing the weather rather than millions of dollars. "We are launching new products and the other team's strategy is fucking us over." The frustration in her voice is palpable. She takes her time and, over the loud noises of the pub, explains the situation further and the wheels start spinning in my brain.

"I have to ask this," Miriam says out of nowhere once she makes it back with our drinks, holding something red I assume is a Negroni. "Do you work with Claudia Di Lauris? Can I meet her?" I can't help but laugh at her brutal forwardness.

Miriam and Sarah's laughter grabs the attention of one of the men sitting at the table with us. He is wearing the team's T-shirt, so I can only assume that he works for them too. His hazel eyes sparkle with curiosity, and a thin-lipped smile graces his face.

"That's what I call the Di Lauris effect!" he mocks with a teasing tone, causing laughter to erupt around us. I guess she's a big deal in the company too.

"We have touched base here and there," Sarah starts. "I had a meeting with her today, but she is generally busy," she adds, going back to our first topic.

"Someone told me they are offering a business course about her in one of those fancy universities," the guy with the hazel eyes says.

"Bummer! I was hoping to meet her and wow her with my amazing personality and great body," Miriam jokes, winking at nobody in particular. Everyone at the table bursts into laughter, and I almost choke on my drink. My face has probably turned as red as the Negroni in my glass.

"Maybe we can work on that. My name is Michael, by the way," he finally introduces himself. The bells in my brain start ringing. I know I have seen this person before, I just can't quite place him.

"Selene," I answer, extending my hand towards him. "I guess it's never too late for introductions."

"Sorry, I had to make sure my team was on the winning side," he explains, pointing with his head towards the soccer match on the TV.

"Manchester City fan?" I assume, watching the score board, the team with the blue shirts leading.

"That's right!"

There is a moment of weird silence. Miriam seems to have hit it off with Sarah, so I continue my conversation with Michael. "Do you work for the team or are you here as a plus one?"

"I am what they call a freelancer. Anyway, I should go. I have an early start tomorrow," he announces to the group, and I notice some people are giving him a knowing look. They know something we don't.

"I think we will go soon too," I tell him. "Hopefully we'll see each other again."

"Here is my number." He hands me a business card, and I grab it as if it were a treasure. "Call me if you are around the track. Maybe we can have lunch." *Is he asking me out?*

"Sure. Have a good night, Michael."

"He's hot," Miriam whispers, leaning on my shoulder.

"Sure, but something feels off," I try to explain. "I'm getting tired. Do you want to go now or....?"

"I am good to go."

"Perfect."

We take our time saying goodbye to everyone at the table, even with the ones who didn't formally introduce themselves. I make a point of taking extra time with Sarah, leaving her for last so I can get some last words with the woman who might hold the key to my future.

"Let's have coffee soon," I suggest. "Bring the numbers for your problem, if you want; I think I have an idea on how we might solve it."

Her eyes shine bright, and I feel like maybe, just maybe, I am a step closer to my dream.

"I will text you tomorrow," Sarah answers, giving me a smile.

CHAPTER THREE

I wake up, feeling restless and disoriented, beads of sweat clinging to my body. It's that damn recurring nightmare, the one that has been keeping me up at night for a while now. I toss and turn in bed, searching for a dry, cool spot on the sheets.

My breath quickens, and I can feel the nausea in my gut. I know what's about to come. With urgency, I cast the sheets aside and bolt towards the bathroom. The pain is blinding as I kneel in front of the toilet. This isn't new. It's happened before, countless times. I am used to it by now. Throw up, breathe, stand up, brush my teeth, drink water, and move on.

The room is still cloaked in darkness when I leave the bathroom. My nightstand clock reads four in the morning. I could stay in bed, but I know the memories will haunt me if I do, so I toss on some workout clothes and head to the gym downstairs.

My body goes tense again as soon as I make my way through the house only to encounter my wall of trophies, glittering reminders of my career, the person I once was, young and naïve, versus the person I have become. I keep walking, avoiding looking at the trophies. But the flashbacks are already filling my mind.

The gym is where I find my solace and escape from the ghosts of the past. I begin to warm up, doing some breathing exercises, trying to channel that thing they call 'positivity.' I have never believed in all that meditation nonsense, but Michael insists on me doing it, and I know he wants what is best for me. I hear my thoughts, *thirty-seven is still young, I still have some good years ahead of me*, and nothing but myself can stop me from achieving my goals.

Yet, when I open my eyes and meet my own gaze in the mirror, doubts creep in.

"You are so full of bullshit," I tell my reflection, which is the one of a disheveled eccentric hosting an unruly mess of disheveled black hair with some white strands already in it. "No wonder the press made me their villain. I look like one," I joke, bitterly.

Flashes of the press headlines from the past flood my mind, painful reminders of the vilification I have endured throughout my career. I have never been the fan's favorite, never had the charm of the golden boy who could do no wrong. Things got so bad, at one point it was me against my team instead of me against the other nineteen drivers racing in the competition. They craved a poster child, but they couldn't get rid of me so easily. I was too good for that. So, they had to push me, sabotage me, and force my hand until I left.

I walked away from F1 years ago and ventured into other racing categories, behind the wheel of some of the fastest cars the world has ever seen. My talent was never the problem. My personality, perhaps. In my years away from Formula One, I conquered Dakar, Le Mans and Indianapolis. I have driven them all, and yes, I have won them too.

Many have argued that I am done, that I am too old to race, but I disagree. I might not be in my twenties anymore, but I still have it in me. That kind of raw talent doesn't go away that easily. I have taken the last season for myself, to be away from the racing tracks, only so I could focus on my mind and health. But now? Now I am ready. Ready to win. Ready to fight.

"Guess I was right to show up early," Michael's voice penetrates the gym, startling me. "Nervous about the weekend?" The question hits harder than it should. Nervousness courses through me, it's why I woke up in the middle of the night after all.

I roll my eyes and immediately snap, "You could have come later if all you are going to do is ask stupid questions."

The words spill out, and I instantly regret them. "I didn't mean it like that."

Michael deserves none of my anger, he is just an easy target. We have been working together for almost a decade now. He's been by my side, never once judging me the way others do. He deserves better than a snarky response just because I am pissed, and my anxiety is all over the place.

"I know you; I know when to take certain comments seriously," he assures me. "Want to talk about it?"

I shake my head. "I'd much rather box it off."

Michael smiles at me, as if he was just waiting for me to say those words. Quickly, he retrieves the boxing gear from its shelf, and we set everything up as quickly as possible.

"Take it slow," he warns before we start, knowing that I won't. He lifts his arms, showing me where to direct my punches. I bounce on the mat, rolling my shoulders and head. I approach before jabbing my right hand forward while guarding one side of my face.

"Good job. Now cross," he instructs, and I throw the second punch, landing it right in the center of his glove.

We continue like that for forty-five minutes, during which Michael offers clear instructions of foot and arm placement. By the time we're finished, my mood has improved significantly.

"You are getting slow with those combos," I tease, enjoying the kick of the endorphins hitting my bloodstream.

"You could only dream of beating me," he jokes. "Let's train your neck, then we can call it a day."

We spend what feels like an eternity working out, but it's only half an hour more, during which we focus on strengthening the muscles in my neck with weights attached to the band around my head. People don't fully realize the importance of having a strong neck in the sport. Strike that. People don't know about the importance of having a strong physique in this world. Many do not consider it a sport simply because we sit and drive in circles, but they have no idea how physical it is. Nobody sees the struggles drivers go through. The world thinks that we just go to the track to put on a show, but it is so much more than that.

Michael's voice pulls me out of my thoughts. "What time do you have to go to the track?"

I check my wristwatch. "I will be there around ten."

"See you in a couple of hours," Michael says as he heads for the door. "Philip, don't think too much about it, it will be fine and if it's not, we will deal with it."

CHAPTER FOUR

I open my eyes, the Saturday morning light filtering through the curtains. My excitement bubbles over, and I can't wait for qualifying to start. Miriam and I are so eager to enjoy the weekend, we get to the track three hours before the session starts.

My phone buzzes, and I feel my heart racing when I see the name on the screen. In a reflex I grab Miriam's arm, catching her attention while I start typing with my free hand.

Sarah: Morning. Are you at the track already?

Me: Yes, I'm around

Sarah: Join me! I will share my location.

Sarah: Let me know when you are here. I'll pick you up.

Me: Will do!

Miriam glances at me, curiosity in her eyes. "What did she say? Do I have to get jealous of another woman?" she teases.

"You also get jealous of men too," I chuckle. "She wants to meet me. Do you want to tag along?"

Miriam arches her dark brows dramatically "Is that even a question? Stay here and miss the chance to possibly meet Di Lauris who will become my future wife? You must be joking."

Right in that moment, a message with Sarah's real time location pops up on my screen. Excited, we navigate the sea of fans who make every step of the way a challenge, but luckily the hospitality suite isn't too far away. It only takes us about five minutes to get there. I type on my phone quickly, letting Sarah know that we are waiting for her.

"How do I look?" I ask Miriam.

She looks at me, scanning my body from head to toe, "You are slaying the game as usual! She is giving professional power woman, ready to take over the biggest team in the F1 business. She is giving marketing queen at 12PM and take over the world at 17PM!"

I am about to answer when Sarah emerges from the hospitality area, wearing Cavaglio Nero's signature yellow and black colors, in a jacket that is probably two sizes too big for her.

"Hello, girls. Sorry for the rush, I don't have much time today," she greets us.

RHAE AEDEN

"I hope it's okay that I brought Miriam with me, I didn't want to leave her alone."

Sarah smiles warmly. "Not a problem. Follow me." We walk through the entrance, arriving at a door marked 'hospitality,' where two security guards stand watch. "They are with me. Please make sure they get upgraded guest passes," she tells the guards.

My jaw almost drops to the floor. "Did we just get upgraded to VIP?" I whisper to Miriam, trying to keep my composure.

"I think so?" she answers with a delighted smile.

We walk two steps behind Sarah passing by a series of corridors, all of them adorned with the Cavaglio colors. Eventually, we make it to a small room where Sarah addresses Miriam. "You can stay here. Someone will come shortly with a pass for you."

"I'll see you later," I tell her, but she is already making herself comfortable on one of the couches.

Sarah and I continue our walk, until we make it to what I assume is her office, where she gestures for me to take a seat in front of her.

"Let me fill you in," she starts. "We're launching a new clothing collection next week. In short, we want to sell more than just merch. We announced the release date for the collection last week, and yesterday, the assholes from Volpella announced that they are having a huge sale on their apparel.

The prices are extremely competitive, and this sale is going on until our launch date."

"Correct me if I am wrong, but I follow the team on social media, and you just announced that something would be coming, not what, right?" She nods. "You need to find your mole. Someone told them that you were launching a fashion line."

Her eyes widen. She probably hadn't considered the possibility that someone from the inside was screwing them over.

"Do you have the prices of the items for their sale and the expected margins for your products?"

Sarah searches through the disarray on her desk, eventually locating the right spreadsheets with the information I need to see if my plan can work.

"These are the prices." She points to the first sheet, and I scan it carefully, taking my time. "And here are the current prices of items that Volpella has on their website." She hands me another excel sheet, red numbers and percentages all over the place.

"They really went over the top," I mutter to myself. "You have to buy them out."

"What do you mean?" Sarah asks, perplexed.

"You *must* buy them out of the market," I repeat. "If you buy all the stock progressively, they should run out of it by the time of the launch."

"That is going to cost us a lot of money," she points out.

"Correct, but according to these numbers, you would still be making around thirty-seven percent profit, and once the sale is over and the collection is out, you can return the items."

"How did I not think about this?" She sighs.

"It helps to have an outsider's perspective," I say with the satisfaction of a job well done.

"I am so mad they didn't hire you."

"I promise to keep applying."

"I'll call them and show them your idea. There is no way they won't want you after this." Her words excite me, but I try to wave them off. I don't want to feel disappointed again. "I have to start making calls and fuck Volpella up, but I will stay in touch with you."

"I just hope it works out." I smile, getting up from my chair. I can feel my knees shaking from the excitement of sitting there like a big girl with big ideas, but I manage to stay steady. "I will see you around."

I leave the office, closing the door behind me, and then practically sprint to the nearest bathroom. I need a moment for myself to process everything that just happened.

"Oh. My. God." I blurt out when I make it there. "I did it, I am here!" I cheer in a sharp voice with the brightest of smiles displayed on my face.

But that doesn't last too long.

HAMMER TIME

Someone flushes the toilet and right after a guy emerges from one of the stalls, opening the door aggressively. The smile washes off my face, and instead of being happy, I'm embarrassed.

I can barely see the guy's face, but his presence alone is intimidating. He is wearing a full black outfit with a fitted T-shirt that shows off his lean muscles. On his head rests a hat with the yellow racing horse from Cavaglio and big dark shades cover most of his face.

"What are you doing in the men's bathroom?" The man's deep voice rattles me. I almost feel scared, but there's a strange pull I can't quite place.

"You are in the women's bathroom!" *Asshole*. I keep the last part to myself, giving him the courtesy he obviously lacks.

He takes a step forward, standing almost face to face with me and making me feel so small. And if that wasn't enough, he has the audacity to look down on me, like I'm a mere insect in his way.

"Move." His command is so strong that I stumble out of his way. "Check again, Sparks."

"Who do you think you are, talking to me like that?"

"I heard what you said. You know who I am. Now get the fuck out of here or I will call security." He turns around, facing me again. I try to see his eyes, but his shades are so dark, it's impossible.

RHAE AEDEN

Attempting to create some sort of space between us, I cross my arms over my chest.

"Call them. Then we can tell them that there is a man in the women's bathroom terrorizing me." I give him a distasteful look.

"I'm not the stalker here," he retorts, and I'm left wondering who this guy thinks he is. Probably one of those celebrities teams bring for the Grand Prix.

"I don't know who you think you are, but I recommend you get to planet Earth from whatever ego trip you are on… Or better yet maybe fly right into the sun and get a good burn."

"Say whatever you want." He shrugs. "You are just one of them. Thirsting behind us." He strolls past me, on his way outside, his bare hand brushing mine, sending an electric shock up my spine.

"¡Que te den, gilipollas!" *Fuck you!* I scream as soon as I hear the click of the door behind him. When I finally make it outside of the toilet, I check again which bathroom I was in.

Fuck.

He was right.

On my way back to the lounge, I spot Michael's brown hair and impressive figure, talking to one of the guards posted at the door.

"Look who's here. I didn't know you had VIP passes."

"Sarah hooked us up," I fill him in.

"That makes sense." He nods. "I just saw her. Did you have something to do with how happy she looked?"

"Just a bit of teamwork," I reply, smiling.

"Is it called teamwork when you are not part of the team?" Regret flashes in his eyes as soon as the words escape his lips "That came out wrong. I mean, I am technically not part of the team myself."

"Then what are you doing here?"

"Looking for my client, who is part of the team."

"Sounds mysterious." I raise an eyebrow intrigued, craving more information than he is probably willing to give.

"I have an NDA signed… can't say much."

I nod, but now I'm even more curious than before.

"I was disappointed when you didn't call," he flirts, trying to change the topic.

"Careful, Michael." I twitch my nose at him, as if sniffing the air surrounding him. "I can smell the desperation." Both of us burst into laughter.

"I deserve that one… Anyway, I have to run. Hopefully I will see you around."

The first thing I see when I make it to the hospitality is Miriam holding a glass of white wine, enjoying the direct view of the track. "Don't get too comfortable or we'll end up broke getting VIP passes every weekend."

"Or you just get a job here, and we can get them for free," she teases. "How was it?"

"I think we solved the problem, but I can't tell you much," I reply, taking a seat next to her on the couch.

"Did they make you sign a fancy NDA?"

"No, but it's sensitive information, so I'd rather not talk about it."

"Next topic," Miriam says. "You are going to have an aneurism when you find out who's here."

"Just tell me who it is. You are dying to say it."

"Philip Burton!" My jaw drops.

Is my heart still beating?

Am I even breathing?

"How do you know? What is he doing here?"

"I said you would get an aneurism," she says, amused. "They just showed him on the TV walking around the garage."

"He hasn't come to a Formula One race since he retired. There has to be a reason why he came today. Maybe he is coaching someone…" I start ranting, my thoughts coming out faster than I can process them.

Philip is the reason why I am here today. I'm not his biggest fan, not anymore. But I admire his achievements. He has that kind of pure, raw talent that only shows up once in a generation.

"Calm down. They said he will give an interview later, so sit down, relax, and enjoy the show."

She's right. She always is. I sit down in the lounge, get myself a drink and start enjoying the weekend.

Life is good.

CHPATER FIVE

Philip

The paddock buzzes with activity as the crews scurry around, making last minute preparation for the qualifying session. Being in the garage sends my heart racing. I have looked everywhere, seen every face, but there is something I am avoiding having direct eye contact with.

The beast. The car.

Starring at it seems like tempting fate. Sometimes, I am convinced that a dark cloud hangs over my head, and I am not willing to risk it today of all days. My time in Silverstone has been marked by so many challenges. I've made history here over the years, winning races that seemed impossible, and I want to keep making it.

I allow myself to fantasize about the endless nights strategizing with the team, working on the car to get that extra second, the overtakes on the track, and the podium celebrations. For a brief moment, I forget the reasons why I left.

"There you are. I have been searching for you. The interview starts in ten minutes." Michael's voice drags me back to the present.

"The set is twenty steps away. I think I will make it in time." I wave him off. "Is Mancini meeting us there?" I ask.

"He's already there with the PR team."

Shit, that's a problem.

"Well, what are you doing standing here? Let's get going," I urge, hiding my anxiety. I've become quite skilled at concealing my emotions, but Michael has been working with me for long enough to know there's more beneath the exterior.

We walk in silence side by side to the interview spot. I can't help but think about the driver pair-up at Cavaglio this year, and how they have been burning out. Recently, they have been causing more problems and drama instead of wins, and for a team of Cavaglio's caliber that's unacceptable.

Things have only gotten worse since the team refused to name one of them as the number one driver. The result is that both are competing with each other on track instead of going against the other drivers. The younger driver has even disrespected direct team orders, and at this point he's just making a fool of himself. The lad has potential, but he needs to learn his place.

Any pilot would kill for a seat on the team. Everyone is a Cavaglio fan, even the guys at Volpella are a Cavaglio fan. It's everyone's dream to be a part of the team's legacy. Little boys in Karting? Their end goal is having a seat in this team, drive the black car, hear it roar and drive the beast to its full potential. But only the best can achieve that, and only the best can win championships in this team, and the drivers are not living up to the expectations. They are not up to the standard that this team needs, and nobody really wants to admit the big fuck up they made by hiring them without having a real number one.

Changes are needed, and I am here to give them.

Finally, we make it to the improvised set where everyone is already waiting for us.

"Ciao ragazzi," I say in Italian, knowing that it's a must to speak the language when you are part of this team.

"Ti stavamo aspettando." *We were waiting for you.* Mancini greets me in Italian. He's a man in his early fifties who looks no older than forty, emitting youthful energy. He's slim, and his strong features offer a glimpse of the person he probably was when he was younger.

I'm not exactly a fan of his. There's something off about the man, but I have never been capable of figuring out what it is. However, he hasn't done too bad as a team principal since he joined the team, at least if we don't consider this year's driver pairing. I do respect his work, after all he has won some championships with the team since I departed, and to be fair, it's hard to be the boss of a couple of twenty-year-olds with egos bigger than the moon. Try telling them to follow team orders when they are driving a car at high speed with adrenaline hitting their bloodstream... yeah that doesn't always work right.

"This is Sarah. She's part of the marketing team," Mancini introduces a petite woman with curly blonde hair who greets me with a handshake. "This is Jessica," he continues. "She's going to be working with you during this interview." A petite girl next to Sarah throws me a look.

Jessica looks like she just finished college. Her cheeks are red, betraying how nervous she is. Her hair is in a ponytail, so tight that I wonder how she doesn't have a migraine right now. For some reason, she reminds me of the girl with the red hair in the bathroom.

Wait, why the fuck am I thinking about that stalker?

One lesson I have learned the hard way is to never date fans, especially not the ones who pull crazy stunts like that. Those are the worst, and before you know it, you find yourself having to put a restraining order on them because one day, they decided to violate your privacy and start sharing your entire life.

"Pleasure," Jessica chimes in, her tone suggestive, something that doesn't go unnoticed by the crew. "I'm looking forward to working with you." She grins.

"Likewise. What is the approach today?" I keep my voice neutral, hoping she'll understand I am not interested in her. Not like that.

"Sarah and Jessica are working on trying to give you a better angle, but for today, we will just make the announcement together."

Sarah takes a step into the circle and looks at her phone where she probably has notes for the interview written down.

"The idea is to say that we are facing a new season with challenges and changes. But we remain a team, and we are happy about the news. The classic 'teamwork makes the dream work,' and we're working hard on the new car. You know how it goes."

"Any off-limit topics?" I ask, mentally preparing a list.

"Avoid discussing the other drivers." It surprises me that she only has one thing on her list of restrictions. She might not know who she is working with.

"Works for me."

"Then everyone is happy," Mancini says with a satisfied smile.

"Not me," Sarah protests, waving her hand at him.

"Is it about that girl again?" Mancini replies. "We have been over this before. The visa…"

"I don't care about her visa. Look at these numbers." Sarah hands him some spreadsheets with numbers all over the place. "She solved our headache. Do you know what that means? More money is coming in that you can use for your car. Reconsider it because another team will end up hiring her if we don't, and that will be a big loss."

Mancini retrieves his glasses, scans the numbers, and finally concedes. "She did a good job here… let's talk about this later. The interviewer is here" he says, handing the papers back.

A petite woman with short blonde hair approaches us, followed by a camera crew. Her face seems familiar. I'm pretty sure I've seen her before, I can't remember her name.

"Hi, everyone. Are we ready to get started?" Mancini gives her a nod. "Our colleagues at the studio will do a bit of an introduction to the interview. That way we can directly start with the questions here."

A groan escapes me. I hate the press.

"Are we already rolling?" she asks the cameraman in front of us, who gives her a thumbs up. "Thanks for allowing us to do this. We are lucky to interview a legend like Philip Burton and Cesare Mancini with us today. Philip, you have many seasons under your belt. What are your thoughts about the current situation of the team?"

Bold question.

"They're working as hard as they can," I lie, just the way I was instructed to.

"What do you think about the driver pair-up this year?"

I inhale, then exhale, and try to bite my tongue.

But it doesn't work.

"They need to learn the consequences of messing up on the track. What they have been doing this season is unacceptable, especially if we consider that they have one of the best cars out there."

Jessica looks terrified at my words.

"There are only twenty spots," I continue. "Right now, they're blocking the path for other drivers. If they can't keep up, then they should step aside and make room for more talented drivers." Mancini coughs as a warning, and I try to backtrack, hoping to salvage this thing. "But, as a former driver, I understand that the season is long, and there's still time for improvement. I know both of them have talent and will achieve great things."

"Encouraging words for the current drivers. Mancini, how do you feel about the next year considering the changing regulations?" I have never been so thankful for the shift of attention.

"We are optimistic and confident about delivering a stronger car. There are also internal changes underway to ensure that we win next year. In the meantime, we are staying focused on the present while keeping an eye on the future." He looks at me from the corner of his eyes.

"Both of your drivers' contracts are up by the end of the season. We still haven't heard about possible renewals. Are you considering a different line-up?" The question lands at the perfect time, and I can see the gates of hell swinging open.

"We are content with our current pairing. Nevertheless, we believe there's more to achieve than we have in the past years, which is why we've invited Philip here," Mancini answers.

"Are you returning as a coach?" the interviewer asks.

"No, I am coming back as a driver. And I will win the championship next year," I declare, looking right at the camera.

Everyone has a target on their back next year.

The plan is on.

CHAPTER SIX

Selene

Grand Prix weekends are always crazy. It's part of the media circus. There are things you are already expecting when you are a fan. But my Grand Prix weekend has already had many unexpected twists. I didn't see Philip's comeback announcement coming. And what hit me harder was when I realized that he was the stranger from the bathroom.

It hit me when he removed his shades at the beginning of the interview, showing the world his famous dark-blue eyes. I can be honest and admit that, even though he's an egocentric asshole, he looks good.

"I need a drink," I declare, heading towards the catering table.

Shit. Holymotherfuckingshit.

HAMMER TIME

I pour myself another glass of bubbly champagne, sipping it down all at once, hoping it will soothe my nerves. I fill it to the top once again and when I turn around to make it back to the couch, I collide with what feels like I wall, spilling my drink all over my white blouse.

"Damn it!" I curse.

"Seems like you could use some rearview mirrors to see what's behind you, Sparks." The nickname infuriates me, and heat radiates off my body from anger.

His blue eyes collide with mine when I look up at him.

"Keep your distance, and I won't need mirrors. Besides, there is a thing called personal space, and you are invading mine. Who is the stalker now?" I retort.

"I thought I would give you a taste of your own medicine after the stunt you pulled before." he shoots back.

"You two know each other?" Miriam intervenes.

"What is going on?" Michael chips in at the same time.

"Your stalker tendencies are starting to bore me." Philip grunts, and then I lose it. My blood boils, and my body begs to lash out and scream at him. But I would never do such a thing.

"You. Are. Such. A. Diva," I mutter through gritted teeth, trying to maintain my composure and not make a scene. "Philip Burton, remove that stick from your ass and stop acting like the world still revolves around you, because, newsflash, it hasn't for years." I don't recognize myself when the words fall from my lips. That burst of courage to call out a legend of the sport I respect seems so out of place. But, at the same time, a part of me is clapping and cheering, proud of the fact that I decided to stand up to this asshole of a man.

I don't care if he's a legend; his attitude is precisely why nobody wants to deal with him. Nobody except Cavaglio... The team I dream of.

I am never going to get that job anymore, am I?

Michael whistles. "I have been trying to get that through his thick skull for years, but I have a feeling this time it will finally sticks."

"You are his coach, aren't you?" Miriam realizes.

"You also know her? Is she one of those who goes through the whole team?" Philip comments, without even bothering to look at me.

"Yes," I reply firmly. "But only to become your boss."

"Considering you are in this room without a badge, I'd say that you still have a long way to go." Philip sneers. I see red at his words, and I feel like I won't be able to continue with my life if I don't murder him.

"About that—" someone starts, but I don't care.

"Not everyone has everything handed to them on a silver platter. Some of us have had to work hard every step of the way, from the bottom to where we are now. So just sit down and enjoy the show because eventually, I'll be coming for your head, Philip." It's a promise, and it's going on my motivational list to achieve my dreams.

"One could argue that I am the show, judging by how much you know about me." He smirks.

"You used to be," I admit, not bothering to hide it, though I wish I had never admired this man. "But I think I have just lost the little respect I had left for you."

For a moment, there's a glint of hurt in his ocean blue eyes, surprising both of us. Me, for being able to hurt him, and him, for showing emotion. But that fleeting vulnerability is quickly replaced by anger.

"Bring it on, Sparks. Make it before the next season starts."

"Challenge accepted."

"I'll see you around then… What's your name?"

"You will see it when you put your signature on a contract next to mine, Philip," I reply with a devilish smile. "Enjoy the weekend. I know I will."

"Let's go to the garage, Michael. Obviously, the lounge is not what it used to be anymore," Philip says, walking away as if nothing ever happened.

I clench my fists, determination burning inside of me.

I will never bow to him.

CHAPTER SEVEN

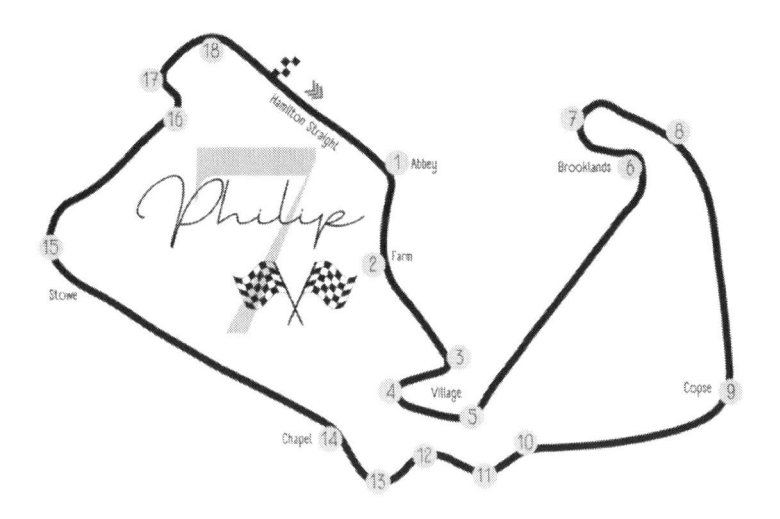

"What was that back there!?" Michael demands, exasperated. "And why did you treat Selene like that?"

I almost stop dead in my tracks when I hear her name. Selene. Like the goddess of the moon. Fitting her looks, but her personality matches more Ares's. I can't deny that I'm intrigued by her. Not many dare to go on a round of verbal sparring with me.

"Are you even listening?" Michael continues.

"Huh? Sorry, I wasn't paying attention," I admit.

"No shit, Sherlock," he says. "What was that? She's the girl Sarah wants to hire."

"What?" I might have underestimated the little spark.

"You are an arrogant dick," Michael points out, a hint of frustration laced in his voice. "You had to mess up the interview and then antagonize the nice girl."

I raise my eyebrow at his newfound concern for someone who I have just found out about.

"How do you even know her?"

"Sarah invited her to the pub last night," he explains.

"Seems like you care a lot given that you only met her twelve hours ago."

"It's not about the girl," Michael insists. "You just announced you'll be returning next season to the sport. You can't be a prick like you always are. Not to the press, the team, the fans, or anyone. Sometimes I don't understand you, mate. If you'd just let people see the real you, then you'd be—"

"Let me stop you right there," I interrupt him, my tone firm. "Our relationship might be more than professional. You are a friend. You know my reasons. Being an asshole to her is a kindness, and you know it. Second, and most importantly," I continue, my voice steady, "all I want to do is race. That's it. That's my life, and that's the reason why I'm back. I don't care about the public, and I don't care about the media. All I care about is that car and how fast it runs." I take a deep breath, trying to keep my emotions in check. "Do you understand that?

Michael nods.

"Good."

RHAE AEDEN

We walk in silence the rest of the way until we make it to the garage, where everyone is getting ready for Quali. The room pulses with energy. One of the drivers is still warming up, jumping rope before getting in his car. I spot Mancini in one corner, and he signals for us to come over.

"Boys, we have Philip here," he announces. "You already know the news, so let's give him a warm welcome to melt his icy heart. Hopefully, he'll bring us a bit of luck today."

People start clapping in the garage, but I notice one of the drivers shooting me a glare filled with anger. João, that's his name. He's the younger one of the teammates, racing for Cavaglio for the first time. He has the most to lose next season, and I can tell he's not thrilled with my return, as his contract is coming to an end next season, and chances are I will be the one to take his seat if he doesn't end over Munguia in the standings.

Mancini gestures for me to get into the back of the garage where the TVs are and the IT guys work. I always found myself at peace here. I sit at one of those large tables in the corner from where I can see everything.

João gets ready to climb into the car, pulling his suit up and removing his headphones before putting on his helmet. He's about to get into the car when he looks in my direction, throwing me a look loaded with all types of emotions and challenges. The mechanics start dancing around the car, tightening his security belts and making sure that everything is in place. João doesn't hesitate. As soon as the tire warmers are off and the mechanics are done, he drives out of the garage.

The time for Q1 is already running, he has eighteen minutes to position himself amongst the fifteen best or be disqualified in the first round. Through my headphones, I hear his engineer giving him instructions.

"Don't wear the tires out too soon, this is just Q1" and "Remember to warm them up properly."

On the screen, I can see the car turning into the corners, doing a bit of a warmup while other drivers are setting their times. Munguia, the Mexican driving for Cavaglio, has just finished his lap and has positioned himself fourth.

Not bad, but also not good.

João, on the other hand, is about to cross the start line and start his fast lap.

3…2…1… The clock starts ticking.

Eighteen corners to go.

He crosses the Abbey in a breath. Corners one and two pass almost simultaneously, the zigzag follows, and with that, the time for the first sector is almost set. Then follows the straight, up until the sixth corner. He's setting good times, and, if he keeps this up, he could set the fastest lap of Q1. The DRS zone gives him some extra speed too.

Two more kilometers to go.

RHAE AEDEN

The second sector of the track is nearly over after he passes Copse in turn nine, then drives down the straight until he enters the DRS zone in the tenth corner where Maggots starts, followed by Becketts, then Chapel. He paints the sector purple and then his car becomes a blur as he drives through the third sector, only slowing down when he makes it to Vale so he can get better traction at the exit in the last turn.

His time is set.

Time's up, and he's in first place.

For now.

Munguia is also attempting a second lap. He's already in the second sector and achieving better times, but he loses control of the car two turns before the speed trap. He manages to recover the car and avoids what could have been a nasty accident. The garage falls silent, and the tension becomes palpable. Some members of the team seem to be holding their breath as they watch their driver's lap. Nevertheless, Munguia finishes it and makes it to the third position.

"Ask them to come back to the garage; this is a good lap," Mancini instructs through the radio. Both drivers follow the instructions, and João makes it back first.

"The medium tires are the better choice. The degradation with these is bad. We won't be able to keep up like that," Munguia suggests to his strategists, sparking a discussion among them.

"Any recommendations?" a strategist asks me.

"Be better at your job, then you won't need to ask for recommendations," I huff without even looking at him. Michael's expression is far from happy, and I know that I need to do better. "Ask him to warm them up properly. The tires have memory, they are degrading too quickly, which means he's losing grip in the first laps already."

"We have been trying to tell him that… but he's not listening."

"Your problem."

The second part of qualifying passes quickly. Another five drivers are eliminated, and João is in second place, with Munguia in third.

Now, the real game is on.

"Time to prove yourself," I mutter quietly, secretly hoping that João will outperform the driver sitting in first place. I know he can do it if he stays level-headed.

He leaves the garage before the clock starts running and positions the car right at the exit of the pit lane. Munguia follows him with a couple of other drivers close on his tail.

Two minutes to go.

I press one of the buttons on the table, giving me direct access to Mancini.

"Can I talk to João?" I ask, earning a confused look from him. I don't judge him, he probably thinks I'm crazy, but he still gives me a thumbs up.

"João, you're doing just fine. The tires are working well. Forget about the rest. You can score pole position," I assure him.

"Thanks," he replies through his radio.

Mancini nods approvingly, and Michael claps me on the back, impressed that I even had it in me to try and be nice for once. "You do have a decent bone in you after all."

"Don't be naïve. This is for my benefit because he's the better driver."

"Ah, I should have known." Michael tone is sarcastic.

The clock ticks down, and João drives out of the pit lane the second the red light turns green. He starts his warmup lap before going for his fast one. But he's forced to abort it when he loses control in a corner.

Meanwhile, his competition sets a fast lap, painting all the sectors purple.

João doesn't give up easily and tries again, zipping through the first sector, right into the second straight. But there's a slower car in João's way, one on its slow lap and it's obvious that João doesn't see the car right until the last turn. He tries to avoid a collision, but instead, spins his own car.

The gravel does little to slow him down, and he slides further before crashing into the safety wall. I can feel the impact of the carsh in my bones. I can feel it almost as if I was the one in the car.

"João, are you okay?" his race engineer asks anxiously, but there's no response.

Please, let him be okay.

"Try to give us a thumbs up if you are listening."

Nothing happens.

Seconds feel like minutes as we all wait for a sign, anything that shows that he's okay. Then, finally, heavy breathing noises come through the radio, and on the screen, I can see João slightly raising his thumb.

He's okay.

I'm not sure that I am.

CHAPTER EIGHT

Selene

Watching a driver crash is not your average Saturday afternoon entertainment. Formula One is like a Russian roulette. With every lap that passes, the drivers risk their lives, and you never know which will be the lap that could kill them. The fans don't know any of the drivers personally. We just get glimpses of what they allow us to see. Nonetheless, we're still invested in their lives, especially their well-being. So, here we are, glued to the TV screen, hoping for a reassuring message to pop up.

It feels like an eternity until something happens.

And then, there it is. Heavy breathing and a thumbs up. There is a collective sigh of relief in the hospitality room.

"That was chilling," Miriam says, and a shiver runs down my spine. "It didn't look that bad, we have seen worse, but wow, that was scary."

"Do you think he will race tomorrow?" I ask, still not taking my eyes off the screen, watching the paramedics carry him to the ambulance.

"They do have a reserve driver for cases like this, but I wonder what happens now that Philip is back on the chessboard," Miriam says. Philip rejoining the grid is going to destabilize so many things, but it's also going to be worth every single penny invested.

"May your delulu come trululu." I sigh. It will be nice once Philip starts racing again next year, but he is not getting in the car tomorrow, no matter how good he is. "They will tell us later if João or someone else is driving."

"Well then, I guess that's it for today. Should we go for a drive or something?" Miriam asks.

"We can do that and grab a bite," I say, standing up from the couch. "I'll just go to the bathroom really quickly."

"I'll wait here," Miriam says, already distracted by her phone.

On the way to the bathroom, my mind keeps wandering back to Philip. His face replays in my head when I find myself double checking for the women's bathroom sign. A smile appears on my lips.

Not everyone gets to say they had an epic encounter with an F1 driver in a public bathroom.

A strange noise comes out of one of the stalls. "Are you okay?" I blurt out. I press my palm against the stall door, expecting it to be locked, but it swings open, revealing a man with jet black hair hunched over the toilet, retching.

"Get the fuck out!" It's not just any man.

It's Philip.

Realization dawns on him when he spots me, but before he can utter a word, his body spasms again, almost hitting his head on the toilet. Most people would walk away, but for some reason, I inch closer, placing my hand on his sweaty forehead and pushing his hair back. Surprisingly, he doesn't protest and lets me help him, and from the way his body grows even more tense, I realize he's not used to receiving help from others.

"It's okay," I whisper almost inaudibly, trying to comfort him. I remove my hand from his forehead as soon as he regains control over his body again. "Wait here," I order and sprint to grab some paper towel.

When I return, he's sitting on the floor, leaning against the wall. I hand it to him, and he takes it without hesitation, wiping his mouth.

"Thanks," he says, his piercing eyes locking onto mine.

"I didn't think you knew that word," I tease, hiding a smile.

Philip smirks, and I take a moment to appreciate the man. He has aged like fine wine, with a chiseled jaw hiding beneath stubble. If memory serves me right, he's in his late thirties, almost fifteen years older than me, and still, he looks better than most men my age.

"Want to take a picture and sell it to the tabloids, or why are you still here?" he challenges.

"Saying thanks is nice, but being thankful would be nicer."

"Has anyone ever told you how annoying you are?" he shoots back in that defensive way of his that says he's hiding some sort of vulnerability. He's scared. But of what?

"On occasion," I joke, trying to lighten the mood. "But I bet nobody's ever told you what an asshole you are."

"On occasion... Michael tries to keep me grounded when he can." He smirks. A laugh escapes him, and I realize I have never heard him do that in all the years I have followed his career. It's a new side of him, and I get to see it.

"He is miserably failing at that," I retort, hopefully with a mischievous glint in my eyes. "Want to tell me what happened?"

"Why would I? You're a stranger. For all I know you could still be a crazy stalker." I can see him putting a façade on again, the lines of his smirk fading as he becomes the person he has constructed for the rest of the world.

"That line is getting old, Philip."

"That's because I'm old, Selene." He purrs my name in a way that sends a little shiver down my spine, and then I remember, I never told him my name. "Michael did," he says, as if he could read my thoughts.

"You obviously don't feel that old if you're making a comeback," I say with a smirk. His blue eyes filled with doubt. "If it makes you feel better, sometimes talking to a stranger helps. I promise I won't judge."

"Of course you wouldn't." The irony in his words is thick enough to cut with a knife. It makes me wonder what he's been through to become this bitter. Or was he always like this and he never showed the world this side of himself?

"I don't care enough about you to do judge."

"Ouch." He clutches his chest in mock pain. "You're breaking my heart."

"You don't have a heart to break, don't pretend otherwise," I bite back.

"Touché, Sparks." He chuckles, and I hate the way my body and mind react to the combination of the nickname and the raspy laugh. "You still could be a stalker, waiting to uncover my deepest secrets and sell them to the press," he continues, revealing his trust issues.

"Well, if it makes you feel any better, I did admire you once," I reveal with a sly grin, relishing the shock on his face. "Back when I was about six years old, and you were at the peak of your career. You were the reason I fell in love with the sport, the Spaniard who made Formula One popular in my country."

I can see him mentally calculating our age difference.

"How old are you?"

"Old enough to tell you the truth you seem to not want to know," I tease, although my words are honest.

"And old enough to have a bite." He smirks, his eyes scanning me from head to toe. *Is Philip Burton checking me out?*

"Just when it comes to you." I smile.

"What a pair we make." We look at each other and burst into laughter. "Sorry to be a disappointing childhood hero…"

"It's a good thing you sell yourself as the villain and not the hero then."

"Who was your hero?" he asks, but before I can answer, the bathroom door swings open, and Miriam walks in.

She's about to say something when she takes in the scene in front of her – Philip on the floor and me standing over him. The confusion is written all over her face.

"I wanted to make sure you were okay, but I didn't expect you two to be having a party in here. Guess bathrooms are your thing, huh?" Miriam quips, leaning against the door.

"Sorry for keeping her away from you. I needed her here," Philip says as he gets up. We're standing closer now, and I have to tilt my head to look him in the eyes. He's ridiculously tall for a driver. "Selene," he mutters. "I guess I'll see your name on my next contract."

RHAE AEDEN

With that, he leaves the stall, and I can't help but feel a twinge of something like loss as he walks away.

CHAPTER NINE

Philip

"How is João doing?" I ask Mancini as I stroll into the garage on Sunday morning, before the crew has even rolled out of bed. Mancini runs a hand through his mop of white hair, then stirs his coffee, looking utterly defeated.

Please let him be okay.

"He's at the hospital." My heart drops at those words. "He's conscious, and everything seems fine, he's just really shaken up."

"You never learned how to give good news, did you?"

"I just know how to congratulate world champions on the radio," he retorts, and I can't help but chuckle.

I remember the first time my team principal told me I was a world champion. The goosebumps, the rush of adrenaline, and the people screaming on the radio, *'Philip, you are the world champion! The world champion!'*

Ah, those were the days.

A shiver runs down my spine at the memory. Those moments are my happy place.

"É tu? Come stai?" *How are you?* Mancini switches to Italian briefly. "Michael told me you had food poisoning." Note to self, thank Michael for being a helpful son of bitch.

"Catering food does not agree with me," I lie, trying to dodge the real issue. It's enough that Selene saw it all and even had the audacity to help me.

"You better get used to the catering," he warns, pointing a finger at me. "I will not go over the budget cap for some fancy cook." His accent gets thicker as he gets angrier, and the Italian in him takes over. Always so temperamental.

"I can afford my own private chef with the amount you're paying me," I joke, even though we both know the paycheck I'll be cashing is no joke. Who would have thought that at thirty-seven I would be one of the highest-paid drivers?

"Prove me you are worth every single penny."

"I'll be so good that acquiring me as your driver will seem like a bargain when the cash starts pouring in because of me." I know what I'm capable of. They just need to let me do my thing, and I'll surprise the whole world.

"Did you become a manager for drivers while you were on your retirement trip?" We both laugh.

"I only work with the best because I'm the best."

"Seriously, Philip." His voice drops. "Are you ready?"

"You wouldn't have hired me if you didn't think I was."

"I am not asking you about what you think I think, but how you feel. What if you had to race today?" Mancini clarifies, not beating around the bush.

What if I had to race today?

I haven't thought about it... I have been training and my simulator times are near perfect, but I have not gotten into this year's car yet, and that is a whole different story than doing simulated races.

"I'd say, let's go grab some points." I regret my answer as soon as it leaves my lips. I can score points, that much is clear, but how many is the question right now.

"*Porca troia*, Philip! *Dai*, be honest! "

"I haven't driven a Formula One car in a while. I'm physically ready to drive, but how I'll perform? Nobody knows. That's the beauty of the sport. Can I get a podium today? Probably not. This isn't my car; it's João's and he is the one who should be driving it. But if you ask, I still have it in me to become a world champion. If I didn't, I wouldn't even bother to be here." It's the unvarnished truth.

"That determination," he says, emphasizing each syllable, "is exactly what I wanted to hear. I missed it, Philip." He pokes my chest with a finger and slaps my back with his other hand. I'm not big on touchiness, but I tolerate it because I know how crucial it is to be on good terms with the team principal.

I force a smile. "We've never worked together."

"No, we have not. But you are a legend, and I want that legend on my team."

"You got him," I assure him.

"I talked to the FIA." The mere mention of the federation gets my whole attention. "I asked them to let you drive today." Another bomb drops, and I hold my breath for a second, maybe even longer, not knowing how to process this. I'm so eager to get into an F1 car and start racing again, for a second, I believe I could today. Then I remember how this world actually works, and my dreams get crushed.

"That isn't an option. You have a reserve driver for situations like these. This isn't my season, and my contract only starts in a couple of months. Plus, I don't think the FIA and the press are ready for me just yet."

"Slow down. Nobody said anything about letting you race in the Grand Prix. I was thinking about you driving one of the old cars, one of the relics," he explains and my heart clenches a little bit inside my chest, longing for what could have been.

Despite the letdown, my curiosity gets the best of me.

"What car?"

"The C-08." My face goes as pale as a sheet of paper for a split second before I regain control of my expression. I only allow myself to press my lips into a thin line. "Ten laps before the race."

"You had this planned already." My blood boils.

"Money rules the world, my friend. Everyone will be talking about you, if you do this. It's good PR to start your comeback." He's not wrong, but the idea of driving that car repulses me.

"Next time you need me for a promotional stunt, have the decency to ask me what I think about it first. And also ensure that I am in the right mindset to drive a fucking rocket ship without losing it!" I hiss. This is one of the reasons I left. They turned me into a circus, a pawn for the FIA, a target for the press.

"Sorry, caro mio. I knew you would say no if I asked you. You would be too scared to have to face the press and all the cameras piling up at garage door, so I decided to spare you the hustle. But I will have Sarah or Jessica speak to you next time."

"Talking about Sarah—" I start.

"What about her?" Sarah says as she strolls into the garage, way too early for someone who's not working with the mechanics or engineering crew.

"Hire the girl she asked for," I demand.

"Already giving orders?" Mancini gives me a defiant look.

"A recommendation, if you prefer," I reply.

"What's in it for you?" I appreciate that he's astute enough to ask the right questions and learn my motives, it speaks about his character. But I am not planning on letting him know my real interests.

I'm not sure I even know them myself.

"Why do you care?" I brush him off.

"You were screaming at the poor girl less than twenty-four hours ago," Sarah chimes in, probably sensing that my motives might not be pure. But when have they ever been?

"I thought you wanted her. I'm trying to help you here."

"I won't stop you then," Sarah says.

"*Boh... Chi è questa ragazza?*" *Who is this girl?*

"She is the one who applied for the job in the UK, but management didn't want to sponsor her visa," Sarah explains, filling in some of the blanks. "And she's the one that has saved us millions that you can invest in your next car." A smile covers my lips because not many people would defy their bosses like this.

"What job should I tell management to give her, eh?" Mancini answers, and I can see he's starting to feel cornered by both of us, just how I like it. Let him see who's really in charge.

"Anything related to marketing strategy or planning, or whatever works. If her visa is the issue, then we can simply hire her in the Italian offices and have her come to London every once in a while," I say.

"Why are you invested?" Sarah probes again.

"She is good, and I only work with the best. If you said that she has saved you millions, then she has already proven herself worthy. Plus, those millions are going into the car *I* will drive, and the car *I* will win with. Employ her. End of discussion."

Both of them wear the same expression of surprise, and I don't blame them. Honestly, I'm not even sure where that came from. But after a couple of hours of meticulously stalking her online last night, I stumbled upon Selene's LinkedIn profile. She has experience working with football teams and some famous athletes, like Guillero Maripan or Takumi Minamino.

I found myself inexplicably obsessed. The more I dug, the more I wanted to know. I found her Instagram as soon as I was bored of her LinkedIn. The little information it offered about her personality captured my attention. She might have said that I wasn't the hero in her story, but an old post from years ago revealed she had been following my career since she was a kid. She even had a toy car version of the C-08.

"I propose a deal," Mancini says, interrupting my thoughts. "You'll drive later, and then I'll pull some strings for that *ragazza*." He's putting a bait right in front of me, and it's such a sweet one that I am tempted to take it.

RHAE AEDEN

I'm thinking about it, but Sarah locks eyes with me, her thoughts running faster than my own.

"He'll do it!"" she practically screams, her excitement palpable.

"Done," I reply calmly, giving her a steady look. "Get me a racing suit, and I'll ask Michael to fetch me a helmet."

And just like that, we've reached an agreement.

CHAPTER TEN

Selene

I wake up completely energized right before my alarm goes off. I roll over, getting greeted by the sight of Miriam with her braids covering her face as she sleeps. It's unfair how her skin is glowing while I am always a puffy mess with under eye circles bigger than the moon.

"Good morning, sunshine," I chirp.

"It's not a good morning if I haven't had enough rest," she announces, covering her head with a pillow. "What time is it?"

"It's nine." That same pillow lands in my face. Can't say I didn't see that coming. Miriam is *not* a morning person. "How about we go have breakfast and enjoy an early morning," I suggest, hoping to convince her to get up and start our day.

"I hate you," she mumbles.

"You love me," I counter, slipping under the covers on Miriam's bed and then throwing my arms around her waist, spooning her.

"Be honest," she says, her eyes barely open. "You want to go and see Philip." I grab a pillow and then toss it right back at her, hitting her in the face. Now she is fully awake. "Ouch!" she yelps.

"You're ridiculous."

"You were the one cozying up with him in the bathroom, not once, but twice. I am just stating the obvious."

"Technically, the first time we were arguing...I think?" I'm still not sure what to make of it. "I didn't even know it was him. I mean, I'm not sure how you'd categorize that. And the second time, I was just helping him out."

"Oh, is that what they call it nowadays?" Her words drip with sarcasm, making me chuckle.

"Don't start," I warn her.

"Hey, I know what I saw," she says, jumping out of bed.

"And what did you see, hmm?" I answer.

"He likes you."

"And you got that all from a three-minute interaction? One that you witnessed only for five seconds, maybe ten?"

"Call that intuición femenina" *Female intuition.* She says in Spanish, repeating the words I have taught her in the past.

"Your pronunciation is improving," I point out, trying to steer the conversation away from Philip Burton.

"No thanks to you," Miriam protests.

"How about we have this discussion over breakfast and then go to the track?"

"You realise that we are pretty much staying at the track, right? Look outside the window, you will probably smell rubber burning and fuel." *The best smell if you ask me.*

"They should make that scent a candle," I muse.

"Yeah, sure, and then we'll all get cancer from inhaling fumes. Whatever, let's get going. Nobody's going to stop you today," she finally gives in.

"Thanks," I say, giving her a warm hug.

I rush into the bathroom, wash my face, apply some makeup, and attempt to salvage my hair. When I step out of the bathroom, I find Miriam already dressed in jeans and a black shirt from Cavaglio Nero, with yellow accents on the collar, complementing the gold beads and rings in her braids shine.

"Are we going matching?" she asks, looking at herself in the mirror.

"I have to think about what to wear," I mutter, scanning the contents of my luggage, quickly deciding on washed jeans and a plain black shirt that matches the Cavaglio Nero cap.

"You look good in the Cavaglio Nero colors. They suit you," Miriam tells me when she sees my outfit.

I smile at her, but sadness creeps into my heart.

"What's wrong?" she asks.

"I always knew getting a job in this industry would be hard, and I have only attempted a couple of times, and I am still young and—"

"Get to the point," she cuts me off.

"I thought I had it this time, you know? I was certain, and my dreams got crushed by an email. And yesterday I got a taste of what the job feels like, even though it was only for thirty minutes... They were the best thirty minutes of my life," I admit, realizing how steep the fall can be after you've had a glimpse of heaven.

"You'll get it. You're so close. Sooner or later, you'll be presented with the right opportunity, whether it's with Cavaglio or another team." Miriam cups my face gently with her hands, her forehead almost touching mine.

"I love you." Miriam is not only a friend, she's family.

"I love you, too. Now, let's get going, I am starving."

We make our way down to the breakfast hall, and to my surprise, many team members are already enjoying an early morning coffee. I scan the room, and I notice someone waving in our direction. It's Sarah, inviting us to join her and Jessica at their table.

"Up so early, ladies?" She says.

"Someone couldn't contain her excitement about today and dragged me along," Miriam grumbles.

"Guilty." I shrug. "How are you doing?"

"Tired." Sarah sips her coffee. "This is my fourth cup already. Please sit with us," she instructs, pointing at the two free seats between her and Jessica.

"Isn't it too early for a fourth cup of coffee?" Jessica asks. I think this is the first time I have heard her speak. Her voice is insufferably sharp and high. It's not exactly screaming friendliness.

"I was up at five with Mancini at the garage. Philip was there too," Sarah informs us. Jessica's ears perk up at the mention of Philip's name. *Fan alert, perhaps?*

"Ugh, he is so handsome," Jessica drools. *Yup, fangirl.*

"Piece of advice? Dating a racing driver is hard but dating Philip… absolute no-go. Plus, you work with the man now, don't shit where you eat."

The warning is clear: no dating team members.

"He has been assigned to you?" I ask, surprised.

"Jealous?" Jessica bites at me, almost territorial.

"Ha!" Miriam laughs. "I think Selene is done with Philip Burton for a while."

"Pardon?" Jessica gives me a puzzled look.

"I met him yesterday," I explain, not wanting to give her any the details.

"Would you like to join me in the garage before the race?" Sarah asks me, moving on from talking about Philip. My eyes go wide in surprise. Only VIPs are generally allowed there. "There will be an event with Philip. I thought maybe you would like to see it."

"We would love to join," Miriam responds before I have a chance to say anything.

"Perfect. Meet me around ten and bring the passes from yesterday. If anyone says anything, just tell them to call me," she instructs, as she gets up from her seat, taking another cup of coffee to go.

"Thanks for this. And for everything. You've taken this experience to a whole new level for us," I say. Sarah has been nothing but a kind soul in a world that is known for its fierce competition.

"Think of me as your Formula One fairy godmother. Honestly, it's the least I could do." She pats my shoulder gently. "I've got to run now, but I'll catch you later."

Sarah hasn't even left the breakfast hall when Jessica starts glaring at us as if we have just committed a crime. "So, Philip," she says, attempting to bring the conversation back to her favorite topic. Miriam shoots me a loaded look, and I already know what she's about to do.

"Well, we'd better hit the track if we want to get our daily dose of fuel fumes." My friend stands up, interrupting whatever gossip session Jessica was about to kick off.

"We'll catch up with you at the track," I say, waving at her as I am getting dragged away. Breakfast will have to wait.

"Bye." Miriam waves at her, smiling like the Cheshire cat. "Just grab a croissant or something," she whispers as we pass the catering table filled with pastries.

"You didn't need to run for your life like that," I reprimand her while I grab a crispy croissant. To be fair, I'm thankful she got us out of there before things could get out of control. Something tells me Jessica wouldn't react well if she found out I spent some time with Philip.

"Are you sure I didn't?" she retorts, taking a bite out of the croissant in my hand. There are no boundaries between us. What's mine is hers and the other way around.

"She can't be that bad," I say. Maybe she's just obsessed with him but is a nice person when it comes to other things in life.

"She's one of those girls who gets territorial about a person they don't even know," Miriam counters.

"Fair enough," I give in. "Come on, let's get going."

There's not much to do around the track this early, except maybe spot some celebrities and socialites. A few paparazzi attempt to corner us, desperate to know who we are and how we ended up in the paddock. They get way too close, completely ignoring the concept of personal space.

I can't help but put myself in Philip's shoes, picturing him dealing with this circus day and night, enduring their harassment. I remember how they treated him when I was younger, and from the short time we spent together yesterday, I'd guess that not much has changed. I can't imagine what it's like, becoming a product instead of a person, having your entire life exposed when all you want is a bit of privacy. No wonder the guy has so many trust issues.

We arrive at the garage just before ten, and my heart races with anticipation. I'm about to step into a garage. Not just any garage, though. It's the Cavaglio Nero garage, where magic happens. This might be the best day of my life.

I am prepared to see the car of this season, the CN-23s in the center of the garage, but what I find is Philip's striking yellow C-08. I'm starstruck; it's the car that ignited my passion for all of this. And even though I'm amazed, something else catches my attention.

Philip is standing in a corner wearing a Cavaglio racing suit, looking every bit the part of a racing driver. The suit hangs low on his hips, giving me a tantalizing view of his back, which is clad in a black fireproof undershirt adorned with sponsor logos. I catch myself biting my lip, appreciating how it accentuates his back and arm muscles. I think I need one of those fireproof shirts, because I might be close to catching fire.

"Do you need a napkin?" Miriam teases.

"What?"

"To wipe away the drool from your chin," she mocks.

"Shut up," I hiss.

Philip turns around, his blue eyes locking onto mine. It's as if he's looking into my very soul, but I don't flinch. I tilt my chin up defiantly and meet his gaze in the distance, flashing a smile that throws him off balance. This man is so starved for human connection that a simple smile leaves him stumbling.

I ignore him and find Sarah, who's standing with a group of people, one of them being the team principal of Cavaglio Nero. She signals for me to join them. I stride towards her like I belong in this world.

The problem is, I don't.

"Good morning. I'm Selene," I extend my hand towards Cesare Mancini, and he meets it with a firm handshake. "I hope I don't sound like a fangirl, but it's a pleasure and an honor to meet you," I say with my best smile.

Philip takes a step towards us, joining the group, curiosity in his eyes.

"*Ah, Sarah me ha parlato di te.*" *Sarah has told me about you,* he says in Italian. I am not sure who this is meant for, but I decide to use it to my advantage.

"Aspetto solo cose buone." *Hopefully only good things.* "É stato un piacere lavorare con lei questo weekend." Philip's eyes go wide at my use of Italian, mirroring Mancini's reaction.

"Sei italiana?" *Are you Italian?* Mancini asks surprised.

"No, spagnola," *No, Spanish,* I reply.

"No, you are lying to me." He switches to English. "With that accent you must be at least half-Italian. Father or Mother?"

"Mi dispiace, I am one hundred precent Spanish. Both my parents are from Spain, but I learned Italian a couple of years ago," I reply, thrilled to impress the team principal of Cavaglio.

"Look at that, she's like you, Philip."

"I am half-Spanish," Philip says nonchalantly. "Born and raised somewhere between Spain and the UK, with bits of Milan, I guess." His gaze remains locked on me, even as he speaks to Mancini.

"Her Italian is better than yours," the team principal teases. "What other talents do you have?" I can't help but feel like the star of the show, with all this attention directed at me.

"We could have coffee, and you can discover them. I can't reveal all my tricks at once," I say, hoping that he will take the bait.

"*Brava.* I like her," he says to Philip, who finally diverts his gaze from me to focus on his boss.

"Happy to hear you say that," Sarah tells him.

HAMMER TIME

I feel tension between both of them, some sort of unresolved business, and I am certain that Mancini is about to say something when Jessica strolls into the garage, positioning herself next to Philip, who seems incredibly uncomfortable with her proximity.

"Philip, are you ready for today?" she asks, batting her long eyelashes at him.

"Sure." He doesn't even look at her, which seems a bit excessive, but then I recall the way she acted at breakfast, and I kind of feel sorry for the man. "Anything you need from me besides the ten laps?"

"A photographer will be taking some pictures around the garage, and afterward, the press will want to speak with you." Jessica's sharp voice pierces my ears again.

"Did you not organize a press session?" Sarah asks. "Sports News should give him some screen time for the sponsors."

"I didn't realize—I—I—" Jessica starts to stutter.

"Please, don't tell me you forgot," Sarah says when Jessica seems unable to come up with an answer. "Do you know how packed their schedule is now? It's going to be impossible to get an interview."

"I have a friend at Sports News. Maybe she can help? I can give her a call," I offer, earning a look of pure disdain from Jessica. She's going to bite my head off the first chance she gets.

"You mean Sasha?" Miriam, who joined us without me noticing says. She instantly knows who I am talking about, as Sasha is a friend of us both.

"Sasha Valine? The commentator?" Mancini asks, his black brows shooting up his forehead.

"Yes," I confirm. "We worked together for a while. It's worth giving it a shot." Sasha isn't just a commentator or a journalist. She is *the* one. Everyone knows her and respects her. If you want to appear everywhere, she is your girl.

"Please, call her and let me write you a check for everything you have been doing this weekend," Sarah practically begs.

"Don't worry about the money, I'll call her right now."

"Take your time," Philip says without any enthusiasm.

He really does hate the press.

Ignoring his comment, I spin around and head back in the direction we came from, my phone in my hand as I dial Sasha's number. As soon as I find a quiet spot, away from the noise, I press the Call button.

Beep. Beep.

"Priviet!" Sasha's voice blasts though the phone. "Look who finally decided to call me. How are you doing?" she says in the cool tone that she is known for.

"Hi, S! Sorry, work has been quite overwhelming, you know how it is," I say, not feeling the need to explain what has been going on in my life the past couple of weeks.

"Tell me about it. I can't wait for the summer break to stop traveling from one country to the other. We're drowning in work here since the silly season started," I smile at the mention of the silly season. It's honestly one of the best moments of the year, when the drivers, team principals and other important players of the sport start transferring teams, and there are crazy rumors and announcements every two seconds.

"Talking about the silly season… I wanted to ask you for a work-related favor."

I explain the whole situation to her, without sparing any detail. Sasha quickly grasps how this could turn into a win-win situation: she gets an exclusive interview with Philip, and I get my moment to shine with Cavaglio.

"The offer is tempting. I'll get in touch with the on-track crew; they should be able to arrange something. I'll text you the details as soon as I know more," she assures me.

"You have no idea how much I love you right now," I can't help but gush.

"Consider it payback for everything you've done for me."

"Bye, S. Thanks for everything."

The weekend couldn't have gone any better if I had scripted it. I close my eyes briefly, pressing my back against the cool wall, trying to calm my thoughts and racing heart. My cheeks hurt from smiling.

"Are you okay?" a familiar voice asks me, and I open my eyes, stepping away from the wall to see Michael standing in front of me.

"Yes, all good. I just needed to process what's happening, but everything's fine."

"I know the feeling. What are you doing here?"

"Sarah invited us to join you guys in the garage. What about you?" I'm genuinely intrigued by the comings and goings of Philip's coach.

"I—damn it, I was on my way to bring Philip his helmet, and I totally forgot," Michael mumbles while patting his pockets, searching for something. "Ah, crap! Can you give this to him?" He extends his hand, clutching Philip's helmet. "Tell him I'll be back as soon as I can!"

"Sure," I say, confused, but I doubt Michael even hears me.

I take a moment to appreciate the helmet. It's not one I recognize from Philip's collection. The onyx-colored piece sports the Spanish flag on one side and the British one on the other. At the front, there's the yellow horse emblem of the Cavaglio Nero team, and at the back, a subtle matte black inscription that reads, *'Fear is your best motivation.'*

I stride back into the garage, where everyone is standing just as I left them, except for Philip, who has his headphones on and is warming up next to the car. He doesn't notice me, and I attempt to be as invisible as possible, not eager to engage with the beast.

"Good news," I announce upon returning. "I talked to Sasha. We should get at least ten minutes with her, but they've demanded exclusivity and I have given it to them. Sorry for making the call without your confirmation, but I figured it's better to ask for forgiveness."

"You did well, a strategist indeed," Mancini applauds me, and I find myself biting the inside of my cheek once more to contain my smile.

"She'll send me the crew's phone numbers soon. I can just share them with you." I offer Jessica a warm smile, hoping to extinguish any lingering animosity, but if looks could kill, I would be six feet under.

"The photographer is here," Jessica announces.

She walks over to welcome him, and I use that opportunity to hand Philip his helmet.

"Hey." My heart starts racing, probably in terror of talking to Philip.

"What do you want, Sparks?"

"Rude, I thought we were besties now." His eyes dart to the helmet hanging from my hand. "Michael gave me this. He said he'd be back soon." I take a step closer, lifting the helmet with both hands and tilting my head to look at him.

RHAE AEDEN

Click.

Our heads snap toward the photographer, who's pointing his camera at us. Suddenly, I feel self-aware, wanting to hide every inch of my body and everything surrounding me. I grow tense, and I can see Philip noticing it. In a way, his eyes show concern, probably because he has experienced firsthand how terribly uncomfortable, I must feel.

"Did you get her consent before taking her picture?" Philip asks the photographer with his usual snarky tone.

"Sorry, I thought she was a girlfriend or an influencer," the photographer mutters, not bothered in the least by Philip's cutting tone.

"She's more than just somebody's girlfriend," Philip snarls, but at this point, I guess that's all the man can do. Why be nice when you can act like a caveman? "Next time, ask for permission," Philip scolds, his tone undeniably prickly.

The photographer only nods at us, pointing his camera towards the car and giving us some semblance of privacy.

"The helmet," I remind Philip, noticing it's still in my grasp. I hand it to him, and he grabs it without hesitation.

"Thanks."

"You know you don't have to be a total jerk to every person wielding a camera and a microphone, right?" I snap.

"A thank you would be enough."

"Just saying," I continue, unfazed. "Maybe if you tossed a little love the press's way, they might reciprocate," I quip, wondering why I even care about his public image when he so obviously doesn't.

"All I do is speak the truth; not my problem if people can't handle it," he responds, methodically working on fixing his racing suit. I find myself focused on the precise movements of his hands.

"There's a thing called sugarcoating," I say, watching as he wiggles into the suit, shaping it to his body. Somehow, we end up inching closer to each other, and I can't help but feel that pull again.

Philip puts on his helmet in one swift move and opens the visor, allowing me to peer into his eyes. I notice his zipper is only partly done, and out of reflex, my fingers rush to it, helping him pull it all the way up.

I hear another click, and I remove my hands from his body, just realizing how intimate this moment was.

What is going on with me?

"Let him do it. Those pictures won't see the light of day anyway," he reassures me, grabbing my wrist with his hand and placing it back on the rebellious zipper.

"You know, fear isn't the best motivator," I whisper, my eyes fixated on the sponsors plastered all over his chest.

"I bet you think love is," he teases.

"No, dreams are the best motivators," I reply.

"I guess so." His gaze briefly shifts away as he sizes me up.

"You used to have dreams of becoming a world champion, and you got them. You are back here because you dream of another title," I whisper.

"Touch both sides of my helmet," he abruptly interrupts.

"Wait, what? Why?" I cock my head, perplexed. This guy's mood swings are going to be the end of me.

"Just do it," he urges.

Complying, I place my hands on the flags on either side of his helmet and look up at him. His head tilts slightly, bringing our heads so close that I can feel the cold radiating from his helmet.

"It's for good luck," he whispers.

"You don't need luck. You're Philip Burton," I murmur as I close the visor of his helmet, getting him ready to head onto the track.

CHAPTER ELEVEN

Philip

Selene's words hit me like a bag of bricks, putting me on edge. I move my arms and legs, trying to shake off the strange sensation that's crawled under my skin.

My eyes are drawn to the vintage yellow beast at the heart of the garage. I take a moment to remind myself that nothing else matters once I'm behind the wheel. My focus narrows, zeroing in on the car. I am one with it now.

Without a second thought, I leap into the cockpit of the single seater, shimmying around my seat and getting reacquainted with the sensation of being in this car after so many years. It feels like yesterday when I drove the C-08, snatching my first championship title.

Memories of my early seasons flash through my mind like a sped-up movie. I recall my mom putting me in my first kart in Spain when I was four years old. Then the move to the UK to chase my racing dream. Dad leaving us for good after too many years of coming and going. My first contract in a lower Formula category. Mom getting sick.

We lost her too early, but her efforts weren't in vain. I made it into F2 and shortly after, I scored my first win, impressing the teams in F1 so much that I was offered a contract almost instantly. My father showed up after, coming to see if he could cash a check from his prodigy son after he was done draining his family's fortune. He didn't even know that mom had died at the time.

The first pole position came soon after in the season and a podium followed. As did the first rivalry with a teammate, and the never-ending battle with the press. Beating their golden boy didn't agree with them and so the vilification began.

I became the favored driver for Cavaglio Nero in my second year, after finishing second in the world championship. I won my first title the following year. I was crowned the youngest winner in history. But I was still far from becoming anyone's favorite.

That was also the last year I raced under the Spanish flag. The team who used to work there back then suggested I use my double nationality and change to the British one to gain extra points with the press.

It was a shot in the dark. Thing started going downhill, and the team didn't know how to get rid of me after the press went against them for having me as their driver instead of that blonde British boy.

That's when the first sabotage came.

If I wasn't going to leave, then they would force my exit.

Accidents happened, the car was undrivable, the press impossible. It was the beginning of my downfall and I still managed to win another two world championships until I decided to leave. I couldn't take it anymore.

Fighting nineteen other drivers? That was easy.

The press? I could ignore them.

But fighting my team was what really messed me up. I became paranoid not knowing if I would have a crash because someone had manipulated the car. So, eventually, I left.

So, if things were so bad why did I come back?

Cavaglio Nero is the best Team in F1, no question about that, and I am willing to suffer ten times more to get another world championship, even if I have to compete against my own team. And things have changed since I came. The team is a complete new one, and I hope that this time they will work with me and not against me,

"Radio check," comes through my earpiece, and I force myself to focus on the present.

"Check," I respond.

Mechanics secure my seatbelts and ensure everything in the car is in order. I thank God for my helmet that's hiding my face so they can't see my expression.

"Perfect," comes through the radio. "You have ten laps in the C-08. You know the drill," the engineer tells me, making it sound like I'm about to enter a real race rather than just putting on a show.

"Ciao, Philip," Mancini's voice chimes in over the radio as well. From the cockpit I can see him at the pit wall with the rest of the engineers. "Have fun and give them a show."

"Understood," I reply, wasting no time.

I press down on the throttle and speed out of the garage. The light at the end of the pit lane is already green when I cross the safety line, then go full throttle. I warm up the tires, which feel different from the last time I raced in a Formula 1 car. I take it easy on the first laps, trying to get a feel for the vehicle again.

By the third lap, I press down on the throttle as much as possible. A thin smile covers my mouth, brushing my lips against the inside of the helmet. I zoom past the pit lane at nearly three hundred kilometers per hour, navigating The Loop with increasing confidence. It's an easy and fast ride until I make it to the sixth corner, where João had his accident yesterday.

"Fear is the best motivator," I tell myself and stomp on the throttle in the second sector, as if trying to escape a ghost. The corners come and go, and in the blink of an eye, I'm in the third sector.

"How's the car?" an engineer asks after a couple of laps.

"Next year's car will be better," I say playfully.

"Copy."

I go for one more lap, giving it my all. How satisfying would it be to post better times than the qualifiers yesterday in this vintage beauty?

"Let's go, baby girl," I encourage the car.

Back at Abbey, I tap the brakes lightly to navigate The Loop and open my DRS as soon as I hit the straight. But as I cross into the second sector, my mind betrays me. I lose control of the car, and images of João flash through my head again as I spin in a double 360. Miraculously, I manage to regain control before things get out of hand. My breath comes out in heavy bursts, my heart racing faster and harder. I want to stop, but I keep driving, as though I can outrun my problems. But I can't. They follow me wherever I go, no matter how much I try to escape.

I complete the rest of the laps, driving more carefully than usual. The crowd roars nonetheless, and they go wild when I finish the last lap, performing a donut before returning to the garage where the mechanics stand ready to attend to the seatbelts and headrest.

I just want to break free.

"Don't," I tell them. "Don't touch me right now." I try to be polite because my state of mind has nothing to do with them. They are just doing their job. "Where is Michael?" I ask as soon as I'm out of the car, not wanting to remove my helmet yet.

"I'm here," his voice calls out from beside me.

He rushes towards me, holding a towel. I catch Mancini's gaze from across the room. I know what he's thinking.

Is it worth the trouble?

Yes, it is, and I know it.

I walk towards the back rooms of the garage, Michael following me. I only allow myself to relax when I find a spot where cameras aren't allowed. Finally, my legs give in, and I collapse onto the floor with my back against the wall and my helmet still on.

Michael squats in front of me.

"What happened?"

"It's just going to happen all over again," I mutter.

"Explain," he demands, a coach and friend all at once.

"Everyone's just waiting for me to mess up, so they can prove I'm not good enough," I say, tired of spiraling. I don't want to deal with the press, the circus, any of it.

I just want to drive.

"But you *are* good. You are the best. You won two championships, even when the team was sabotaging you. You are a legend. You are Philip Burton."

I smile to myself and decide it's time to take the helmet off. "I am Philip Burton," I repeat after him. "And I am the best driver this generation has ever seen."

"You are humble too," Michael adds, laughing.

"What if history repeats itself? What if another young Brit, who can't even drive to save his life, comes back and things get out of hand again?" I ask myself more than him.

"For now, focus on yourself. We'll cross that bridge when we get there."

"Everyone's just waiting for me to fuck up, so they can prove I'm a total screw-up." I groan, sick of this endless mental loop I'm stuck in.

"Get your head back in the game, just like we practiced," Michael orders.

"It's just…the whole industry went hunting for a villain, and they found the perfect candidate in me. It doesn't matter what I do, what if it happens again?"

"Why don't you try and make amends with the press this time? Try being on their good side. Don't hate on them because they hated on you."

"You know it's not that easy. That's why I stopped racing under the Spanish flag, to try and gain the sympathy, make them see me as one of their own, and you know how that went. I served a purpose in the story, and they know the power my name has in their headlines." I heave a sigh of relief, feeling grateful that Michael's got my back. "At the end of the day, all I've got is this car and all that matters is winning that shining silver trophy by the end of next season."

"You've got more than that. You have me." He winks.

"I know," I admit, feeling thankful. "I just want to taste victory again. One more title to shove it right back in their faces. Show 'em that I've got the skills."

"You'll get there. We all believe in you. That's why they can't stand you. Deep down they know exactly what you're capable of."

CHAPTER TWELVE

Selene
Two months later

"I barely see you anymore. You're just drowning in your work," the person across the table from me complains. "Why don't you just stay home? I make enough to cover both of us. There is no need for you to work once we get married." Not just any person.

Mark.

We have been dating for a couple of weeks now. A couple of weeks too many if you ask me. I was initially attracted to him because of his appearance – those dark, short locks, brown eyes, and a body that was built for late night fun. The fact that his schedule was busier than mine was another plus on the list. It meant no strings attached for either of us. But the words he's throwing at me right now indicate something's changed or maybe he misread my signals.

RHAE AEDEN

"Are you even listening to me?" he snaps as I sip my wine, praying nobody around us can hear this conversation.

"Oh, I'm hearing you, Mark." I raise an eyebrow. "I've always been crystal clear about what I want from this relationship." I gesture between us. "And if you're having a change of heart about our arrangement, maybe it's time we go our separate ways."

"You don't want to split up. Do you even know me?" Heads turn around us, looking at the scene he's causing.

"I've known you for two months," I retort. "The same amount of time you've known me. In that span, you should've figured out that I won't be a stay-at-home wife, not now, not ever."

"You're thicker than I thought." For the first time tonight, I'm mildly intrigued by whatever he's about to say. "With your grandiose dreams of working for a Formula One team. Let's be real, your ultimate goal is to bed one of the dri-"

"Allow me to stop you before you make a colossal mistake." I scan the restaurant, and when I lock eyes with the waitress, I signal for the bill.

"You're crazy if you think you're breaking up with me."

"I can't break something that never existed. Now, don't make a scene." The waitress approaches us with the bill. "Card, please," I instruct her without a glance at the tab.

I can foot the bill, even if it's an extravagant amount for two glasses of wine and a small plate of food that's left my stomach feeling emptier than my post dinner wallet. *Ah, the joys of living in Monaco.* I pay the bill and stand up, making sure my little black dress sits in the right places. I pivot on my heels and walk towards the exit, with the intention of getting a cab as soon as possible.

I might have kept my cool inside the restaurant, but I am not above being scared of what a man can do when his ego has been hurt, so I reach into my purse, discreetly retrieve the pepper spray, and dial Miriam's number, ready to call her in case things get bad.

I find a taxi and am about to make a run for it when Mark catches up to me.

"You'll regret this, Selene," he snarls, grabbing my arm.

I'm momentarily stunned by his grip.

"Release me. Now," I demand, my voice laced with anger.

"What will you do without me?" His hold tightens, and he whirls me around. He's so close that I can feel his breath on my face. "I'll make sure your life becomes a never-ending nightmare. You can kiss any job prospects in Monaco goodbye." I remain composed.

Out of the corner of my eye, I spot a man in a suit nearby. At least I'll have a witness if something goes wrong. Mark also spots the approaching individual, his hold loosening a little bit. I take advantage of the distraction to twist my arm and break free from his grasp. Before he can react, I aim the pepper spray at him, and the liquid hits him in the eyes.

"My eyes! I can't see!" he shouts, but I don't stick around to watch the show. I hurry away in my stilettos, nearly running on tiptoes, all while Mark's enraged threats echo behind me. "You bitch, I'm going to kill you!"

"Only if I don't kill you first," the man in the suit blurts out, his voice familiar.

"Philip?" I turn my head to see his dark blue eyes glaring at Mark. It's been two months since I last saw him, but I'd recognize that voice anywhere. Philip doesn't acknowledge me, instead, he casually taps his phone screen as if there wasn't a maniac threatening me.

"Is he the reason you're leaving me?" Mark screams, one hand still covering his stinging eyes, the other pointing at Philip. *Has he always been this unhinged?*

"She could only upgrade after dating you," Philip retorts with a smug grin. "Now, do us all a favor and leave before you lose whatever dignity you have left." He puts his phone to his ear and speaks to someone on the other end. "Please send security. We have a man who needs to be escorted off the premises."

A tall, bald security guard emerges from the restaurant and approaches, ready to handle Mark.

"This isn't over, Selene!" Mark's words echo as he's led away.

Philip steps closer to me. I can't help but take in his appearance. Maybe it's the shock or maybe it's just that Philip could easily be a person spoken about in Greek mythology, but he looks even better than he did two months ago. His slightly longer hair frames his face, and his suit emphasizes every muscular contour. He looks good, denying it would be pointless.

"Hello, Sparks," he purrs, his mixed British and Spanish accent heavier than the last time I saw him.

"What are you doing here?" I ask.

"Thought I'd play the part of a gentleman for once and rescue a damsel in distress." He smirks, taking a step closer.

"Too bad I'm neither a damsel nor was I in distress." I lie about the second half, moving towards him and standing so close that I need to tilt my head up to meet his gaze. A familiar position we've been in before.

"It's okay to admit you need help." I recognize my own words leaving his mouth. I said this to him when we met in Silverstone.

"Kettle meets pot," I tease.

"Touché, darling. I hope this was a first?" he asks, nodding towards where Mark had just been.

"With him, yes."

The cold of the night sweeps over my skin as the adrenaline wears off, and I feel the urge to cover my naked arms with my hands, but I remain in the same position, clenching my teeth so they won't chatter.

"What do you mean 'with him'?" His jaw tenses.

"The dating scene is rather bleak," I confess.

"Did you drive here?" Philip changes the subject abruptly and swiftly removes his jacket.

"I walked." He steps behind me and drapes his jacket over my shoulders, standing as close as possible. I inhale his cologne involuntarily. "You really don't have to give me your jacket," I protest, though I secretly relish the warmth it provides.

"I did. You're shivering."

"Thank you," I murmur.

"Come on. I'll drive you home."

CHAPTER THIRTEEN

Philip

We make our way to my car in silence. As soon as the valet hands over my keys, the car's lights illuminate as I unlock it, and I catch Selene muttering a soft, "Wow." I don't even have to glance her way to know that her eyes are as wide as they can be when she sees the yellow Lamborghini Aventador I'm driving.

Usually, I stick to my Cavaglio Nero, but it has circled around the media a million times by now, enough times that fans and haters are able to recognize it when I'm in town. So, whenever I want some privacy, I take this car. Enough people in Monaco have the same model so that it goes unnoticed by most.

"Cierra la boca te van a entrar moscas." *Close your mouth, flies will get inside.* I tell her in Spanish while holding her car door open.

RHAE AEDEN

"Wait, what?" Her astonishment intensifies at my use of Spanish.

"Never forget it's my second mother tongue." I can't help but ogle her as she hops into the car, her already short dress riding up her thighs.

Focus, Philip.

"Where do you live?" I ask, diverting my thoughts from the inappropriate images popping into my mind.

"Les Revoirs," she responds softly, almost as if she'd prefer it if I didn't know. It's a neighborhood close to the French border, about a fifteen-minute drive from where we are.

"That's quite a trek by Monegasque standards," I remark.

"I'm not a superstar, celebrity, or married to one, so there aren't many options for me in Monaco," she replies with a shrug. It's clear she doesn't want to delve into her living situation any further.

"I expected to see your name on some of the contracts I've signed recently." I switch topics, wanting to put her at ease.

"I haven't applied for anything since Silverstone."

"Why?" I don't usually care about people. But, for whatever reason, when it comes to her, I'm uncharacteristically curios. I'm still annoyed at Mancini for not offering her the job as he promised.

The little snake...

Then again, maybe it's for the best, especially given the unexpected bulge in my pants whenever I steal glances at her bare legs.

"There hasn't been anything in my area lately." Her stomach rumbles, and she quickly looks out the window, but her crimson cheeks give away her embarrassment. "Sorry."

"Why are you apologizing for being hungry?" I chuckle. "It's absurd how much we pay for restaurants here, considering the minuscule portions they serve. I always leave feeling like I've been on a hunger strike."

"You're paying for the ambiance and the people, and of course, the quality. But yes, portions could be more generous."

"When did you move here?"

"A little over a year ago. I've been working with the football players of AS Monaco." One of her hands clings to the door handle when I start accelerating through the empty streets of Monaco. Her knuckles turn white from her firm grip.

Is she scared?

"I've seen them," I say in a hushed tone, easing my foot off the gas pedal and noticing how her grip instantly lightens. "A rather lackluster team with extravagant salaries."

"You really don't have a filter, do you?"

"Not everyone appreciates the truth." As we stop at a red light, I take a moment to glance at Selene, who is now massaging her wrist, probably tired from the tight hold she just had on my car. "You do know I'm probably one of the best drivers on the planet, right?" I nod subtly towards her hand.

"I'm not a good passenger. I rather drive," she explains right when her stomach rumbles again. For whatever reason, anger courses through me at the fact that she's hungry, and I feel the urge to put an end to that.

What is wrong with me?

"I'll take you out for dinner."

"There is no need for that," she declines.

"That wasn't a question; it was a statement," I retort.

"My statement is that I don't want you to take me out for dinner," she insists, but I've already made up my mind and am driving in another direction, rather than to her house.

"Your body needs food, Selene. Please let me make sure you get something in your stomach after the night you just had."

Glancing at the time, I contemplate where to take her for dinner, somewhere we can have some privacy and actually fill her stomach with some substance.

"It's getting late. Any dietary restrictions? Vegan, gluten intolerant, or anything like that?"

"No, why?" she asks.

"There is a place with the best burgers in town nearby."

"You really don't have to," she protests.

"I want to."

We continue driving in silence through the city streets for another five minutes until I spot the burger place that I have been coming to for as long as I can remember. I pull up to the drive-through and position the car next to the menu board so Selene can look over the options.

"Take your time," I tell her.

"Don't you want to check the menu?" she asks when she notices my eyes haven't drifted from her face once.

"I've been here so often I practically have the menu memorized," I admit. "Do you know what you'd like?"

"Yeah, I'm ready to order."

Selene

We both opt for cheeseburgers, Coke, and a side of fries. It's somewhat reassuring to know that even top tier athletes appreciate the simple pleasures of carbs, just like the rest of us mortals.

"How's the prep for the season going?" I ask around a mouthful of fries.

"Do you genuinely care, or are you fishing for a headline?" Philip shoots back, his trust clearly lacking.

"I wouldn't say no to the right offer," I tease. "You're aware I could've spilled the tea from Silverstone, right? Your name hasn't escaped my lips since then," I lie with a straight face. I have talked about him more often than I would like to admit.

"Too bad." He smirks. "I rather enjoy hearing my name from your pretty lips." I feel my face going crimson at his words, and my mind drifts to wild places, picturing the sexiest instances in which I would say his name.

No, no, no, no. Don't go there.

"How do you manage to pull that off?" I ask.

"Elaborate, please," he says, his tone playful.

I let out a frustrated huff. "Being a world class jerk and an egocentric ass without breaking a sweat."

"Years of practice, I suppose." He smirks again. "But I don't hate the entire world."

"Your parents excluded," I tease, only to immediately regret it, remembering that his mother passed away a long time ago.

"I do hate my father," he admits before I can apologize.

"It makes sense," I reply, and he looks at me with a mix of curiosity and surprise. "You've never really talked about him the way you've talked about your mother publicly," I add when he keeps staring at me.

"He abandoned my mom." Bitterness taints his voice.

"I'm sorry to hear that," I offer softly.

"Why? It's not your fault that he's a piece of work."

"No, but I obviously steered this conversation into a topic you'd rather avoid."

"I see," he says, a smile appearing on his face. "Not only do you hold a degree in economics and a master's in marketing, but you're also a licensed psychologist?"

"You are the most exasperating person I've ever met." I grunt and attempt to open the car door to escape this conversation. But Philip gently places his hand over mine before I can fully open the door.

"Sharing isn't my strong suit," he admits, letting go of me, and I can't help but wonder if that's his peculiar version of an apology. "My mom raised me on her own and provided everything I needed to get where I am. Talking about my sperm donor feels like an insult to her."

"I am—" I start to apologize.

"Don't finish that sentence," he interrupts. "Now eat your food so I can take you home, knowing you won't starve tonight."

Even though Philip's way of ending the conversation is abrupt, I can't help but feel like I've gained a piece of information from him that the world doesn't know about.

"How's work with Jessica going?"

His face contorts in a pained expression. "It's challenging. She's a fan, and, on top of that, she's Mancini's niece… Now, I assume you are done eating." I nod, fixated on Jessica being Mancini's niece. "Let's drive you home then."

Philip is about to turn on the engine, but I put my hand on top of his, shaking with nerves. "I want to ask something, and you can totally say no," I say, seizing the opportunity that's right in front of me. "Can I drive?"

Philip looks at me, a smile playing at the corners of his lips, then glances at the steering wheel and back at me. "You're lucky your house is only three blocks away." He smirks, exiting the car.

"Yes!" I jump out and make my way to the other side. "Are you ready for the ride of your life?" I tease.

"As long as you don't get us killed, I'll be content."

My fingertips tingle with the urge to hug him. But I resist and run to the driver's side, hurrying to adjust everything to my liking. Philip, however, clutches his face in his hands with nerves, probably starting to realize what he has just done.

"You do realize you're more likely to have an accident at work rather than during this drive with me, right?" I reassure him.

"Start driving before I change my mind," he grumbles.

I rev the engine, feeling the car's power surge through me, and speed out of the parking lot, almost drifting at the exit.

"Easy there, Selene," he cautions.

"Oh, don't tell me you're scared," I taunt, zooming through the streets, passing a traffic light just as it turns red. I know the way home like the back of my hand, and I have only a couple of streets left to savor the car.

And savor it I shall.

"This is me," I announce with a grin, stopping the car in front of my place.

Philip quickly steps out of the car, rushing to open my door, ever the gentleman. I exit and realize just how close we're standing. I can see his chest rise and fall with each breath, and the scent of his cologne envelops me. It's a fragrance I doubt I'll ever forget. My body tingles again, and this time, I don't hold back. I touch his chiseled jaw and then get on my tip toes to give him a kiss on the cheek.

"Buenas noches, Philip," I say.

"I'll keep an eye out for your name in my contracts."

"You'd better," I say, feeling happy.

Philip tilts his head slightly down. A part of me feels curious of what might happen if I tilt my head a little bit closer to his, but another feels anxious. But my nerves get the best of me, forcing me to take a step back.

"Good night, Selene."

CHAPTER FOURTEEN

Selene

"I never really liked Mark. I told you there was something off with him," Miriam says as soon as I am done filling her in on the drama from last night.

"You sound like my mom," I say, chewing on some food while scrolling through the work emails that have piled up.

"Good. She always has the best advice," Miriam replies. I hear her talking some more, but my brain disconnects from her words when I see an email standing out from the rest. "Are you even listening to me?"

"No," I admit, my heart racing in anticipation.

Miriam leans in to get a peak of the screen and her reaction mirrors my own. "Oh my god," she mumbles when she sees the screen.

HAMMER TIME

"Are we reading the same thing?" I ask.

```
Dear Ms. Soldado,
The help you offered us in Silverstone has not
been overlooked. The launch was an extreme success
following your suggestions.
We would like to invite you this weekend to Italy
and use the time to come to a possible work
arrangement with you.
Let us know if you are available to join us. If
so, we will arrange tickets and accommodation for
the trip.
Best,
Sarah Parker
```

"Are you reading this?" I ask, perplexed.

Miriam nods, then grins, and a scream escapes her lips.

"I'm not dreaming," I say, still in disbelief.

"You need to reply," she instructs.

I don't want to get too excited. I can read between the lines of the email. They're not offering me a job, but the possibility of finding something for me. Which means I did a good enough job in Silverstone for them to want me around, but still not good enough to have a fixed position. And still, this is a success in my book.

Dreams come true when you fight for them, and I've been fighting for a chance like this all my life.

I type my answer and reread everything, searching for any typos before I press the send button, knowing that one or maybe ten will magically appear the moment it leaves my drafts.

"I'm shaking." I lift my hand toward Miriam to show her how shaky it is. There are no thoughts in my mind, only an overwhelming feeling of happiness.

"Let me open a bottle of champagne. This calls for a small celebration."

"Should we do that? What if we jinx it?"

"Let's just drink to us. We can toast to the future." Miriam goes straight to the fridge to grab a bottle of the cheap champagne we always have at home for any girl's night or special occasions. Live is always better when you have champagne.

I stand up and grab glasses from the cabinet and Miriam loses no time pouring the drinks.

"Cheers to us."

"Do you think you'll see Philip?" I almost choke on the alcohol, caught by surprise at the sudden mention of Philip.

"Why would you ask that?" I say.

"It's Monza, and he's like the King of Cavaglio. It would make sense for him to be around," Miriam says. "And considering that you came home in his car last night, it would only make sense for me to ask. Did you think only the neighbors would hear that engine? I want answers, and I want them now."

"How the hell—" I cut off.

"I was up working late, and I heard the car, so I went to the balcony, and guess who I saw. None other than Philip… with you." She points at me with an accusing finger. "So much for claiming to dislike him. Now, now, time to come clean." She raises her brow and crosses her arms over her chest.

"Well," I start, not sure what to say. "He was there when all the Mark drama happened."

"Wait, what?"

"Yeah, he was at the restaurant, and when Mark followed me outside, he came and helped me, called security and all of that." I can feel my body quiver, remembering the events of last night. "Then we grabbed some food and he drove me home. End of story."

"Well, you definitely were cozying up with that good night kiss." Miriam laughs, and I can feel my face turning the brightest shade of red.

"You are shameless. It was just a goodbye kiss." Suddenly, self-doubt fills my head, was it really just a good night kiss? Do I want it to be more than just that? "Do you think he had anything to do with this email?"

Why am I always like this? Why do I have to think about things a million times instead of enjoying the moment. It's ridiculous. Philip doesn't like me; in fact, he wants me as far away from him as humanly possible.

And still, yesterday he took care of me…

RHAE AEDEN

But no, he can't have had anything to do with this. He can't. What would I do if he had gotten me a job? The road is one of the things that matters most for me. I want to get this job for being brilliant and excellent, not because someone with good connections asked for it.

"Don't think like that. You are good enough, and they know it. You don't need a Philip Burton to make you shine. You are Selene Soldado, you shine with your own light."

"I have worked so hard, the last thing I want is to achieve my dreams just because of him."

"You impressed them before you met Philip. These are the consequences of your own actions. Plus, he kind of hates you. Although, what happened last night is going into our history books."

"Ouch…"

"I'm just telling the truth. Does he still call you Sparks?" I want to wipe that smug satisfaction off Miriam's face, but I know she wouldn't be my best friend if she didn't tease me half the time.

"He does," I confirm.

"Well, there's nothing to worry about. And, if there is, we'll deal with it later. Don't jump the gun, *Sparks*," she says, winking at me, and I burst into laughter.

"Why do you always have to be right?" I sigh because she's usually spot-on, and I can't imagine a world where I couldn't share my life and problems with Miriam.

"Because I'm a wise woman. You should know that by now, little grasshopper."

"Whatever." I roll my eyes and take a sip of my drink.

Later that night, when I'm alone in bed, staring at the ceiling and trying to fall asleep, all I can think of is a wild mane of dark hair and precious ocean-blue eyes that seem to pierce the deepest part of my soul. I attempt to shake Philip's image from my mind, but it's impossible.

He's all-consuming.

CHATER FIFTEEN

Selene

I land in Milan on Friday, excited for the weekend ahead of me. I make it to the hotel Cavaglio has booked. It's an extraordinary place situated right next to the Duomo. As soon as I'm checked-in, I decide to take a shower and put on my blue two-piece suit to go out in search of some adventure in the streets of Italy.

Just like any other tourist, I'm utterly captivated by the city's beauty, constantly turning my head in all directions to take in the breathtaking architecture. I have been here before, but the streets and the people never cease to amaze me. However, Milan is more crowded than usual today. It's almost impossible to move in the streets without bumping into tourists. The city is already preparing for the race weekend and also for the event taking place today at the Duomo.

HAMMER TIME

Some early birds, in Cavaglio colors, are already staking out the best spots to witness the spectacle. I check the time; it's only half-past three, and the event kicks off around five, so I've got time for a coffee.

I walk down the street, following the same path I took to come here until I spot a small coffee place that isn't as full as the others. "Un latte macchiato, per favore," I request, fully expecting the customary glare that a tourist receives after committing an offense as big as ordering a Latte Macchiato at noon.

"Non ho sentito bene. Cosa vuoi?" *I didn't understand you well. What do you want?* The waiter asks, perplexed at the fact that a possible fellow Italian wants this kind of coffee.

"Hai sentito bene, voglio un latte macciato, per favore." *You understood it right. I want a latte macchiato, please.* I tell the guy, whose eyebrows are high on his forehead.

"Disgrazia," the waiter curses as he turns around to put in my order. I make sure to leave him a nice tip before leaving the bar.

With my coffee in hand, I stroll back to the Duomo, and when I see a dark-blue billboard in the middle of the street, Philip makes it into my mind again. It's always his eyes that I envision when I think of him.

What am I even thinking?

Sure, he is a handsome man, a complicated one too. There's so much hidden about him, so much that nobody knows. That's probably a good enough reason to stay away from him. It's impossible to know a man who will never open up to anyone. I don't even think Michael knows everything about Philip, and he's probably the closest thing Philip has to a friend.

My phone vibrates in my pocket, and I fish it out to see the notification, but what catches my attention is the time displayed on the top of the screen, ten minutes to four.

"Damn it!" I curse to myself, stuffing the phone back in my pocket, ready to run through the city as fast as I can while holding my coffee as far away from my suit as possible to avoid any spills.

By some miracle I make it to the location three minutes early, but I am completely out of breath. I take a moment for myself while I look for the entrance. Finally, I spot a security guard stationed in front of some backstage setup, so I approach him.

"Hi! I'm looking for Sarah Parker. She has my pass and is waiting for me inside."

The guy gives me a scrutinizing look as he scans me from head to toe, probably trying to determine if I'm another crazed fan or if I'm telling the truth.

"My name is Selene Soldado," I continue.

"She's with me," I hear a voice behind me and turn around to find Michael in a white T-shirt that works wonders for his figure. I haven't seen him in a while, but his infectious positivity hasn't changed a bit.

"Michael!" I exclaim with joy at seeing a familiar face.

"She was asking for Sarah," the security guard says.

"Sarah invited her, but I also know Selene," Michael explains. "I'll take her to Sarah."

"Sure," the security guard mutters, scratching his neck.

Michael just strides past me, gesturing to follow him.

"Thanks for that," I tell him once we're alone.

"Not a problem. I was thrilled when Sarah mentioned she was going to ask you to join us on Monday." He starts walking ahead of me, clearly in a hurry, probably to get to wherever Philip is.

"On Monday?" I ask, adding the pieces of the puzzle together. I saw Philip on Wednesday. If Michael is right, he couldn't have had anything to do with me being here if she had already decided to ask me before my encounter with him.

"Yeah, she's been trying to get you hired since Silverstone, but HR has been reluctant since all positions for the season are already filled." Well, that's not exactly encouraging.

"I appreciate the effort." My face betrays me, and my lips form the thinnest of lines as disappointment washes over me.

Luckily, he doesn't seem to notice.

"It's what you deserve after everything you've done."

"It was really nothing." I wave him off. "What exactly is the plan for today?"

"Oh, you're going to both love and hate it." He looks in my direction, a mischievous glint in his hazel eyes.

"Sorry, what?"

"Come over here, you'll see." He leads us to an elevated area right in front of the Duomo from where we can view the entire piazza. At that moment, a Formula One car, one I know all too well, zooms past, leaving a trail of smoke in its wake.

Philip

I speed through the piazza, pushing my car to the limit, which, considering the car I'm in, isn't all that fast, but it'll have to do.

"Ready for party mode," the engineer says with an eager tone coating his voice. That's our code, signaling that I can do some tricks now. It's funny how today of all days I don't feel like a monkey in a circus. I'm genuinely enjoying the car.

"Let's give the fans some smoke."

I rev up the power, lock the steering wheel, and push the throttle, ready to spin the car and do some donuts. The fans *love* donuts. I relish the feeling of spinning around. I can hear the crowds outside the car roaring, almost as loudly as the engine beneath me. I stick my hands out of the cockpit while the car keeps spinning, making the shaka, which drives them even wilder. I continue driving around, speeding and pushing the car to its limits. I only stop when I'm ordered to throught the radio.

I bring the car to the front of the Duomo and park it just as Sarah had asked so that the press could have their picture-perfect photo. I take off the steering wheel as I exit the car, standing on top of it and waving my hands to the fans, feeling almost as if I won a Grand Prix.

I jump from the top of the car, my feet hitting the ground, and then jog alongside the barriers, shaking hands with fans. I exchange greetings and sign autographs. It feels nice to have all these people here for me, cheering instead of booing.

I feel almost happy, but then the realization hits me that Jessica probably has me booked with the press. My good mood vanishes before it can fully settle in, and discomfort rules my body. Thankfully, my helmet is still on, hiding the change in my expression from the fans. I continue shaking hands and signing autographs, but I don't stop to take pictures with them anymore. The crowd is buzzing with excitement, but I'm not. Everyone is trying to touch me, throwing things at me.

It feels like too much.

"Philip! Philip! Philip!"

The chants of my name echo in my ears. I step back from the fence to avoid their touch, but they keep extending their hands, demanding more. I start walking away, my steps picking up pace, but their screams grow louder, making me feel more anxious.

I only remove my helmet when I find a private spot behind the stage, away from the view of the fans. Jessica is already there, waiting for me with her ponytail neatly tied up and a wicked smile on her face. I can see her lips moving, but I'm not really listening to her. All I hear is a piercing ringing in my ears.

The world starts to spin, and my vision blurs.

"Are you okay?" she asks. "You look a bit pale."

If looks could kill, the one I just gave her should have done so. "Call Michael," I instruct, attempting to follow some breathing techniques and stay calm.

For once Jessica follows the instructions and runs off, looking for my coach. Michael makes it to me quickly, thankfully without a ponytail following him.

He kneels beside me on the floor, urging me to breathe. I am not really conscious of his words. Instead, I focus on his hand gestures, going up and down indicating for me to breath in and out.

Eventually, my breath steadies and my mind calms.

"Panic attack?" he asks after a while.

I nod, unable to form any words.

"You don't want to do the press?"

"It's this whole circus that I don't want," I mutter, regaining my composure.

"Bullshit." Michael playfully jabs me in the shoulder. There always seems to be something new with me. No matter how hard I work on myself, how many therapy sessions I attend, there is something new that makes me doubt myself and sends me into a new spiral. "Say what you want, but you're only lying to yourself," Michael continues.

"And what beautiful lies I tell." Michael hands me some water, and I take a moment to enjoy its coldness inside my mouth. I can't even explain what triggered this panic attack…

Well, that's not true; it was the crowd, their neediness, their expectations. They wanted me today, but how long until they hate me again?

"That you do," a female voice chimes in, approaching us.

"Go away, Jessica," I snap, not wanting her near me.

"Good thing I'm not Jessica," Selene says, kneeling next to Michael. "Quieres vomitar?" *Do you need to throw up?* She asks in Spanish.

If anyone else had asked the same question, I might have verbally attacked them, or maybe even physically. But I can see the concern in her green eyes, and the fact that she chose to ask it in Spanish shows that she is a discreet person. She's trustworthy, though I already knew that, even if I won't admit it to her. She was right when she said she could have told the tabloids about finding me in the bathroom that day in Silverstone, but she never did.

I chug my water until it's empty, then give Michael a loaded look. "Can you bring me some more?" I ask, hoping he'll get the message. He does. "What are you doing here, Sparks?"

"I was in the neighborhood and thought I'd come annoy you for a bit," Selene says, tilting her head and scanning my body as if searching for any injuries. *Is she worried about me?*

"Mission accomplished. I guess it's your presence that makes me feel sick," I tease, recalling our second encounter.

"If I recall correctly, I was nowhere to be seen last time. But I'll go if my presence makes you feel that way." She begins to stand up, and I instinctively grab her wrist. Her gaze goes straight to where my hand touches hers and then her green eyes lock onto mine.

"Don't. Stay."

"If I didn't know better, I'd say you like me," she teases. I can work with that. I can work with anything if it means she stays for now, even if that makes me a selfish asshole.

"I never said I disliked you. I tolerate you," I lie.

"That works for me." She settles beside me on the floor, her back against the wall, and my hand still on her wrist. I am not sure if it bothers her, but she doesn't complain, so I decide to leave it there for now.

"What was it this time?"

"What do you mean?" I feign ignorance, but nothing escapes her.

"You know exactly what I mean," Selene says bluntly. It's astonishing how she always tries to extract answers from me. Only Michael has ever done that.

"Maybe I don't want to talk about it." I rarely indulge others when they try to get answers from me, especially if they are the kind of answers that involve me to talk about what goes on inside my head. But with her, I'm tempted to give her pieces of the puzzle. Maybe it's because until now she hasn't attempted to judge me.

"So, you're not just a pro at dodging cars but also things that make you uncomfortable." The sarcasm in her voice doesn't escape me.

"Who says I'm uncomfortable?" She looks at me, her dark brows furrowing, then offers me a smile that leads to both of us bursting into uncontrollable laughter. "I can't remember the last time fans cheered for me."

Selene looks at me with a sad expression.

"Is it really a bad thing that they are doing it now? And how will you feel if they continue to do so next season when you start racing again?"

"Are you psychoanalyzing me?"

"According to you, I only have a degree in economics and a master's in marketing. I could never do that." She uses my own words against me, and there's something especially painful about it, but I like this kind of pain.

"You're smart enough to do that without a piece of paper saying you can." It's the truth. I know she's capable.

"Okay, now I really am worried about you." She looks at me with a hint of concern. "That's the closest you've ever come to giving me a compliment." She laughs wholeheartedly.

"That's not true. But if it were, then it would be a good thing I complimented your brains before your looks," I can't help but tease. "However, I've already told you that you have pretty lips."

And damn, those lips... The things I'd do to her mouth.

I notice her cheeks flushing with the cutest shade of red, and I can't help but wonder what shade of red they turn in the privacy of the night, when the lights are out.

"I think I'll take the compliment about my intelligence." Selene looks away from me for the first time since her arrival, attempting to hide her blush.

I gently lift her chin with my hand, forcing her to meet my gaze. "You shouldn't be afraid of your beauty," I whisper.

She's incredibly young, which naturally comes with a certain level of vanity, but it's saddening to think that maybe she can't see herself the way the rest of the world does. She's amazing, every single aspect of her.

"Who says I am?" she retorts with a tone of defiance. That's what she does, contradicts and challenges me whenever she gets the chance.

"Here's the water!" Michael shouts from the end of the corridor, rushing in our direction. "Sorry, I had to search everywhere." I guess he didn't understand my look, after all.

"That's my cue." Selene attempts to get up, and I realize my hand is still around her wrist. It's time to let go. "I'll see you guys around. Don't overthink it. Enjoy the butterflies, and learn to savor the nerves," she whispers before planting a kiss on my cheek.

I grasp her neck, not wanting to release her.

"I hope to see your signature soon, Sparks."

She only chuckles in response, doing something incomprehensible to me.

When she finally leaves, Michael shoots me a knowing look. "Not a word," I warn.

CHAPTER SIXTEEN

Selene

My heart has been pounding ever since I woke up. The morning routine is a breeze: wash my face, brush my teeth, apply some makeup, tame the unruly copper waves, and get dressed in another two-piece suit, this time a black one, that I decided to pair with a yellow top. My morning routine is a breeze: wash my face, brush my teeth, apply some makeup, tame the unruly copper waves, and get dressed in another two-piece suit. I choose a black one this time, pairing it with a yellow top.

I decided to rent a motorcycle yesterday to avoid the traffic, and just as the GPS predicted, I make it to the track in twenty minutes. The pass I have been given for the weekend makes my life so much easier, allowing me to bypass the long queues.

HAMMER TIME

The track is crowded. Drivers and staff are all over the place, some heading to interviews while others rush to the garage, making sure everything is perfect before qualifying today. Ahead of me, I spot João, the Brazilian driver who had the accident in Silverstone. He recovered remarkably quickly to fight for his seat on the team next year. However, Munguia's stellar performances have made the decision far from simple.

Who would Philip prefer as a teammate?

I would think João is the perfect candidate. He's one of the youngest drivers, giving him more years to compete in the sport, but lately, the decision doesn't seem as straightforward. You need a clear number one in a team, that's one of the problems Cavaglio encountered this season, and having João compete with Philip might cause problems. One is young and ready to win his first championship, the other wants to keep adding records to his career.

"Are you going to a funeral?"

I'm torn out of my thoughts only to see Jessica in front of me.

"Nice to see you again." I force myself to smile, but my tone is sharper than usual. I don't know why, but I can't read her like I do other people, and her obsession with Philip makes me uncomfortable. I am pretty sure that Philip likely shares my sentiments, given the edge in his voice whenever he mentions her name or how he reacted when I asked him about her.

"I wish I could say the same, but I have to do damage control thanks to you," she says, pointing at me with an extraordinarily long, gelled nail, almost poking my chest.

"Excuse me?" I ask, taking a step back.

"Don't play dumb. It's all over the news." She tosses her phone in my face. I remove my sunglasses to scan the screen.

"Dammit." The curse slips out involuntarily.

"Yes. Dammit!" she continues in an infuriating tone, but I'm not listening to her. All I see are tabloid photos of me and Philip, beneath the headline in bright colors: 'NEW WAG ALERT.'

I recognize one of the pictures from Silverstone, where I had my hands on his helmet. But then there's another from Monaco from earlier in the week when we were in his car, and another from yesterday when we were sitting on the floor.

"You can't even imagine the headache this is giving me. Why is he even dating you? It's not as if you were pretty, skinny, or someone important to make up for your lack of good looks," she starts ranting, but I can't even muster the energy to be bothered by her attempt to insult me. I'm more concerned with what to do with these pictures. "Why is he dating you?" She almost screams.

"We're not dating," I correct her. "We met in Silverstone and crossed paths two times since."

I hand her the phone before putting my shades back on, trying to come up with a plan to do the damage control she's clearly incapable of. Jessica is more concerned about her client's personal life than the task at hand.

"If I were you, I'd be more interested in figuring out who's following your client rather than who he's dating. If you'll excuse me, I have to find Sarah now."

I don't give her a chance to say anything else as I walk away, only one thought in my mind: I need to fix this.

What if the team thinks I'm not a good choice to hire after these photos?

What if people assume I'm only here because I'm dating a driver?

I'm not even dating a driver!

I rush through the paddock, trying to escape my own thoughts, but the images keep haunting me. Almost running, I make it there in a couple of minutes, only to stop abruptly in front of the Cavaglio Nero motorhomes. I try to clear my head while taking in the sight of the massive motorhomes. This is where I belong. Nothing can stop me. Everything is going to be okay.

Taking a deep breath, I step towards the facilities and press my identification card to the reader on the side of door. As soon I step inside of the building, the receptionist points me in the direction of Sarah's office, telling me she's waiting for me. I walk through the corridors, navigating through the waves of employees who are rushing to get things ready.

Finally, I make it to the office. Usually, Sarah's curly blonde hair is the first thing I notice when I see her, but today, it's her big, warm, motherly smile that grabs my attention, showcasing her perfect white teeth. Her smile is exactly what I need after the news I just received.

"Hello there, darling." She stands up from the other side of her crystal-clear desk and welcomes me with open arms. I really need that right now, to feel like at least someone is in my corner. "I see you're eager to wear the team's colors," Sarah observes, eyeing me up and down after our embrace. "Spoiler alert: it gets boring after a while."

"It's good to see you too, Sarah." I sigh, still managing to smile through the million thoughts racing through my mind.

Does she already know?

"Please, have a seat. Do you want some water, coffee?"

"I'd appreciate some water, please."

Sarah retrieves two bottles from a small fridge in the corner of her office. "I wish we were meeting under better circumstances."

"Sarah," I start. "I'm so sorry about that. There's nothing going on between Philip and me," I start babbling, unable to bite my tongue. But I quickly realize my mistake when her eyes go wide at what just escaped my mouth.

"Excuse me?" Her surprised question confirms my suspicion.

I fucked up.

"There are pictures of Philip and me going viral," I confess, feeling ashamed, unable to meet her gaze. "Some tabloids are labeling me as his new girlfriend."

"Oh." She puts on her glasses and types something on her keyboard. I can see pictures of myself being reflected in her glasses. My face turns pale while she scrolls through the internet, assessing the situation. "Are you dating him?"

"No, not at all. We've met twice since Silverstone, and both times were a coincidence. Nothing has happened, and nothing will," I state.

"It's none of our concern what the drivers do in their free time or who they date, as long as they're not bad people. There's also no strict policy about employees dating each other in this line of work, and technically, you're not employed by us," she says, studying me carefully. "But I wouldn't recommend starting a relationship with *that* driver. Philip is great, but he needs to learn how to deal with his fury and his trust issues before he starts a serious relationship. And let's not forget about the fifteen-year age gap between the two of you."

"Give or take," I correct her.

"What you do in your private lives is your own business. But I like you, so my advice is to stay away from him," she says bluntly. "He's trouble, the kind that is emotionally unavailable."

Her harsh words hit me personally, even though they're aimed at Philip. A part of me yearns to protect him from the way she thinks about him.

The man has trust issues, anxiety too, but that doesn't mean he's a bad person. It means he needs therapy, which is nothing to be ashamed of because everyone needs help at some point. That's a part of life when you have a mental illness or things like trust issues, and there is nothing wrong with getting it.

"With that said, let's move on to our work matter."

I sigh in relief, eager to move on from Philip and focus on what really matters to me. If everything goes right, I might leave this weekend with a working contract under my belt.

"I was intrigued by your email, and I'm ready to listen to whatever you have in mind," I reply.

"We won't employ you." Her statement feels like she dumped a bucket of cold water on me. "However, we'd like to collaborate with you. We don't have any available positions at the moment, but we'd like to offer you something."

"I'm all ears," I say, pushing away the disappointment.

"We'd like to hire you but in a freelance capacity," she explains, and things instantly start to make sense.

"What would that entail?" I ask, even when my brain is already reading between the lines. They want me, but they can't have me right now, so they're ensuring I won't work for their competition by giving me this opportunity.

"Think of it as 'we'd like to have you around until we have a permanent position.' How does that sound?" Sarah asks.

"I'm interested," I answer sincerely, not feeling the need to play a game of poker with her. I appreciate transparency, and she probably does too. "What exactly would you require me to do?"

"We'd ask you to assist us during certain campaigns, and perhaps Jessica can work with you." she says, and I flinch at the mention of her name before she adds, "as well as provide some consulting services, similar to Silverstone."

"That's a lot to think about. I'd like to take the weekend to consider it." Because this feels like a significant step. If I accept their offer, I won't be able to join other teams for a while. It can only be Cavaglio for me.

"I expected that. It's a big commitment and decision, and you are no fool, Selene. Enjoy the race weekend and come back to me during the week."

"Sounds like a plan." We both stand up from our chairs and shake hands.

F1 2023 DRIVER LINE-UP

PHILIP BURTON
OLIVER MUNSUTA

JOÃO QUERINHO
NANDO FERNAN

LAWSON SROLLER
MARCUS VERSTEEG

EMI SAITO
ALEX SAUD

CHAPTER SEVENTEEN

SIX MONTHS LATER - BARCELONA TESTING

I glance out of the plane window, relishing the silence and calmness on my flight to Barcelona. Summer has rushed by, with a few events sprinkled here and there as part of my team obligations. Before I knew it, winter was upon us, marking the end of the season, and the beginning of the new one. I still have some time for training and getting two hundred percent ready for the season.

One hundred is overrated, I need more. I crave more.

Car testing in Barcelona is just two weeks away, which means I need to put in as many hours in the simulator as possible to outperform my new teammate, Oliver Munguia.

For the past months Selene has been a persistent presence in my thoughts. I have spotted her at the team's headquarters a couple of times since our last encounter. She was working as some kind of consultant – I think –, gradually making her mark in the world.

I am happy for her, but I have made it a point to keep my distance. She has the potential to be a distraction I don't need.

"Sir, we'll be landing in fifteen minutes," the stewardess informs me, touching my arm a bit too friendly. I take a moment to take her in: platinum blonde hair, thick fake lashes, brown eyes, and lips painted in a shade of red lipstick that guarantees to leave its mark wherever it touches.

I grin at her, allowing her to see how my eyes travel over her curves. "Thanks. Hopefully, you'll have some time to relax after this flight instead of overworking yourself."

The woman smirks at me, letting me know that whatever my proposal is, she's in for the fun ride.

Game on.

Barcelona is a paradise. Anything can happen during the first sessions of testing before the season starts mid-March. Testing stands as one of the most anticipated dates on the calendar. It's when everyone gets a glimpse into what the other teams have been cooking up during the winter break:

Who has found the gray areas in the regulations?

Who has elevated their car into new heights?

Who is bringing innovations?

Everything is possible, and all ten teams will have a couple of sessions to find out who got it right and who failed miserably. There will be a total of three days, divided into morning and afternoon sessions, for us to figure everything out and then go back to the factory to improve everything again.

Cavaglio has decided to split our driving sessions evenly. Oliver takes the morning while I claim the afternoons. Thankfully, the press was preoccupied this morning, busy ogling the shiny new cars, leaving me to enjoy a day free from their probing questions. Although I know it's just a temporary break, they will come back eventually.

For now, the agreement stands that when one of us is driving, the other has to spend quality time with the press and the rest of the circus. But, right now, it's my time to shine and enjoy the car for the first time.

I'm already in the car, surrounded by the staff. One of my racing engineers is showing me the engine mapping, which is basically a set of instructions for how the engine should work during a race. As a driver, I don't make any changes directly, but I have always loved the data and things that help me be more efficient during a drive.

Then, we review the strategy for today, what exactly we want to test in the car, which tires we want to use, and so on.

Once everything is in place, a mechanic dressed in black and yellow, standing outside the garage, right in front of my car, gives me a thumbs up. I lose no time and make my exit, cruising through the pit lane at precisely eighty kilometers per hour.

"Radio check," the familiar voice of my racing engineer crackles over the radio.

"Check," I respond.

"Go easy on the tires and monitor their degradation. Let us know how the car feels after a couple of laps and give us any important remarks when you are back in the garage."

"Copy."

For the first few laps, I obey my engineer's instructions and drive smoothly, reveling in the feel of the car beneath me. The simulator sessions give you a pretty close feeling to how everything works, but nothing beats the real deal, how the car glides through the corners, the way the engine roars underneath me. I can feel everything working like clockwork machinery.

"Option A or D for the next laps?" I inquire. We have to be cautious with our radio exchanges, as they're shared across all teams. We know we have a competitive car, but the question is whether we want to flaunt our prowess or play a game of smoke and mirrors to keep our rivals guessing.

"Option A, for ten laps."

I push the throttle, increasing the speed, not wasting any time. The Barcelona straight is exhilarating, and I can feel the wind's force over my helmet. The aerodynamics of the car have changed since my last race. Some argue it's for the worse, but I can tell that it's a positive difference.

A few laps later, the radio crackles to life once more.

"Can you go faster? Question."

"Yes," I respond with determination.

"Okay, box first. We'll try a different compound."

I steer the car into the pit lane where the crew is already waiting with softer tires for a pit stop. They treat it as a training exercise, changing everything within seconds, as if it were in a real race. It takes me two laps to warm up the new tires. As soon I see the start line, I start pushing as if I was racing against the whole grid instead of doing some training.

Back at the beginning of the circuit, I navigate the first two corners with precision, pushing the car to its limits, perhaps even too much, but I want to find its every flaw so that we can work on them before the season begins.

Determination courses my veins. One thing is certain. I'm going to fight for the world championship trophy this season.

I keep pushing the car, but I sense something is wrong before I make it into the fourth corner. The car loses grip on the front right tire, and my heart races even faster than before, realizing what's happening.

The are no clouds in the sky, something I can't help but focus on as my car flips itself upside down over and over. Strapped into the cockpit, I can't do anything but cling to my steering wheel. Adrenaline courses through my veins as my car flies across the track. Eventually, everything stops spinning as my car settles on the hard gravel, but the momentum of the crash pushes it straight into the barriers.

RHAE AEDEN

For a moment, I see nothing but darkness, and I fear I've lost consciousness. A piercing buzz invades my ears, and gradually, the world blurs into view, and my breath comes out in heavy pants.

"Philip, are you okay?" I hear the concern in my engineer's voice, but I can't muster a response. There are no coherent thoughts in my mind.

Except one.

"I need to get out," I manage to blurt out after an eternity.

Only now do I realize my car has landed on its side, and a wave of claustrophobia envelops me. My body still trembles with adrenaline and fear as I struggle to release the seatbelts. It takes longer than usual, as I'm falling to my side, but I finally unlock them, tumbling out of the car.

Once outside, I bend over, hands on my knees.

The world darkens, spinning more and more, and there's nothing I can do to stop it. I feel my head hitting the ground.

Is this what dying feels like?

CHAPTER EIGHTEEN

Selene

The past few months have been a rollercoaster, with some challenging experiences. While I've been involved in a few projects for Cavaglio as a freelancer throughout the season, they haven't required my physical presence at the office or at the track yet. It's something I despise. I yearn to be where the action is, more than just a name hidden behind an email signature.

Life has been hectic, so I decided to spend a few days in Madrid with my parents around the time when pre-season testing was scheduled. Deep inside, I was hoping that by some miracle they would call me to come in and work on some last-minute project. However, reality is far from expectation. The Barcelona tests have concluded, and I'm still at my parents' house, with no opportunity of seeing the Cavaglio team any time soon.

On Wednesday, I sit on the couch, scrolling on my laptop and reading articles about Philip's crash. It's impossible to take my eyes off the footage of the accident. It's nothing short of a miracle that he managed to get out of the car himself after flying in the air and crashing right into the wall. The image of the car, resting on its side and crumpled against the safety wall, turns my stomach.

Dad leans over from behind the couch, peering at the screen. "Have you seen the headlines?" he asks.

"Which ones? There are many."

"The ones claiming he's finished before even starting, and the ones suggesting he was never talented enough to win a championship." Philip has always been one of dad's favorites. I remember my father defending him during dinners with friends when I was younger. Philip might not be my hero, but he was his.

"He must be furious. It's so unfair. It wasn't even his fault that the tire wasn't properly adjusted. It has nothing to do with his talent!" I respond, my irritation surfacing more than it should. I hate how strongly I feel about him sometimes.

"Someone's definitely upset about it." Dad smirks, raising an eyebrow at me. "Have you been in touch with him?"

"Not you too." I roll my eyes and let out a sigh. "I've already told you that those pictures were taken out of context. I don't even have his phone number."

HAMMER TIME

"Of course, cariño, whatever you say," Dad replies. He leans down and plants a kiss on my head. "When are you heading back to Monaco?" he asks, shifting the topic.

"Tomorrow afternoon. Miriam is driving up from Seville. We've decided to take a little detour and spend some time in Barcelona before returning to Monaco."

A short vacation before diving back into reality.

"That sounds like fun. I don't think I tell you nearly enough how proud I am of you, Selene." His words warm my heart, a reminder of how fortunate I am to have him in my life.

"I know you are, Dad. I love you."

"I love you too, corazón."

Miriam picks me up from Madrid as planned, and together we drive up to Barcelona, arriving just as the sun is setting. Streetlights make it seem as if it's the middle of the day when we leave the hotel in search of an adventure. Miriam walks a few steps ahead of me, twirling on her feet with a radiant glow about her.

"I love Barcelona," she says with a dreamy tone.

I catch up to her and grab her by the waist, hugging her tightly before planting a kiss on her cheek.

"I love seeing you happy and taking some time off. You've been working way too hard lately."

"We should go clubbing tonight," she says, and I release her instantly, letting out a groan, never one for parties.

"The things I do for love," I mutter, wanting to make her happy. "I assume you've already found a club?"

Miriam doesn't miss a beat and shows me a rooftop bar in the city center on her phone. "I did my homework. It's popular, but not too wild, and the music seems promising."

It's then that I notice Miriam has more makeup on than usual, and she's dressed only in an oversized black blazer, paired with stockings and high platform boots. I look down at myself and feel a tad insecure about my outfit, which isn't necessarily screaming 'party girl.'

"I've got something for you," she says, reading my mind. Miriam pulls a white blazer and a golden choker with matching earrings from her tote bag. "Are you wearing a white bra?"

"Yes?" I reply.

"Perfect! Follow me."

Miriam grins, excited about the promise of a night out. She grabs my wrist and pulls us inside a slightly crowded bar, making her way through the people to get to the bathroom.

"Put this on." She hands me the blazer and I get inside the stall, following her instructions. "Leave your bra peeking out a bit," she adds.

It takes me a couple of seconds to undress and put on the blazer, which is a bit bigger than intended for me, yet I like the look it creates. I unbutton the blazer to showcase a bit more cleavage. As soon as I leave the stall, my attention drifts to my reflection above the sink. I smile, feeling confident.

Miriam elbows me, excited and happy.

It's still early, so we order drinks at the same bar – negronis, and a mysterious sweet concoction I can't quite identify. An hour passes, and I'm feeling pleasantly tipsy.

"Let's head to the club!" Miriam shouts over the music.

We pay for our tab and practically run through the streets, stumbling over our own feet, laughing uncontrollably, and relishing the quality time.

The club is bursting when we finally make it there. We grab another drink and head onto the dance floor. I let go of my inhibitions, enjoying the night out in a city where I can be whoever I want. No one is going to recognize me or take a picture of me here. We sing, scream, laugh, and dance, losing ourselves in the music. It's precisely what we needed – a night of carefree fun.

I close my eyes for a few moments, soaking in the pulsating beats of the music. Minutes pass, and I enter a trance-like state. When I reopen them, I spot Miriam kissing a petite blonde girl right next to me. A smile spreads across my face, and I can't help but wish I could find someone to enjoy the night with as well.

Miriam opens her eyes, probably sensing my gaze on her.

"I'm going to bar!" I scream over the music, trying to give the girls some privacy. Miriam gives me a thumbs up and then she goes back to kissing her new lady friend.

At the bar, I settle down on the last free stool. I'm starting to feel tired, but the night is young. The menu in front of me displays a variety of cocktails and drinks that capture my attention. I am ready to order one of them when I notice someone approaching me from the side.

"Someone wanted to get these for you, miss," a waiter says, gesturing to glass of champagne and a bottle of water.

"I'm sorry, what?"

"These drinks are for you," he repeats.

"For me?" I echo, skeptic.

"Yes," he responds, impatience creeping into his tone.

"From whom?" I inquire, untrusty of whichever creep decided to send these drinks in my direction. It's not uncommon to spike girls' drinks and I am smarter than to take drinks from a stranger.

"The guy over there," he says and with his free hand points towards the VIP area.

Across the room, a blonde girl in a glittery golden dress sits on top of a man dressed entirely in black. I can see him nursing a glass containing some mysterious dark liquid. My gaze continues to travel up the man's body only to find the most beautiful shade of deep blue eyes I have ever seen staring back at me.

Philip motherfucking Burton.

CHAPTER NINTEEN

Philip

A wave of emotions courses through Selene's face; surprise, distrust, fear, astonishment, disgust, and finally hatred. She takes the glass with the bubbly drink from the man's tray and walks towards me, her white blazer riding up her legs distracts me for a second from the expression of fury and determination on her face. Suddenly, I catch Sofia shifting on my lap, a reminder that she's been here this whole time. No wonder Selene is looking at me as if she could rip my head off of my shoulders.

Am I really that drunk to forget someone is sitting on my lap?

"Should you be getting shit faced like that, or is that just your regular face now, Philip?" Selene says, anger lacing her voice.

It's been months since I last saw her, and even though this situation isn't exactly what I envisioned happening when I sent the drink her way, I'm still happy about the sparring session that's building up.

"Ouch, you hurt my feelings, Sparks," I quip, placing my free hand over my heart in a theatrical gesture.

"You don't have feelings, or a heart."

"And who are you?" Sofia interjects with disdain.

"His biggest nightmare," Selene answers, glaring at me.

"Then better go away. Do not upset him."

I have to bite my tongue to avoid saying she's the one disturbing here, but I enjoy watching Selene's anger and feeling like part of that might be jealousy.

"I would, but I wanted to tell your boyfriend that he can keep his drinks to himself, or even better, buy them for his new girlfriend," Selene says.

"Excuse me?" Sofia leaves my lap only to stand in front of Selene. Sophia is way taller, towering almost a head over Sparks. But I know Selene doesn't easily get intimidated.

I stand on my feet as quickly as my drunken state allows, attempting to intervene when I sense the tension and notice Sofia's intention to slam her hand on Selene's face. But Selene beats me to it. She raises her hand in the air and grabs Sofia's wrist before it lands on her face.

"Don't you dare put a finger on me," Selene says.

"Philip, do something!" Sofia pleads like a petulant child.

"Security," I call out to the nearest guard. "Please escort this woman out," I instruct him, casting a stern look in Sofia's direction.

"What? You've got to be kidding me! You can't do this!" she yells as the security guard firmly ushers her away, leaving me alone with Selene.

Selene starts to walk away, but I seize her wrist, pivoting her around before she can leave. It happens too quickly, nearly causing her to trip, but she avoids the fall by placing her hands on my chest. Our proximity is uncomfortably close, and I can't help but take a deep, intoxicating breath, inhaling her tormenting perfume.

She always smells so damn good.

"Let go of me, Philip."

"Going so early?" I ask.

"I don't appreciate being put between you and your girlfriend. Now let go," she insists, her arm rigid, yet she doesn't struggle against my grip.

"Are you jealous, Sparks?" I release her wrist slightly, not wanting to make her uncomfortable, or at least not more than she probably already is.

"You wish I was, don't you?" she teases without knowing how close to the truth she really is.

I relinquish my hold completely, but instead of darting away from me, Selene remains in place, gazing at me. "I would be a liar if I said I don't enjoy seeing you getting angry," I say, attempting to get a reaction from her.

"Why did you do it?" she asks calmly.

"Would you believe me if I told you I forgot she was there?" I respond honestly.

"Are you really that drunk or are you just dumb?"

"Both. But being drunk heightens my stupidity," I admit with a chuckle.

"I'm leaving now. You should too."

"The night has just begun, Selene."

"I don't care. I need to find Miriam. We came here together."

"I'll help you find her. After all, we don't want you to get into more trouble, do we?"

"You are the reason I am always getting into trouble," she huffs.

"Indulge me."

Selene rolls her eyes at me, eventually giving in to my selfish request. She walks in front of me, leading us onto the dance floor, trying to spot her friend, when a girl hits her boyfriend on the arm as soon as she sees me. Another one takes out her phone, and I try to cover my face as best as I can right when she flashes her device at us. Thankfully, Selene is oblivious to the circus. She would probably have a panic attack if she noticed people starting to stare at us.

We search together for her friend, but after a couple of minutes, it's clear she isn't around. I grab her hand and squeeze it, trying to get her attention.

"What?" she screams.

"Are you sure she's here?"

Selene shrugs.

"Check your phone," I suggest.

Quickly, she fishes the phone out of her purse, her eyes scanning the screen and then rolling to the back of her head. "She left with that girl she met."

I chuckle.

"Come on, I will drive you home," I offer.

"You are too drunk to drive," she points out. She's right. I shouldn't drive right now, even if I can already feel the effects of the alcohol fading.

"Dance with me. It will pass soon, then I can drive you."

"I could just get an Uber."

I don't like that answer. I want to be with her.

"Come on! No Uber can drive better than I can. Besides, you are young, you should be dancing the night away, not staying in bed." I inch closer and dance around her, trying to make her laugh. The grin she gives me is priceless.

"Maybe you are too old to be having this much fun," she jokes.

"I can behave like a child if you insist on behaving like an adult," I say, taking her hand and spinning her around, only to pull her closer to me. "Please stay for a couple of songs?" I beg.

"You get two songs."

"Five," I counter.

"I'll give you three. Take it or leave it."

"Deal."

Before she can reconsider, I turn her halfway around so that her back is pressed to my front and my hands on her waist as we move together, lost in the music.

At some point, her head settles on my chest, and I use the chance to press my chin against her soft hair.

What is happening to me?

The next song starts, and Selene jumps in place, singing to the lyrics.

"I love this song!" she screams, turning around with a big smile on her face. I stay put, hypnotized by her movements and the look of happiness she's wearing. I try to spin again, but one of the guys around us takes a step back, causing her to trip over her own feet.

I manage to catch her just before she hits the floor.

"I got you, Selene." There's barely a sliver of space between us now. I am hovering over her, with my head slightly tilted down.

"Your good reflexes are paying off, after all."

My hand decides it's a good moment to start acting without my permission. It ends up resting on her neck, using my thumb to caress her cheek. Selene shoots me a surprised look, but she doesn't pull away from my touch. Instead, I would even dare to say she leans in the slightest bit.

"There are more perks to that," I joke.

Selene lets out a laugh. I have seen and heard it before, but there is something about this one, the combination of the alcohol perhaps, or how the lights shine on her making her look even more seductive. Whatever it is, it makes my dick twitches inside my pants, and that's all my body needs to make a move. I tilt my head to the side, painfully slowly, giving her enough time to react and step back if she wants to.

Thankfully, she doesn't, and instantly, her small hand ends up on the back of my neck, pressing her nails into my skin.

"Excuse me, sir," someone scoffs. "Here is the water you asked for." I close my eyes and take a deep breath, realizing the magic of the moment has just vanished.

Selene takes a step back, her face as red as a tomato. It doesn't take a genius to figure that she's ashamed.

"I will get an Uber. Have fun."

HAMMER TIME

I nod, knowing that no matter what I say or do she will not end the night with me, and a part of me knows it's for the best.

After all, we do hate each other, right?

CHAPTER TWENTY

Selene

It's been over a month since the Barcelona incident, but the memories still cling to me. Try as I might, I can't seem to shake him from my thoughts.

Meanwhile, the season has started, and Philip's been performing like a champ. He's already in second place in the championship, even if he hasn't bagged a win yet. He's been giving his rivals a run for their money, pushing the car and himself to the limits.

Naturally, he's still the press's favorite target. Not a word he utters or a statement he makes escapes their notice, especially since he has been criticizing the federation, stewards, other teams, and even drivers. In return, they've all been swinging back. The FIA has been handing him sanctions and penalties, and the press has run some pretty ridiculous headlines. But even with the whole world against him, he keeps on fighting.

HAMMER TIME

Recently, he sparked the eternal debate of whether Formula One is more about the driver's skill or the quality of the car by commenting on the lack of talent from the latest race winner. Some have tried to use his words against him, claiming he only succeeds because of his car, but Philip's track record and trophies from other motorsport categories speak for themselves. He's a true winner, both on and off the Formula One track.

On my end, work, in all its forms, has become my escape from thinking about him. But it's not proving all that helpful considering the projects I'm tackling.

"Miriam! Can you turn down the music?" I holler from the office space we have built in our apartment for when we work from home. The noise comes to a stop almost instantly.

"Are you busy?" she asks, her face poking through the door without entirely crossing the threshold.

I take a look at her and force myself not to burst into laughter when I see half of hair is done in perfectly styled braids while the other half is still puffed up and undone.

"New hair?" I mock.

"Ha. Ha. Soooo funny." She sighs.

"Well, I like how one half looks. Will you show me once it's finished?"

"At the pace I'm going, I'll be done by tomorrow. What are you up to?" she asks, coming closer to my desk.

"I'm having a meeting with Sarah to discuss some ideas."

"What are you working on this time?"

"Hopefully, my pitch to become a permanent team member," I say before adding, "but I don't want to jinx it. Do you need help with your hair later?" I say, inspecting the gorgeous braids that are cascading over her shoulders.

"Only if my hands fall off." We both chuckle, knowing that even though I've tried to learn, I'm still miles away from being great at braiding her hair.

"Sounds good. I should be done in about half an hour."

"Okay, I'll leave you to it. Good luck!"

I double-check my slides, searching for any possible mistakes, methodically ensuring everything's in the right place. I review them a couple more times before finally deciding to call Sarah, who picks up almost instantly.

"Hello!" she greets me, with a broad smile on her face. "How are you, darling?"

"I'm doing well, you?"

"I'm fine."

"Are you at the office?" I ask, noticing the faded black Cavaglio logo in the background of her screen.

"Yes. We arrived in Italy last night. We'll be working from here this week, you know, Italian Grand Prix and all."

"I see. I don't want to take up too much of your time. I bet you need every extra minute you can get."

"You're right," she agrees.

I swiftly share my screen and present the slides I've been so nervous to show her – a set of graphics that could help shape the company's marketing strategies.

Thankfully, everything goes according to plan, just as I've rehearsed.

"To conclude, the sport is entering a new era, and as a company, you should evolve with it. The demographic analysis I've prepared makes me wonder if we're truly tapping into our full potential to reach our new target audience," I finish, my heart pounding so loudly, I fear Sarah can hear it too.

"Mmm... Could you send me those slides, please?"

"Of course, give me a second."

"What's your availability like this week?"

"What do you need me to work on?" I ask.

"I want you to join us tomorrow in Milan and present this in person to the board. Can you do that?"

"Sure," I say, somehow managing to contain my excitement. "I need to arrange a few things, but I can make it."

"Perfect. Someone will book your flights and accommodation. Also, if it's alright with you, stay until Monday and join us for the race."

"That sounds great." I'll never turn down attending a race weekend.

"In the meantime, please touch up slides four, seven, and eleven. I want to see more revenue figures, and if possible, add geographical data too. I'm not sure how much access you have to our database," she says, jotting down notes in her notebook, the gears already turning inside her head.

"I can handle it, but I'll let you know if I need help."

"Great, in that case, I'll see you tomorrow. Someone will send you all the details. Excellent work, Selene. Keep it up!"

"Cheers, Sarah," I say just before she leaves the call.

I close my laptop and let out a victorious scream, my feet kicking the ground as I sit on my chair. My scream must've pierced the walls because Miriam bolts back into the room, her hair still partially undone.

"What's going on? Why the war cry? Did you get a job?"

I only grin, my cheeks aching from the pent-up excitement.

"I'm off to Milan tomorrow," I announce.

"I knew it had to be something major. I am so happy for you," she says, placing her hands on my shoulders and squeezing tightly. I don't mind the pain at all, it feels great.

"I can't believe it."

"You're doing it, S! One step closer to your dreams," Miriam says, her hand covering her face, mirroring my own astonishment.

"Cavaglio, here I come." I release a shaky breath.

"Do we still have champagne?" Miriam asks.

"I think there's a bottle of Aperol in the fridge," I offer instead.

"Can we do Negronis?" Miriam inquires.

"I can mix some Spritz Aperol while you finish your hair if you'd like?" I suggest, eyeing her still unruly hair.

"Now you're talking." She's about to leave when she changes her mind and hugs me from behind while I sit in my chair. "I'm so proud of you for everything you are achieving."

I hug her back, fighting tears of joy.

Ever since I met Miriam, she's been with me every step of the way. Sharing these cherished memories that I'll carry with me forever is priceless to me. It's always her and me against the world, and I don't think I will ever be ready for her to leave my life.

Miriam leaves my side and I make it to the kitchen, only for her to appear there a few minutes later, carrying in her hands an assortment of supplies, including brushes, adornments, and hair extensions for her new braids.

"Got a hot date or something?" I ask.

"What makes you say that?"

"You always give your hair a makeover for special occasions. And since there haven't been many big career moves lately, that leaves us with a personal life event. Am I right?"

"Well, I might be catching up with Anastasia later," Miriam confesses.

"You're trading me for another girl?" I tease. "Ouch! I thought I was your one and only."

"Come on! Don't be such a drama queen."

"Me? A drama queen? Never," I say dramatically while pouring some of the orange drink into the glasses on the kitchen counter. "You have gone on a couple of dates with her after Barcelona, right? Does this mean things are getting serious?"

"Meh." Miriam shrugs. "She's been traveling a lot since she left Ukraine, and I think she just wants to have some fun." There is something in her voice, combined with a glint in her eyes that gives away she's not totally happy about the arrangement.

"Are you catching feelings for her?"

"She's great. Interesting, ambitious, and fun. But I feel like we're in this weird zone that isn't the friend zone but isn't a relationship either. It's like a situationship where we're both comfortable but also not?"

"So, yes?" I ask.

"I'm not sure." She sighs. "The sex is amazing, like multi-orgasms kind of amazing, and our friendship is good too, but I'm not sure if I am ready and willing to commit to more than that right now."

"Sounds complicated."

"I guess. Honestly, I feel like neither of us wants a relationship, but we just click," Miriam explains, but I feel like she isn't being completely honest.

"Okay, well as long as you're happy, I'm happy. But if she hurts you, I will hurt her." We both laugh, our sister-like bond at its best.

"How about Philip? I saw photos of Barcelona again."

"Do you think they will ever stop?"

Some people at the club in Barcelona decided to take our picture, and the image spread like wildfire on social media. A bunch of tabloid headlines popped up on my feed: *'Burton's new girlfriend,' 'Driver during the day, player at night.'* The shittiest of them all was *'Second place for a second driver.'* This last one featured a picture of Philip with Sofia and then one with me. I was so thankful that my face wasn't too visible.

"I guess it comes with the territory," Miriam says.

And what a shitty territory it is.

"He is not my territory though," I clear up, knowing that in Miriam's head, eventually I will be marrying the guy. That couldn't be further from the truth. "We were just drunk."

"Has he called you since Barcelona?"

"He doesn't even have my number."

But he could get it if he just wanted to, the intrusive voice in my brain claims.

Besides, I don't know how I would have reacted if he had. I am still figuring out whether Philip is an absolute dickhead, brainless, or the most complex man I have ever met. I don't know which one scares me more. "Either way, it doesn't matter. He doesn't like me like that. He was just drunk."

"Does that make it easier?" Miriam says with a frown.

"What do you mean?" I ask.

"Lying to yourself. He likes you, and you like him. At least enough to check him out whenever you have a chance. You only need to see the way you look at each other in those pictures."

"What you see are sparks of anger. He's an arrogant ass, with a god complex that makes my life harder than it already is. I don't need someone like him in my life."

"Whatever you say, *Sparks*." She winks.

I roll my eyes. Sure, he likes to call me Sparks, but he's also the only person in this world able to ignite me like that. I didn't know that side of me existed until I met him, and he forced it out of me. The worst thing is that Miriam isn't completely wrong. He makes me angry and my blood boil like nobody else, but he also sends jolts of electricity through me.

HAMMER TIME

He is an intense rollercoaster of emotions, but damn, it's an exhilarating, intoxicating ride.

CHAPTER TWENTY-ONE

Selene

I arrived in Milan yesterday, ready to meet everyone at the headquarters. Sarah and I worked on my presentation, constantly thinking about the looming presence of the executives joining us today.

As I approach Sarah's office in the early morning, nerves send a slight tremor wash through me. Yet, I enter the building with a smile, ready to impress everyone who will listen to my presentation today. Once there, I see Sarah engrossed in her laptop, oblivious to my presence behind the crystal door of her office. A gentle knock on the glass draws her attention, and her warm, maternal smile greets me. I cross the threshold and make it inside.

"Ready for the big day?" she asks.

"Always," I reply with enthusiasm.

"That's exactly what I wanted to hear," she responds. "The floor is yours, darling. Let me gather my things, and then we can go to the conference room."

"Please, lead the way." I gesture towards the door once she's organized her belongings.

On our way there, she asks if I'm nervous.

"Not really," I say, but the truth is evident in my tone.

"I'd be terrified." She chuckles.

"Well," I begin, my confidence rising. "I have studied and prepared this presentation as thoroughly as possible. So, yes, I'm as nervous as anyone should be, but I also know that I've given it my all. As I see it, if something goes wrong, it won't be for lack of giving it my everything."

"Well said. That's exactly the attitude I want you to have. Not many think as pragmatically as you, Selene. It's quite refreshing, especially in a person your age."

"I'm twenty-five, it's time for me to start acting like an adult," I reply with a shrug.

"Never lose that enthusiasm and never give up," she says in dreamy tone, maybe remembering her own start in this world. "It doesn't matter how many times they tell you that you can't do it, always keep pushing."

I nod in gratitude for her valuable advice. These past few months, she hasn't only been a boss to me but also a mentor, who has taught me how this world really works from the inside and who has given me any opportunity she could to show everyone my value.

We continue walking in silence, making our way to a spacious conference room. Sarah asks about my computer, and I nod, retrieving it from my bag.

"Perfect, please begin setting it all up. I will let everyone know that they can join us," she instructs.

"Of course. I'll wait here," I reply, starting to prepare in the meantime.

My heart is fluttering when the first person joins, and slowly the room begins to fill with people. Most of them are middle-aged white men, and I can't help but anticipate that they'll dismiss me as a mere novelty act. They probably just see me as someone who they have to put up with for the next hour only to say they are open for more women to join the company.

"Is there anyone missing, or can we start?" Sarah asks, making everyone look around the room to check if their colleagues are all in place. "Okay, the stage is yours, Selene," she says when nobody answers her.

I take a deep breath, gathering my courage, and rise from my seat to move to the front of the room, becoming the focal point of attention.

"Good morning, everyone. For those of you who may not be familiar with who I am, my name is Selene, and I've been working as a freelance consultant for the team during the current season. Over the past few months, I've had the opportunity to collect some data as the sport is currently experiencing one of the most significant surges in popularity it has ever seen.

"This surge has resulted in a transformation in our demographics. Our fan base is becoming more diverse and younger. Gone are the days when our primary target audience was predominantly in their early thirties and overwhelmingly male. We are entering a new era. Our audience spans from young children, all the way over teenagers, to adults beyond forties and beyond, and the viewership of women has seen a dramatic rise. But what exactly motivates fans to watch our sport?"

"Well, what is it?" a man says, interrupting me.

"That's an excellent question," I respond with a forced smile, concealing my frustration at his interruption. "Regardless of gender and age, fans are drawn to our sport by the thrill of competition, the excitement of racing, and the innovations in technology. However, even though the competitive aspect is a significant motivator, each fan selects their favorite teams based on personal factors that later influence their consumption behavior."

"Why is this tied to demographics?" I bite my tongue as another man poses a question that should have been self-explanatory if he could have waited five minutes instead of interrupting me.

"Well, traditionally, the sport has been perceived as a 'men's sport,' and that perception still lingers. However, as you can see from the slide, this is evolving," I explain. "Women's viewership has surged by nearly forty percent in just one year. They are becoming the primary consumers of our content outside of the actual races."

"What does that mean?" Sarah interjects, trying to help.

"Men tend to consume the sport differently. They watch the races and often forget about us until the next racing weekend," I elaborate. "On the other hand, women not only watch the races but actively engage with the content. They consume it voraciously. Post race interviews, podcasts, YouTube videos, and various other forms of media—they are the predominant audience right now. If you look at the trending Formula One content, you'll find that it's mostly created by women. They are the driving force behind the current surge in popularity, and it's essential that we acknowledge and cater to this significant and growing demographic."

My statement echoes through the room, making it abundantly clear that we can no longer afford to neglect this crucial audience.

"What do you suggest we do then?" inquires one of the younger men, his curiosity seeming genuine, yet I can't help but feel cautious.

"We should take measured strides in their direction," I reply to the room, prepared to provide a practical example.

"Could you provide an example?" he presses on, prompting me to move to the next slide, eager to illustrate my point.

"You're investing significantly in Cavaglio Nero merchandise and a fashion line, but there's an issue," I begin. "All the patterns and sizes are either gender-neutral or tailored for men, yet it's women who are predominantly purchasing and engaging with these products, as we have seen earlier in this presentation. We must start considering their needs more seriously, and that begins with something as straightforward as offering merchandise sizes that cater to them and patterns that complement their bodies. The 'boyfriend look' can only be appealing for so long," I conclude, with a touch of humor. To my surprise, a few women in the room laugh, and even some men join in. Sarah applauds enthusiastically, and others follow suit.

"And you're just a consultant, correct?" the same man who asked questions earlier interjects, his tone slightly combative, causing the applause to fade and the air in the room to change, everyone suddenly becoming uncomfortable.

"Yes, solely because the board has yet to approve a more substantial role for her," Sarah explains, her tone a mix of support and defense.

"Mmm... Why do we have a marketing team if a consultant must address this?" the man continues, seemingly poised for confrontation.

"That's a brilliant question, one I've asked myself, Nicholas," another man comments, heightening the tension in the room.

"I suppose an outsider's perspective brings a breath of fresh air sometimes," I respond with a gracious smile, concealing the simmering fury within me.

"I assume you're seeking a permanent position within the company?" the same man presses again, maintaining his discourteous tone throughout the meeting.

"She not only seeks it; she deserves it," Sarah snaps.

"Selene has clearly made a compelling case," another man finally chimes in, offering support.

"She has grasped something the team overlooked or didn't find significant," a fourth man adds, hinting at a glimmer of hope that my words may be heeded.

"Well, perhaps we should consider hiring an entirely new team if our current one is so inept that an external woman has to step in and—" one of the men from earlier starts.

"Excuse me what's your name?" I interrupt him.

"Oliver Arnoult," he responds with a forced French accent. The name rings a bell, and I instantly recognize him from news articles.

"Pleasure to meet the director of the board," I begin. "I must admit, I disagreed with your recent article on leadership in the sports industry, but it is an honor to meet you. Now, if I may speak my mind without interruption."

A vein pops on the man's forehead, and by the way he is looking at me with furious eyes, I can't help but feel that he might be ready to burst any time now. He's probably not used to people contradicting him, especially a young woman.

I am not one hundred per cent sure if he has an issue with me on my work, but whatever it is, it makes me feel small and diminished. I have always dreamt about working in a world that is dominated by men, and I have always known that my dreams would come attached to uncomfortable situations. In secret, I always hoped that I would be able to avoid them, but it seems I won't. That's fine. I'm fine working my ass off and doing extra hours if in the end I achieve the respect I deserve.

"While the company is still in a favorable position, much of that can be attributed to its historical status as a top team. Regardless of whether you adapt to the changing market, you will continue to generate profits, but those numbers will decrease year by year. The plan I propose could boost revenue by a staggering thirty-seven percent. You, Mr. Arnoult, are a man of numbers. Contemplate the significance of that increase and where those resources could be strategically invested. Advancements in car technology, innovations in street cars—the entire company stands to benefit from these transformative steps, and this is just one of many ways."

CHAPTER TWENTY-TWO

Philip

"Philip, you need to start working on your relationship with the press," Mancini says. I have been sitting in one of the offices at the Milan headquarters for hours now, enjoying a lovely strategy session on the upcoming events of the season, which of course include press tours that I am not eager to do.

"Why? Embracing the role of their favorite villain has its perks," I quip, fully aware of the merciless treatment we've received from the media this season. We are not even halfway through the damn year, and they have already treated me worse than they did in all my past years in the sport combined.

Munguia huffs, crossing his arms over his chest and chimes in with a pointed question. "Why are you so keen on playing their villain?"

"I'm not," I respond, drawing skepticism.

"You are, Philip. You seem hell-bent on being their villain, to the point where you don't even attempt to correct their misconceptions," Oliver continues.

"You wouldn't understand," I brush off his accusations.

"Then why did you tell them that João got kicked out because, and I quote, 'he's not good enough for Formula One,' yet you secured him a position at Volpella, and now he's third in the championship?" Munguia confronts me and I have to hide my surprise.

Nobody is supposed to know I made sure João stayed in Formula One. The kid has the talent to become one of the big ones. He's just not ready yet. Give him one or two years, perhaps after I retire for good, then he will show the world what he's made of.

"If you invested as much time in the simulator as you do in finding out what I do behind closed doors, then perhaps you'd be as good as you think you are," I retort, standing up and adding, "Now, if you'll excuse me, I have more important matters to attend to."

As I exit the office, Munguia hurls an insult at me, but I ignore it. If he seeks confrontation, he won't find it with me. I have enough of that every day with the press, the last thing I want to do is to be that person in my personal time too. I make my way to the seventh floor, searching for a quiet refuge. For a moment, I believe I'm losing my mind when I catch a glimpse of copper hair.

HAMMER TIME

My obsession with Selene is spiraling out of control.

I blink, expecting her image to fade or to realize that it's another person standing nearby, but instead, the image becomes clearer and when she turns around to start a presentation in front of the board, I realize it really is Sparks.

I stand there, captivated by her professionalism when the dinosaurs from the board start acting like caveman who can't conceive a woman showing them something new. It doesn't surprise me that she maintains her composure on the outside. As someone who has gotten the best out of her in the past few months, I am able to detect the hint of frustration in her flushed cheeks before spewing facts that show how right she is. Selene remains calm, putting each one of them in their place with precision.

That's my… No. Don't you dare. She isn't yours.

People begin to leave the room, and Selene starts bidding Sarah and some of the other members farewell. I attempt to slip away before she notices me, hoping to find the peace I was seeking earlier

"Where do you think you're going?"

"Hmm?" I turn around, feigning surprise as if I hadn't been standing here for who knows how long, enchanted by her words.

"What did you think?" She approaches me, her perfume enveloping my senses in an intoxicating haze.

"About?" I feign disinterest.

"Don't play games. I saw you here."

"It was an intriguing approach," I admit.

"Is that all you have to say?" She raises an eyebrow, her tone now laced with irritation, the same one she always seems to use after a while of talking to me.

"What did you expect me to say?"

"Well, typically in situations like these, someone in your position might say, 'Great job! Interesting ideas!' I suppose you're different," she remarks with a bitterness.

"On that, Sparks, we can agree."

"You're impossible, Philip." Selene exhales in frustration and attempts to walk away, but my reflexes get the best of me, and my hand grabs her wrist. "Let go of me."

"I will, but don't leave," I beg, allowing her some space to retreat. "What's really bothering you?"

"Besides the fact that you have a permanent stick up your ass?" I attempt to hold back a laugh, but it slips out, earning a smile from her. "Today was quite something."

"You were exceptional," I admit, hoping to offer her some sort of consolation. My words catch her by surprise, and I can't blame her for raising her eyebrow at me in skepticism.

Selene's hand moves to my forehead.

"Your temperature seems fine, so you are not having a fever," she jokes. "Are you feeling unwell, perhaps? Should I call an ambulance?"

"I can acknowledge excellence when I see it," I say.

"Impressive." Selene whistles.

"I can be pleasant sometimes," I whisper, moving closer.

"So, you just don't play nice with me?" Her tone and posture changes, and very subtly, she takes a step away from me.

"What's that for?" I inquire, confused.

"Does Barcelona ring any bells?"

Of course it does. Barcelona has been everything I have been thinking about since I last saw her and trust me when I say that I have tried to forget that night as hard as I can.

"Tell me what's bothering you, Sparks." I step towards her, closing the space between us. Thankfully, she doesn't move, but the closer I am to her, the closer I also want to be, and every time we meet, resisting the pull gets harder.

"Did you see how the press treated me? You know how they can be, and you didn't lift a finger to help me. You could have at least called to find out how I was dealing with the spotlight. I am not like you, Philip, I am not used to being their target."

I did see it, and I did try to protect her identity. They still wrote about her, but no one truly knew who she was, and I made sure it stayed that way. I was especially cautious about keeping her connection to Cavaglio a secret, otherwise, they would have torn her apart, making up stories about her climbing the easy ladder. That couldn't be further from the truth.

"I managed the situation as best as I could. I apologize if some stories got out." There is no need for her to know I went out of my way to help her. She would blame herself if she found out I threatened certain journalists to ensure her safety.

"And you couldn't have told me this?"

"How?" I ask.

"Ever heard of a phone? I know you're old, but it's this thing that you can make calls and send texts with it," she says, mocking me.

"I am not that old. Besides, you're the one who left me in Barcelona. Why are you angry with me?" I say. After all, she was the one who walked away, the one who pulled back.

"I don't know," she whispers in frustration.

"Come on, Sparks, use your words,"

Selene touches her forehead, massaging it with two fingers, her eyes closed, allowing me to scan her beautiful features. "I think I need a break from my feelings after the meeting."

"They'd be idiots not to hire you after that," I say.

"They've already proven themselves idiots." She smirks.

"Good point."

"How is Sofia?" Her unexpected question catches me off guard, and her wide eyes tell me that it catches her by surprise too.

"Does it matter?" I reply, even though I haven't seen or thought about another woman but the one standing in front of me right now for the past months.

"I guess it d—" The elevator doors open, and Jessica bursts through them. Her signature long, black ponytail swings from side to side, following the rhythm of her hips.

"Philip, darling." Her high-pitched tone makes my ears ring in pain. God, how I hate working with this kid.

"Jessica," I respond.

I realize too late that her hand is gripping the side of my face as she plants a kiss on the corner of my lips. I attempt to pull away, but her grip is surprisingly strong, her nails scratching the side of my face where her hand is.

"Mancini is looking for you," she says before I can reprimand her behavior.

"I was about to leave anyway," Selene chimes in. "I suppose I'll see you on the track."

I want to chase after her, explain that this is far from what it appears to be, and that Sofia isn't a part of my life either. But instead, I remain where I am, watching as the elevator doors close in front of me.

RHAE AEDEN

And Selene slips away once more.

CHAPTER TWENTY-THREE

Philip

The Emilia Romagna weekend kicks off on a high note. It's my first pole position of the year, and to top it off, I've shattered the track record, setting the fastest lap in history. This achievement brings back memories of my final year in Formula One, when I set the previous record before retiring.

I've noticed Selene sitting in the VIP lounge as Sarah's personal guest, just as she has been on other occasions. However, we haven't exchanged a word since our most recent encounter. I have been resisting the urge to go to her and clarify that Sofia and I are nothing all weekend long, and that Jessica has concocted a delusional scenario in her mind. But I refrain, opting instead to compile a list of reasons why I dislike her:

1. *She smells so enticing, it's nearly nauseating.*

2. *She's exceptionally intelligent, perhaps too clever for her own good.*
3. *She constantly challenges me, as if she's determined to be my nemesis.*
4. *I'd wager she adores Christmas…*

I give up after the fourth point. Is that even a valid reason? What on earth do I mean by *'she loves Christmas'?* There's clearly something wrong with me; perhaps I should schedule another blood test soon.

Shaking my head, I redirect my focus to the upcoming race day. We're in a strategy briefing, and my focus should be here and not on her. The weather conditions remain stable, suggesting a race without many surprises. Some might label it boring, but fate tends to flip a coin every time we race, and more often than not, the coin lands on its edge, transforming the race into one of the most captivating of the season. I, for one, am banking on that.

"Philip!" I hear the voice—the dreadful high-pitched voice. *Why, oh why, must I endure this every single weekend of the season?* "Philip!"

"What?" I snap, whirling around abruptly.

"Hi," she says, smiling while batting her long, fake eyelashes as soon as she has part of my attention. "You have a press appointment in ten minutes."

"With whom?" I ask, receiving what might be the worst news of my life from the least competent member of the team.

Leave it to Mancini to make the ill-advised choice of hiring family and friends for crucial roles within the team. I have started to notice he's buddies with Arnoult, a man who I am not very fond of. I can't help but feel suspicious of him. They say that none of his assistants last longer than a month on the job, and it's not for lack of competence.

"That interviewer from..." She checks her notes to determine which channel we're dealing with. I wouldn't mind her invasion of personal space if at least she could perform her job competently, but she has proven multiple times that she isn't capable.

"Sphere Sports," Munguia says before Jessica can find it. I grunt in frustration. "We both have it."

"Then we'd better get going," I reply. Sphere Sports is perhaps the worst of them all; they care more about sensationalism than the sport itself. They are the yellow press of Formula One.

"Try to take a few breaths and leave the caveman act behind. No one wants to see you pissed off like that," Oliver nudges me, Jessica trailing behind.

"Nobody wants to hear your opinions, but here we are," I retort, feeling the anxiety rising, which only makes me more short-fused. I know Oliver is right, but I've lost my patience.

RHAE AEDEN

The press is a battle I have lost and have no intention of fighting anymore.

I pick up my pace, trying to walk away from Munguia and his uncomfortable truths, hoping he will take the hint and leave me alone. But, of course, the Mexican doesn't get what I'm trying to do.

"Pinche gringo, espera wey!" *Fucking asshole, just wait there!* Munguia shouts from the distance, and from behind me, I can hear him speeding up. Eventually, he reaches me and grabs my shoulder, bringing me to a halt.

"Take your hands off me," I say in an icy tone that genuinely startles him for a moment.

"Wey, I can't do this anymore. Why do you have to be like that?" he asks, horrified by my actions, as if he's never witnessed this side of me before.

"Like what?" I snarl, my patience running thin.

"You're acting like a jerk! But you're not one," he says.

"Don't pretend like you know me. You don't."

"I don't, but I see you and the things you do."

"And what do you see, Oliver?"

"Someone hiding behind a facade of indifference when the truth is, you care more than you would like to admit."

"What if I do?"

"Then show it, for heaven's sake!" he says, losing his temper for a brief second. I don't think I have ever seen him this irritated.

"What good would it do to show that, huh?"

"You claim to be one of the greatest drivers of all time, maybe on the track you are. But you're so full of nonsense that you don't even comprehend how your image on camera impacts the team."

"I signed a contract to be a driver. I'm not a circus monkey," I remind him.

"Newsflash, that contract has a clause about media and publicity obligations that need to be fulfilled. Just performing on the track is not enough."

"And here I thought they only hired you to do that job."

"Don't forget I'm standing in front of you in the championship, Philip." Not for long, *cabrón*.

"Enjoy your standing while you can; I'm coming for you."

"I know you are. What you haven't grasped yet is that I'm not your enemy." That part hits home. Deep down, I do understand that he's my teammate and my first competitor, but also my best wing man on track. "I used to respect you, you know? I'm not sure I do anymore."

Those words echo the ones Selene uttered the first day we met, and they stir my insides. I am a disappointment to every person who has ever believed in me.

"Apologies for that," I offer. His eyes widen. "I do go to therapy, you know?"

"We all do," he says.

"I'm aware of my issues, and I manage them as best as I can, trust me. You should have seen me the year I retired. I'm not a complete jerk, even when I act like one."

"Try harder to show it to the rest of the world. Now, let's walk and put on a smile for the cameras."

We approach a woman on an improvised set, her lips adorned with bright red lipstick, a bit of it even smudged on her front tooth. Nobody dares to tell her, and the stain keeps growing bigger while she chews on her gum, making it almost impossible to look anywhere but at the stain.

"Please, have a seat," she says, her strong British accent foreshadowing what is about to come. The press hates me, but that hate reaches new levels when the interviewer is British. "My name is Cynthia. We'll be rolling from now on, and the necessary edits will be made during post-production. This should only take a few minutes," she informs us.

Munguia and I nod in perfect unison. I run a hand through my hair, attempting to tame it for the cameras; Anyone would think that I'm not above caring about my appearance, but what I'm really trying is to distract myself from the creeping anxiety that's settling in.

"Philip, where would you rank yesterday's performance among the ones from the past?"

I don't like where this is headed.

"I believe that Quali was a crucial achievement for Cavaglio, and I'm content with my performance, after all I have pole." I respond, feeling my pulse quickening.

"Joan Benson stated that you should have been disqualified and penalized," Cynthia says, peering at her notes. I have no idea who Joan Benson is, but his name sounds like that of an inconsequential person.

"If those are his thoughts, then he needs a pair of glasses to rewatch the qualifying session and recognize the car's progress and my driving," I retort sharply, my irritation bubbling beneath the surface.

I know by the way Cynthia looks at me that she won't stop until she gets a reaction out of me. "What do you have to say to those who might label your possible win today as a 'dirty' win and who will call you a cheater if you secure that first position?"

I feel my blood simmering but manage to keep my cool. "There are over twenty races this season, and victories are divided among drivers. It's not always the same driver, and sometimes, some people can't accept that their favorite isn't good enough to secure a win, and that someone else is."

When she realizes that I'm behaving as much as I can, she diverts her attention towards Oliver. "Oliver Munguia, thanks for joining us today too. Are you concerned about Philip's position in the championship?"

"Who wouldn't be? He's one of the all-time greats! He deserves a lot of respect," Oliver responds with a strong Mexican accent. There's a subtle double meaning in his tone that doesn't escape me, scoring him a point in my book.

"But he's not currently outpacing you on the track. The team put in extra effort for you this weekend, compromising you to get that pole. Right, Philip?"

"That's your opinion, not a fact," I reply, trying to skirt the issue, but my frustration is growing.

"Well, Munguia had to give up his pole position, didn't he?" Cynthia presses, but I won't give in.

"Do you need me for this inquisition, or should I leave?" Oliver jokes, but his words carry weight.

"Don't you have anything to say about the team's decisions?" Cynthia's questions grow more irritating by the second.

"I'm not sure what you consider team decisions. I made a strategic tire choice, just as I opted for a different strategy. We worked as a team, and yes, I gave him some recoil towards the end, but he'd done the same for me two laps earlier. So, I'm not sure why you're twisting this narrative," Munguia explains. It's strange seeing him defending me; I've never had a teammate do that in the past. It's quite refreshing.

The interview drags on, and I try to endure it with patience and resignation, letting Oliver handle most of it.

HAMMER TIME

Once Cynthia realizes I won't provide anything she was hoping I would, she finally lets us go.

As Oliver opens his mouth to speak, I cut him off with a deliberate slowness. "Not a single word." Then, I stride away, eager to reach the garage, get into my car, and race. I'm nearly running, but I come to an abrupt stop on my heels.

Selene is talking to Sarah near my car in the garage. I stare at her for a moment, taking in her presence. She's smiling, a rarity around me, which seems to be the norm when I am not around her. I find myself drawn to her, our eyes suddenly locking, causing the rest of the garage to fade into a blur.

"I was wondering when you'd show up," I call out. Her smile fades, and her eyes narrow. Sarah says something to her before departing.

"Funny, I was thinking the same," she retorts.

"Great minds think alike," I respond with a wink, a gesture that might melt any other woman, but she remains unimpressed.

"Mhmm, I didn't realize your brain was functioning," she bites back, crossing her arms over her chest, unintentionally giving her breasts a subtle lift.

Don't look down.

"Just trying to impress you with the two brain cells I have left," I say, keeping my gaze locked onto her eyes.

RHAE AEDEN

"Save them; you'll need them to race." A smile finally touches her lips, but it's not the same smile she gave to Sarah. But it's still a smile.

"Please, wait here. I need to change into my suit," I change the topic and leave her looking at me with disbelief, maybe even a touch fury, but she remains in place.

I go to my room, starting with the fireproof undershirt and then the racing suit. When I return, I find her standing where I left her.

"What do you want, Philip?"

"You," I reply, and she snorts at my words.

"I'll entertain that answer. Why?"

"I have a race to attend," I say as I grab my helmet.

"No kidding, Sherlock."

I ignore her comment and focus on securing my helmet. It resembles the one I wore at Silverstone, entirely black but shiny. My racing number, thirteen, is drawn on top in matte black since the three was already taken. The Cavaglio horse is traced in yellow on the front, with both flags—the British on the left and the Spanish on the right—featured on the sides.

"You changed it," Selene whispers in astonishment as she notices the significant alteration. Her fingers trace the letters where it once read, *'Fear is the greatest motivator' but* now reads, *'Dreams are the biggest motivators,'* the same words she once said to me.

"You need to touch both flags," I instruct her. Suspicion gleams in her eyes, and it takes her a moment to comply. But she does. "Consider it our ritual for good luck."

"I didn't think you believed in luck."

"I don't," I reply, gently pressing the front of my helmet to her forehead. "I believe we create our own luck, and maybe you're helping me craft mine."

"Why me, Philip?"

"Why not?" She takes a step back, marking the end of our ritual. "I'm not involved with Sofia, and I'm certainly interested in Jessica. There's nothing happening between us, and there never will be with them."

CHAPTER TWENTY-FOUR

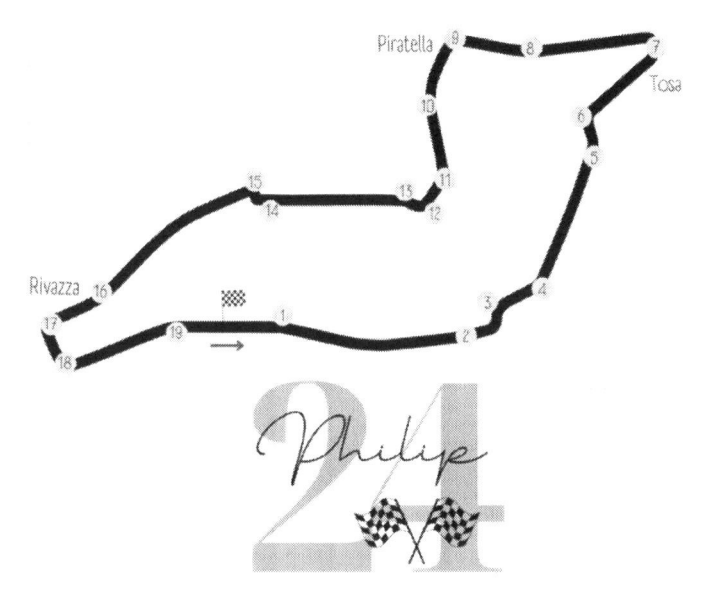

As I warm up the tires during the formation lap, I indulge in a few controlled burnouts towards the end. Munguia is tailing me closely, warming up his own tires. Everyone starts parking in their spot, waiting until all five red lights turn on and then off again. I use this moment to center myself, focusing on my breath.

My eyes widen and lock onto the red lights suspended above me. Each one progressively turns on. I tap the buttons on my steering wheel before all of them extinguish, and I push the throttle, sprinting forward in front of my teammate. In my rearview mirror, I spot João, ready to benefit from any mistakes we make, but our cars are faster on this track, and we should be able to outpace him in a couple of laps.

I maintain my lead, entering the first corner ahead of my teammate.

"Incident in the back," the familiar voice of my engineer informs me over the radio. "Two cars are out. Be prepared for a possible safety car." His voice remains composed, but I can't help but feel a twinge of concern for the drivers.

"Copy," I reply, my mind racing. "Are the drivers okay?"

"Yes, just a racing incident."

The yellow flag is waved, signaling for us to slow down. A few raindrops sprinkle from the sky. Rain wasn't forecasted, but I relish racing in wet conditions, so I wouldn't mind if it started to pour, but these drops aren't enough for a tire change.

We maintain a decent pace. Munguia remains in second place behind me, getting closer with the advantage that the safety car offers, but João benefits from it too. We endure too many laps under the yellow flag, but once the cars and drivers are safely cleared from the track, we resume racing.

Around the eighteenth lap, I notice Munguia's pace gaining momentum, and he closes in on me. He even has the balls to steer his car towards mine while both of us move into the corner, but I see his attempt to overtake me miles away, and so I am able to block it. Not today.

"Oliver has the pace to overtake you," my engineer tells me, and I don't like the sound of that. They are going to force us to change positions. They want me to give him my win. Never.

"No!" I scream, unwilling to accept what he's implying. "Let's at least see how the strategies play out," I demand, growing impatient, unwilling to relinquish my position when we haven't even had a real race yet.

"Copy, I'll get back to you."

I push on, prioritizing securing a lead over Oliver instead of preserving my tires. There is no way he's winning this race. Over my dead body.

"Any updates?" I ask impatiently after some laps pass.

"You both are allowed to race each other."

"Are you serious?" I nearly shout, gasping for breath as I navigate the car through Rivazza before completing another lap in first position. We are going to end up crashing if they don't give team orders. It is not uncommon for teams to let their two drivers' race, after all who would we be if we didn't fight for the first position? Not Formula One drivers, that's for sure. But right now, we're just going to get ourselves killed. We're high on testosterone and adrenaline, chasing the win and neither one of us is going to back down. The risks are too high! We might even crash into each other and fuck the race up for the entire team.

"Keep it clean and don't take unnecessary risks. Munguia has received the same instructions." *Unbelievable.*

"Copy," I say, gritting my teeth and pushing on the throttle. I'd rather voice my frustrations in the garage than waste my breath while racing. If they want a spectacle, then they will get one.

Munguia pulls alongside me, his front tire aligning with the middle of my car, in an attempt to pressure me to make a mistake that will cost me my position. He draws closer, but I refuse to yield an inch. If he wants to pass me, he'll have to take risks. I sense he's hesitant about damaging the car, so he falls back behind before making another attempt in a different sector. Side by side, we race down the straight. Eventually, he activates his DRS and edges past me.

"Fuck!" I scream inside the car, anger consuming me.

As we approach a series of fast corners in the second sector, I push him, positioning my car directly behind his car, pressuring him and forcing him into taking a poor racing line through the chicane. It allows me to take the inside line and recover the first position.

Victory is mine this time.

Oliver remains behind me with João now trailing closer to us. He has taken advantage of the time Munguia and I have lost fighting each other and is now tailing Oliver's car, eager to overtake. His efforts provide a helpful distraction for me, allowing me to stretch the gap between us and make my escape. I catch sight of the standings on the enormous monitor at the beginning of the track. We're nearly halfway through the race.

"Let's shift to plan B," I say through the radio, knowing they'll decipher what I mean by that: to pit and swap my tires on the next lap.

I push the car to its limits, attempting to gain every possible second before my pit stop. A few sectors light up in purple, but not enough to get the fastest lap.

"Prepare the soft tires," I command over the radio.

"Copy."

I guide the car into my designated pit area, halting precisely at the moment the red light above me illuminates. The mechanics are already in place, surrounding the car with fresh tires and the necessary tools. I mentally count to two, and the light flips to green. I dart out of the pit box, but a silver car suddenly appears on my left. I instinctively swerve to avoid a collision and then scream some profanities at him. The silver car hits the brakes, fully aware they've likely committed an unsafe release and will face penalties. At least that's what I tell myself, fully aware that it is probably my team at fault, and I am just praying right now for the FIA to spare me a penalty.

Finally, after the rocky stop, I can rejoin the race.

The whole incident on the stop does cost me a bit of time, but I stay calm when on the screens on the track I see that Munguia has had a shittier pit stop than mine. Seems like they struggled to get the left front tire out.

"Tell me every car's position," I request after I am done warming up the tires in the first part of the lap.

"You're a virtual leader. Munguia is about to make his pit stop," they inform me.

"Gap between us?" I ask, crossing the finish line again.

"Seven seconds."

"Do you want us to race again?" I joke.

"He is on a different strategy," he answers, but I know this race is now mine.

One of the amusing sides of this sport is its unpredictability. You could start at the back of the grid, but if the cars in front encounter mishaps, you might still find yourself on the podium by the end. You never know what can happen in two hours.

"Focus," my engineer reprimands me.

"Always at your service," I playfully respond. I'm eagerly anticipating the race's conclusion and on one of the screens I can see that we are slowly nearing the finish. "Just one more thing."

"What is it?" he asks.

"If I manage to win," I start hesitantly, not wanting to jinx want could be my first win of the season. "I want the Spanish flag to fly, not the British one."

"Are you sure?" There's a hint of doubt in his tone, a familiar sentiment. We all understand the fondness of the federation for their British drivers and the dislike they have shown for me not being one of their golden boys. I might be risking their anger, and some unnecessary penalties in the future with my current wish.

"Yes."

"I'll see what I can do."

"Thanks." The radio falls silent after that.

Selene

Watching a race from the VIP area next to the garage offers numerous advantages, such as the privilege of wearing headphones that allow me access to every radio message from the drivers, not just the ones broadcast to the public. This includes Philip's conversations with his engineer. I don't think I can fully grasp the workings of his mind, how he is racing one of the fastest cars in the world, while working on his strategy and maintaining a conversation all at the same time. On top of everything, he still manages to ask for the Spanish flag if he wins. I like to think this is his particular way of showing the federation a middle finger.

"Where's Munguia?" Philip asks over the radio.

"He's dropped behind João," the engineer informs him.

"Ha!" Philip's triumphant laughter reverberates through my headphones.

Then something happens. Philip loses control of his car in the series of corners at the end of sector two and slides over the chicanes. I can see him struggling to regain control, but it slips from his grasp entirely. My heart skips a beat. The car goes off the track and toward the barriers. Gasps erupt from everyone in the room. I catch them biting their nails nervously, already anticipating the worst of scenarios.

Mancini slams his hands on his desk in a fit of rage, losing his temper. It echoes throughout the garage. But Philip Burton is known for working miracles, and he regains control of the car before crashing into the barriers. He seamlessly spins the car 180 degrees and continues racing as if nothing had happened. There's noticeable damage to the front wing, but that doesn't stop him.

"Everything okay? Is the car still good?" Philip's voice emerges again.

"He's fine," Sarah reassures me as she sees me releasing a breath that I didn't even notice I was holding.

"Yeah… That was scary," I mutter.

"I know. It's extra scary when someone you care about is behind the wheel," she comments. I give her a puzzled look until I decipher the meaning of her words.

"Oh no, no, no!" I repeat, flustered. "It's not like that."

"Of course," she dismisses me, winking slyly. "Your secret's safe with me." My cheeks burn from embarrassment.

I redirect my focus to the screen. Two laps remain. João trails Philip by a mere fraction of a second. João attempts a pass on the Spanish driver, but once again, Philip proves to be the best on the grid. Despite João's fresher tires, Philip's superior speed and skill prevail.

The Spaniard pushes harder, taking more risks in the corners. João tries to keep up with his pace, but his tires wear out before the final lap ends. As soon as the chequered flag is waved and Philip is declared the winner, we all rush to the finish line. Half of the mechanics hang from the steel bars separating us from the track and the cars.

In the distance, I can see Philip's yellow and black car coming into view. The mechanics' shouts make the bars tremble, celebrating the man who just won this Grand Prix.

"VAMOS PHILIP!" I scream my lungs out, knowing that he won't hear me when he flashes past me with his car, but still, I keep screaming, happy for his accomplishment as a tear of joy trickles down my cheek.

CHAPTER TWENTY-FIVE

Selene

I find myself in a sea of people, my head tilted backwards to the point of discomfort, but I don't mind. In this moment, nothing but Philip matters. He is the center of attention. This is his moment.

Munguia emerges first from the waiting room, João follows, each of them taking their respective position. Finally, Philip bursts out, practically jumping with joy. His black racing suit is slightly open, revealing a tantalizing glimpse of his physique, and he zips it back up, adjusting the neck, as he approaches the podium. I bite my lower lip at the unfair allure of his movements. To make things worse, the broadest of smiles is on his face, a rare sight I don't think I have ever witnessed.

RHAE AEDEN

I'm mesmerized as I gaze at him, and the dream continues when Philip spots me in the crowd and looks at me. His blue eyes are shining with happiness, and even over the distance, I can still feel our magnetic pull. He doesn't break eye contact, not even when a man hands him the latest addition to his trophy collection.

It's only when the national anthem begins that he takes his eyes off me, turning around to see which flag stands for him. His smile only grows bigger when he spots the Spanish flag.

The other two drivers pop their champagne bottles, dousing Philip in the bubbly liquid. He tilts his head up to the sky, his eyes closed while the champagne falls on him. His genuine happiness is a captivating sight.

I quickly pull out my phone and capture the moment in a photo: champagne droplets in the air, refracting the sunlight. His disheveled dark hair and closed eyes, combined with the purest of smiles is a sight I do not want to forget. The crowd roars when the anthems are done playing, and I celebrate with them.

"If you think this is wild, just wait for tonight," Michael shouts above the team's cheering.

"What's happening tonight?" I shout back.

"The big party without cameras," he informs me.

I've heard about these parties, and a few videos have been leaked over the years, but there's still much mystery surrounding them. Like how all the drivers gather there, enjoying the wildest nights that imagination can conjure.

"Fancy. You're going to have fun then."

"Oh, you're coming with us," he declares.

"Me?" I point to myself. "Aren't those kinds of parties for team members only?"

"You are part of the family, Sparks," he says, placing an arm around my shoulders in an older brother kind of way. "Besides, we can invite some plus-ones as long as the cameras stay off."

"Hmm, you might have convinced me."

"Then my job here is done. I will see you tonight."

"Sounds like a plan. Will it be here?" I ask.

"Nah, we have reservations in Milan later tonight. I'll text you the details," he says.

"You're a gem, Michael." I give his shoulder a friendly pat as the crowd begins to disperse around us.

"I've got to run," he says as he starts to walk away.

"See you." I wave in his direction.

The hotel room is an explosion of chaos. It's as if a bomb went off. My clothes are everywhere, the bed is barely visible underneath them, and the floor is a minefield of shoes and scattered accessories. The bathroom is no better, with my hairdryer and makeup across the counter. I never considered the possibility of a party while packing for this trip. Consequently, I have no party apparel right now. My suitcase is filled with business suits, blazers, trousers. I'm grateful I even have a pair of heels, considering I'm more of a sneaker kind of person.

All I can do is make an emergency call. I reach for my phone, dialing the number that's already saved on my speed dial. The phone barely has time to ring before the recipient answers.

"I need help!" I exclaim, anxiety coursing through me. Nothing in this room fits, and I need to shine tonight.

"Go on," Miriam instructs from the other end.

"I'm going to a party. I'll fill you in later," I explain before she can ask questions that I don't have time to answer. "I have nothing to wear."

"Why didn't you go shopping?" I tried, but I couldn't find anything that felt comfortable enough. "Actually, don't answer that. What are your options?"

"I've got about three blazers, some suit pants, and a few shirts scattered around," I inform her.

"Didn't you pack that black skirt you wore to the event for that football team last month?" My eyes widen as I realize my oversight. "Wear it with a bralette or something," Miriam advises.

"It's still a work event!" I exclaim.

"I bet Philip will like it." A snort leaves me.

"Him and the other hundred mechanics attending."

"Fair point," she concedes.

"I've got a black shirt; I could use it as a cover-up."

"Sure, give it a try and send me a picture."

"Give me a second." I toss the phone onto the bed. In a hurry, I put on some black lingerie and add the shirt, leaving a few buttons undone to let the bralette peek through. Sliding into the skirt, I stand before the mirror. "It could work," I say loudly, making sure Miriam can hear me.

"Send a picture," she repeats. I grab the phone, put on my heels, snap a few quick pictures, and send them to her. "Oooh, stunning," she responds.

"You're a lifesaver!"

"I'll take that. Now go have fun; your man awaits you."

"You're impos—," I begin, but she hangs up before I can finish. I glance at the time on the lock screen; it's getting late. Michael has sent me a couple of texts with the location, informing me they're already there and waiting for me. I need to rush now.

Milan seems calm at night, and the city is small enough that I am able to reach the party in less than ten minutes. A line has formed at the building's front door, and a heated argument in Italian unfolds between a girl and one of the bodyguards.

I send Michael a text.

Me: I'm here. I'll find you once I'm inside.

Michael: Tell them your name. It's on the list.

I approach the bodyguard who is not involved in the Italian girl's dispute and offer him a warm smile.

"Buonasera, il mio nome è sulla lista," I say, catching his gaze as he scans me from head to toe. "My name is Selene Soldado," I inform him. It doesn't take him long to find it and allow me to enter. "Grazie."

Walking through a dimly lit corridor, I follow the music until I step onto the dance floor. The radiance of the lights blinds me, and I have to blink a couple of times to let my eyes adjust to the lighting. There are at least three floors in this club. I catch myself admiring the crystal lights cascading like falling raindrops when another partygoer collides with me, snapping me out of my trance. They gesture an apologetic 'sorry,' and I respond with a smile.

"SE-LE-NE!" Voices in the crowd scream. I spin around, attempting to locate the source. "SE-LE-NE! SE-LE-NE!"

Someone grips the nape of my neck from behind. "Selene," a voice murmurs over my hair, sending goosebumps racing down my arms. I don't need to turn to identify the voice. He's incredibly close, and I can feel the warmth radiating from his body.

HAMMER TIME

In a swift move, he turns me to face him, and my palms find their way to his chest. I look up at him as he takes a sip from his drink, his Adam's apple bobbing as the liquid flows down his throat.

Damn, he looks good.

I bite my lip, preventing myself from doing something crazy like nibbling his neck.

"How much have you had to drink?" I ask, forcing myself to sound annoyed, even if I am somehow enjoying this. Part of me wants to flee *from him*, while the other wants to flee with him.

"You don't want to know," he quips.

"I want a drink," I announce with a smirk. I spin on my heels and head to the bar, embarking on a quest for the strongest concoction available. Philip stays behind, and I can feel his eyes tracing my movements.

Fortunately, the bar isn't too crowded, and I swiftly place my order.

"Excuse me," I holler, capturing the bartender's attention. "Can I have two shots of Tequila, please?" I ask.

"Anything else?" the bartender replies.

"Yeah, a negroni with prosecco in it."

"So, a negroni sbagliato, right?" the bartender confirms.

"Yes," I reply, eagerly awaiting the shot of liquid confidence. "Thank you!" I shout as the bartender turns to fetch the bottles. He starts with the shots, and I handle them with the ease.

"Do you want another one?" the bartender asks, his eyes shifting toward the shot glass as he serves the negroni. I'm on the verge of accepting when Philip beats me to it.

"Make that two," he orders. The waiter nods and pours two additional drinks next to my negroni. "This is on me," Philip says, extending his card. Typically, I appreciate it when a man covers my drinks at a club, but the situation with him is different, and I don't want to take advantage.

"No," I decline, taking the card from his hand and paying with my phone. "Bottoms up, Philip." I hand him his shot and relish being the one who downs it faster, slamming the glass on the counter without flinching, unlike him. "You might be the best on the track, but definitely not at the bar," I tease.

"Only you would pay for my drink and then call me second best at something," he replies, his tone carrying amusement.

"You've been flying next to the sun for too long, Philip. Somebody needed to show you how to be humble again," I joke, enjoying the banter.

"Flying next to the sun is the price I pay for greatness," he retorts with a gleam in his eye. I can't help but chuckle, and then something hits me. I don't want to play games with him anymore. I don't even know how they started in the first place, but somewhere in between bathrooms and garages, I stopped disliking him.

"You can be great and have an ego half the size of yours," I say, partly meaning it. The laughter that escapes us both rings through the club.

Witnessing him like this, feeling relaxed and with his guard down, is a surreal experience that I am not ready to let go of. Why can't he be this carefree all the time?

While I'm immersed in my thoughts, Philip takes my hand and pulls me towards the dance floor. The space is chaos, with people dancing and jumping everywhere.

Philip whirls me around three times, and I find myself juggling my drink to prevent any accidental spillage before he lets go to take a sip of his newly refilled drink, and then he leans in, softly mouthing the lyrics of the current song while he dances in place.

Drunk Philip holds a unique charm, one that lures me in to letting down my defenses even more. I join his dancing and sing along to the songs.

The night wears on and the alcohol starts settling in my bloodstream. I don't know how many drinks I've had by now, but I am starting to feel the effects of the alcohol. Philip, however, looks as fine as always, even if I know that he has had almost twice as many drinks as me. It's a mystery how the man is still standing. I close my eyes, losing myself in the music, embracing a carefree night. But when I finally open them, I find Philip gazing at me with one of those intense stares of his.

He steps towards me and then leans closer, his eyes never leaving mine. I notice then how the corner of his mouth is turned upwards with mischief. Slowly, his hand moves until it finds my neck, and his thumb applies some pressure on my jaw, not the uncomfortable kind, but the one that makes my center clench.

He grants me a moment to make my move, to give him some sign that I am okay with what is about to happen. But I remain rooted in place, my mind only thinking about the reasons why this can't happen, instead of thinking of how much I actually want this. Philip only draws nearer with my hesitation, pressing our bodies together. Our foreheads touch, I can even feel his breath.

I part my lips with a deep longing, aching for his kiss, but then, in a moment of clarity, I change my mind. I reach out and grasp his throat, choking him slightly. My thumb rests on his chiseled jaw, pushing him back so I can create a semblance of space between us.

He gazes down at my hand, seemingly in disbelief at my touch, "is this what you like?" he teases, licking his lips with amusement. Temptation flits through my mind, and I allow myself a brief moment to consider the possibilities.

"Maybe," I respond in a whisper. I might not be sure of what I want right now, but at least I know that I am not ready to let go of him completely.

"Don't play hard to get, Sparks. Not anymore than you already have," he purrs, and then he surprises me. Reaching out with full force pressing our lips together.

His lips brush against mine, soft and tender at first, like a gentle caress, and then the beast breaks loose, and passion starts consuming both of us. Philip's teeth scrape my bottom lip, tugging on it, mixing pain with pleasure. Our mouths move together in a perfect dance. I don't how long we continue; I just know that I don't want to let go.

That's why it feels extremely painful when I break the kiss.

"Stop." I tilt my head to the side "I am not doing this when we are drunk."

"Why?" he asks, confused.

"Because if we do this, I want to enjoy it, and I want you to remember everything," I whisper, my lips near his earlobe. "And I want consent from someone who can give it, Philip."

Then I give him a kiss on the cheek and surprise myself by walking away from a living god.

CHAPTER TWENTY-SIX

Selene

It's been a week since Emilia Romagna, and this weekend, it's Monaco's time to shine. The city has transformed into a blend of a dream and a nightmare in preparation for the Grand Prix. Half the streets have been sealed off, while the other half hosts grandstands that seemingly sprouted overnight.

Ironically, I've managed to score tickets for several races this year, but not for the race taking place in the city where I live. God must be laughing at my expense.

"Earth to Selene." Miriam snaps her fingers in front of me, pulling me out of my thoughts. I blink, momentarily perplexed. "Are you even listening? Are you going to finally tell me what happened in Milan?"

Surprisingly, Miriam and I haven't spent time together since I came back from Italy. It's been a hectic week. I'm still working on the project I presented, and Miriam's been in and out of the apartment. But today we have finally been able to find some time and go to our favorite coffee place.

"I told you," I reply, still somewhat distracted.

"No way in hell you pulled off an alpha move on the alpha god himself," Miriam retorts, clearly disbelieving.

"Believe it or not, I did," I say, taking a sip of my coffee and feigning indifference, even though I damn well know what I did. I still blush thinking about the way I handled the situation. Philip is probably still coping with me walking away.

"How?" she exclaims, genuinely confused. "How do you manage to stay so cool? Hell, you're my hero now."

"It was the alcohol doing the job for me," I confess. And it really was. I doubt I could ever replicate that move. I'm usually the shy one, but with Philip, I seem to find a new side of myself.

"Alcohol makes me horny, not turn down dirty sex with a deity. How did he react?" Miriam's asks.

"I didn't stick around to find out," I admit.

"Why?" Miriam presses. Part of me had secretly hoped that he'd follow me, chase me around the club, and ask me to stay. But he didn't. "How could anyone reject one of the hottest men in the world?"

"Well, I didn't want to be just another one of his one-night stands. Sex means something to me now," I explain.

I have already had my fair share of wild nights and meaningless hookups, and it doesn't do it for me anymore. I've envied Miriam for her casual approach to sex and her ability to get laid whenever she pleases without having feelings involved, because that's exactly how I used to be in the past – carefree and fearless. But not anymore.

"And he was wasted, like really wasted," I continue.

"From what you are telling me, you were pretty drunk too," she points out.

"Not enough apparently. But it doesn't matter, he probably doesn't even remember anything about last night anyway."

"Why do you think that?"

"Well, he hasn't even sent me a text," I confess.

"Of course he isn't going to text you. *You* left *him*. You need to text him first," she suggests

"Fair point."

"So, are you going to?" She gives me an encouraging smile, hoping for a different answer.

"Probably not," I reply.

"Selene," she groans.

The doorbell jingles, signaling the arrival of a customer.

Miriam's gaze shifts to the newcomer. "Well, look who the cat dragged in.

"If it isn't my favorite party girl." Michael greets me with a smile that practically screams, *'I know what you did.'* I can feel my cheeks blushing, and Miriam's grin only makes it worse.

"I wasn't the only one having the time of my life," I say, remembering how he was dancing around the club and doing shots with everyone at the bar. "Getting ready for the day?" I ask, forcing a change of topic.

Michael stops a waitress passing by us, orders a tea for himself, and then sits down at our table. "Just taking a break away from the team," he explains, his tone sounding defeated, and I can't help but sense that there is something he isn't telling us.

Miriam leans in, her voice hushed. "Is there any particular team member you're trying to avoid? Someone with dark hair, blue eyes, and a perpetual raincloud hovering over his head?"

I huff and give her a kick under the table. "Miriam."

"I've been trying to escape him all week long," Michael confesses.

Miriam pushes further. "Give us the gossip, Michael."

The corporate side of me that wants to make a career in F1 cringes at what my best friend is asking my coworker, but my curiosity gets the better of me, and I lean in as well, ready to hear what Philip's coach has to say about my favorite moody driver.

"One might think that since he won last weekend, he'd be in a better mood this week," Michael begins, "but, of course, that's not the case. He just keeps getting grumpier by the second."

"Any idea why?" I surprise myself by asking.

"That's a question for you, darling," Michael accuses.

"Sorry, I don't understand."

Michael smirks. "He might have been, but I certainly wasn't drunk enough. It would have taken so much more than shots and a couple of drinks for me to not notice what you two were doing on the dance floor."

Miriam bursts into laughter, tears collecting at the corners of her eyes, and I hide my shame behind my hands.

"Please, just tell us what you know. This is too good to be true."

"Honey, you should've been there," Michael continues, relishing the moment. "The two of them were dancing all night, batting their lashes, sharing inside jokes, and spilling drinks. It was a sight to behold. And then." He pauses dramatically. "He tried to kiss her. She leaned in. Lips touched." Miriam's eyes widen, as if she hadn't heard the story. "And what did the redhead do? She pulled away!"

"Shame on you." Miriam practically gasps.

I hide my face behind my hands, groaning at both of them for reminding me of that night, but also at myself for having been so stupid. I don't even know what I want, and I'm so frustrated. No outcome can satisfy me.

"So, he's in a bad mood because of her?" Miriam asks.

"Maybe. Not many say no to him. This one" —he points at me with his thumb— "has got bigger balls than most."

"I'll take that as a compliment."

"Anyway, the press has been nastier since he's decided to race under the Spanish flag again," he comments, sipping his cup of tea.

"Bet Jessica is struggling with that one," I say.

"She'd have to care to struggle, but she's indifferent to all of it. Seems the only thing she cares about is being next to Philip. But she's Mancini's niece, so she isn't going to leave any time soon," Michael replies. "Now back to the important things. Do you like Philip, or what are your intentions with him?"

"Bold question," I respond. "Why would I tell you that? You might run to the enemy and spill what you've heard here."

"I just hope that you know the enemy isn't as bad as he seems. He's just... a complicated man." I'd already gathered as much. "He's dealt with a lot and has overcome even more, but there are still things he's working on." Michael look directly at me. "Give him some time."

"She'll think about it," Miriam intervenes on my behalf. "You could sweeten the pot for him, though." She nudges me under the table with her shoe, and I roll my eyes at her.

"Yes, you could," I play along.

"Pardon?" Michael looks at both of us in confusion.

"Any chance you could score us some tickets for this weekend?" I ask, knowing what Miriam was about to say.

"Ah, that's an easy one, but it will have to be for tomorrow only. No way I can get you in today. I'll ask Philip later for some passes and give them to you this afternoon, okay?"

"Sure, take your time. You have Selene's number, so just give her a call, and we'll be there," Miriam says while Michael gets up.

"Good luck with Philip," I say.

"Oh, I'll need it. Any chance I can bring you along as a peace offering?"

"Sorry, I'm not on the market for that."

Many would argue that Monaco has become a boring race on the current Formula One calendar, and that the only reason why it's still part of it is because of its deep historical connection with the sport. It's like the royalty of races.

But overtaking is rare, and some claim not much happens after the qualifying sessions. João grabbed the pole position yesterday and star from first, with Philip at his heels in second position. Statistically speaking, João stands a good chance of winning this race if he and his team don't make any mistakes. However, it's been pouring all morning long, and it doesn't seem like it's going to stop anytime soon. They've delayed the race a couple of times already for safety, but any moment now, it should be underway.

I've been at the track with Miriam since the early morning. I won't lie to myself; I came earlier than usual hoping to catch a glimpse of Philip. Part of me wanted to do our little ritual, wishing him some good luck, but I haven't spotted him yet. It's disappointing, even though I hate to admit it.

"Are you thinking about him?" Miriam asks.

"Is it that obvious?" I sigh in frustration.

It's been almost a year since I first laid eyes on this man. He frustrates me most of the time, but I can't seem to shake him. Every time I'm on the verge of forgetting him, fate throws us together, making it impossible for me to shake the inexplicable pull that I feel each time I encounter him.

"Your expression betrays you."

"I'm worried about the rain. What if there's an accident and someone gets hurt?"

"Girl, you love races with rain and crashes."

She isn't wrong, I love to see the world burn, as long as they are 'safe crashes' that only destabilize the race with no driver getting hurt. "Monaco is different. There is no gravel here. One mistake and you will drive right into a wall," I say.

"Why don't you go look for him?" Miriam suggests.

"And say what?"

"That's up to you." She shrugs.

"Selene. Miriam." Michael hurries towards us. "I've been searching all over for you. Why are you out in the rain?"

"Michael," I greet him. "I wasn't sure if these passes where for the garage, and we didn't want to push our luck."

"Nonsense. Follow me quickly."

We weave through the crowds, dodging people, cars, cables, and equipment from other teams until we reach the Cavaglio area. The garage is quieter than usual, everyone fully focused and waiting for the news of when the race will start. I find myself scanning every direction. Philip's car is there, but there's no sign of him.

"Where is he?" I ask.

"He's got a private dressing room." Michael winks. "It's right there." He points to a door bearing Philip's name. "You can go to him," he says.

I approach the door with hesitation. I knock, hoping to hear his voice, but there's no response, so I turn around. Michael waves his hand at me, signaling me to open the door.

So, I do.

Inside, I find Philip sitting on the floor, leaning against the wall, his eyes closed. He's got chunky headphones on, playing music so loudly that even I can hear it. He looks peaceful and utterly engrossed in the moment. I don't want to disturb him, not while he is looking so at ease.

Still, against my instincts, I lean against the wall and slide down without him noticing me initially. It's only when I'm sitting next to him and he opens his eyes that he becomes aware of my presence.

"You shouldn't be here." His voice carries the usual edge.

"Happy to see you too, Philip."

"Who said I was happy to see you, Selene?" He huffs out a breath.

"Call it female intuition."

"The last time I checked, you were walking away. So why come back now?" Straight to the point.

"I gave you my reasons. Maybe you were too drunk to remember them."

"I'm not doing this, not before a race." I see him grit his teeth, the strain showing through the muscles of his jaw working.

"Okay," I say, my tongue clicking in frustration. "Sorry, I didn't think about that. I've always imagined you as someone who's got it all together, and I forget that you need your time before getting into the car."

"It's a good facade, isn't it?"

"It is. But you don't need to keep it up with the people who care for you," I say as I stand up. "I know you said you weren't going to do this, but I didn't want to walk away."

Right when I am about to make my way back outside, I notice his helmet on a nearby desk, so I walk towards it and touch both flags for good luck, *our little ritual*.

"Don't get too drunk when you win today. That way, I won't have to walk away."

HAMMER TIME

CHAPTER TWENTY-SEVEN

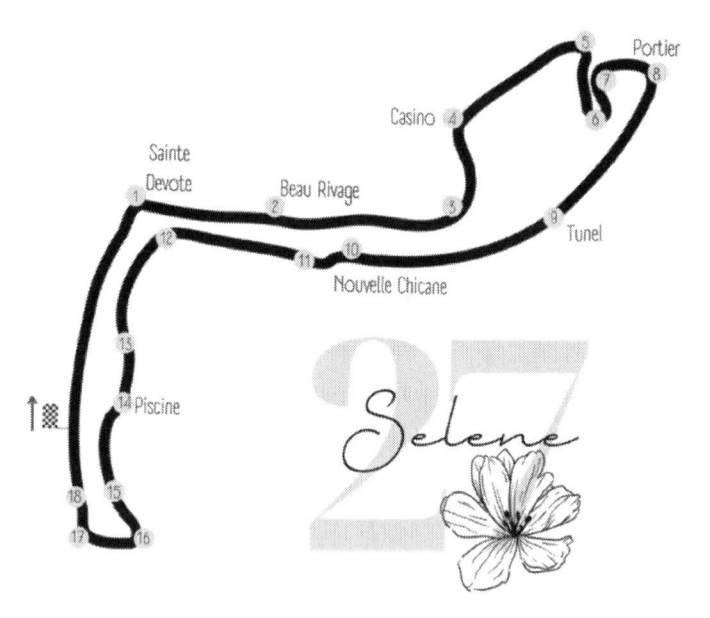

The rain won't stop, so they're forced to start the race behind the safety car, with the promise that eventually it will stop. Worst case, it will finish before anything remotely thrilling happens. The strategists are on their toes, everyone's nervous, trying to make all the right decisions.

When the safety car finally exits, some of the drivers look for openings around Casino Square to pass each other, but the track conditions are still less than ideal. Philip's been testing the waters on the wet road for a few laps now. He's basically become an extension of João's car. He's searching for any opportunity, but João is putting up an impressive defensive game.

RHAE AEDEN

Many people believe you can't overtake in Monaco, but Philip's out to prove them wrong. I can practically hear him saying *'you just need to be talented enough to do it.'*

A driver from the midfield tries to make a move at the entrance to the swimming pool. Philip's engineer gives him the heads up on the opportunity, so he can try to overtake in two different spots. It's a sight to behold watching him push the car to its limits on the track, maximizing every chance. João is aware of this, and his driving is getting shakier with each attempt.

Cars start pitting when the track has dried a little, and Philip does too, hoping to gain the advantage of an undercut. He opts for a set of hard tires, hoping they'll go the distance for the remaining laps. It's instantly clear he's faster than everyone else with that fresh set, but overtaking João remains elusive.

Munguia is in his own world, battling it out with João's teammate like it's the most important race of their lives. He's leading but later loses his position, overtaken near the Casino, with no chance of fighting back. The screen switches to Philip, and we all watch in horror as his car slides across the track. Everyone's hands shoot up in the air. Some mechanics can't even bear to look at the screen, fearing the worst. But Philip, always one for magic tricks, pulls off the save of the season, steering the car back on course before it can meet a safety barrier.

HAMMER TIME

No matter what an incredible race he's putting on, things are looking rather bad for him. There are only ten laps to go, and he hasn't passed João, who might just manage to get his first ever win in Monaco.

"Vamos, Philip," I whisper in Spanish to myself.

"It's hammer time, Philip," says his engineer, and all of us smile, knowing that those words have a powerful meaning. He's going to secure that win by any means necessary.

Philip pushes relentlessly, a constant presence that has João on edge. They both navigate the Casino and power through corners six and seven, barely any space between them. We get a shadowy image as Philip enters the tunnel, with João in front of him, and as they exit, down the straight before the nouvelle chicane, Philip makes his move, overtaking the Brazilian driver.

The entire garage erupts into cheers.

"Sí!" I scream.

He's going to win it.

He wins in Emilia Romagna.

And he's winning in Monaco now.

Philip Burton is the crowned victor of the Monaco Grand Prix.

RHAE AEDEN

The Spanish anthem sounds for the second time this season as Philip stands on top of the podium, gazing up at the sky, savoring this grand moment. His pride is practically painted on his face. When the anthem comes to an end, the crowd applauses, and I can't contain my cheers of happiness.

The heiress to the Monegasque throne strides up to each of the drivers, their trophies clutched in her hand. Philip is the final one to receive his new shiny prize, and she makes a point of taking a longer time with him than she did with the rest, not only does she shake his hand, but boldly kisses both his cheeks, lingering for a while there.

"I hear the princess is inviting him to dinner tonight," Michael nudges me with his elbow.

"Isn't it customary for the winner to be invited to dine with the royal family?" I try to play it cool, not letting anyone see the twinge of jealousy I'm hiding. Why am I even jealous?

"Yeah, but the king is gone on other royal duties, so it'll be *a tête à tête.*" *A tête-à-tête? I'm going to give him a tête-à-tête when I see him.* "Careful, you're flaring up."

"No, I'm not."

"Hmm, how did it go earlier then?" Michael's intentions are genuine, but he's now become my personal punching bag, and I have a feeling that he is used to being that for Philip.

"Considering his shameless flirting with the princess just now, I'd say it went great," I practically growl. Michael eyes me with a mix of surprise and fear. "Sorry, I just... I guess I wasn't expecting him to be flirting with a princess. I can't compete with that."

"You can compete with so much more," Miriam chimes in. "Now, if he's being a jerk and doing it for a reaction, then we'll give him one tonight." Miriam's eyes gleam mischievously. I can practically see the wheels spinning in her head.

"We'll catch you at the party, Michael."

Philip

I'm not one to turn down a princess. God knows I've had my share of invites from stunning celebrities, models, and influencers. I was even remotely interested in what they had to offer. But I can't say I've ever been less intrigued than when Georgina asked me to join her for dinner and *'whatever comes later.'* I found myself more drawn to a certain copper-haired girl, but she bolted right after the celebration. So, here I am, standing in the club, nursing my first beer and waiting for her to make an entrance. But I'm slowly losing hope.

"She'll show up sooner or later," Michael says, almost spilling his drink as he slaps my shoulder.

"I don't know what you're talking about."

"Good, then you won't care about the entrance she is making over there," he says, pointing with his chin towards where Selene and Miriam are making their grand entrance.

My focus zeroes in on Selene, how her short blue dress, a near-perfect match for the shade of my eyes, hugs her curves as she walks down the stairs in the highest heels I have ever seen. She looks utterly stunning, nothing compares to her.

"You still don't know what I was talking about?" Michael teases, and I choose to ignore him.

I sip my beer and remain in my seat, trailing Selene with my eyes from the distance as she makes her way to the bar with Miriam by her side. One of Munguia's car mechanics cozies up to them, and much to my displeasure, Selene seems to be his target. I watch closely, ensuring he doesn't overstep with what's mine.

I monitor the situation from a distance, noticing how he grabs Selene around the waist, and her face twists into a grimace, displeasure written all over her features. If her response was different, I'd have kept my distance. But a nonverbal 'no' still means 'no,' and if he refuses to comprehend it from her, he's about to learn it from me.

I make my way through the crowd to where she stands.

I'm a man on a mission.

"Get your hands off her," I bark at the guy. Selene looks up at me, her face expressing a silent *'thank you'* as the guy raises his hands in surrender.

"Sorry, *fra.*" My blood boils even hotter when he calls my *bro* in Italian. "I didn't know this one was with you." He says with a strong Italian accent.

"This one here has a name, s*tronzo,*" Selene protests.

"No need to get all worked up guys, she is just another tight pus-."

That's when I lose it. I don't let him finish that sentence. Without warning, I punch him in the face, breaking his nose, and blood spills onto the dance floor. Selene and everyone around us gasp in horror. I can see her eyes growing wide as she covers her mouth, surprise written all over her face.

"Show him who's boss, Philip," Miriam shouts, cheering for me with her fist in the air.

"Get out of here. Now!" I bark. The man bolts, not needing a second warning nor another visit from my fist to his face.

"Are you okay?" I ask, gazing at Selene. I find myself scanning her body, as if searching for any damage caused by the jerk. Thankfully, she looks perfectly fine.

"I could've handled it." Her voice quivers, and she stumbles slightly.

"I know, but I wanted to handle him for you." I offer her my hand so she can regain her balance.

"You don't have to fight my battles." I am about to answer, when Selene looks down at my hand, noticing the blood on my fingers. "Let's get you some ice. No point in abusing a hand worth millions." She looks concerned for me, a look nobody has ever offered me since my mother passed away.

"I think I'll survive," I say after she brings me some ice.

We stand still for a while, her hand wrapping mine with the ice she has secured from the bar, while with the other one starts cleaning off the blood from the other guy.

"Where's the princess?" she says, still focused on my hand.

"If you're going to inquire about another woman, at least look at me." I grip her chin with my thumb and index finger, forcing her to look at me.

"So, where is she? Was dinner cut short?"

"Dinner never happened." Her eyes widen, but she quickly adjusts her facial expression to hide her feelings.

"Are you too good for a princess now?"

"Maybe I am," I say. "But I am still working on being good enough for you."

Selene can't hide her shock. Her lips tremble a bit, trying to come up with the right words, but for once, I feel like I have them.

"You don't have to leave tonight if you don't want to."

CHAPTER TENTY-EIGHT

Selene

The message is loud and clear, and I've come to terms with wanting him, but I never expected it to be reciprocated. Not like this. What happens now? What am I supposed to do? The questions start piling up in my head until Miriam interrupts my thoughts, practically stumbling over her own feet in her excitement.

"Sorry to interrupt, lovebirds, but I need Selene," she says, grabbing my hand and dragging us towards the dance floor. She hands me a drink, and before I can protest, she's shouting, "Drink this!"

I chug the suspicious looking drink in one gulp, making my body tremble in disgust when it goes down my throat.

"What was that?" I finally ask.

"Liquid courage," Miriam replies.

RHAE AEDEN

"And why did you drag me away from Philip?" I ask, feeling slightly lightheaded and confused with the aftertaste of Miriam's concoction still lingering in my mouth.

"Well, turns out Anastasia is in town," she says, with excitement in her eyes. But she tries to downplay her emotions, always playing the cool bad girl. I know she's infatuated with Anastasia. "I wanted to ask you if you're cool with me bringing her home tonight."

"Looks like someone is going to have fun."

"By the looks of it, I won't be the only one," she observes.

We both take a moment to glance at Philip, who is standing awkwardly at the bar, watching us from a distance while he still nurses a beer.

"I don't even know," I start, trying to explain the confusion that's brewing inside me.

"What happened? I lost you after he punched that jerk. He has my full support and respect for that."

"He has mine too," I admit, and Miriam gives me a meaningful look. "Stop it. Anyway, you girls have fun and be careful. When are you leaving?"

She looks at her watch. "In like five minutes!"

"Oh. Okay, then, I will see you later."

"Now you go and have fun. Oh, and text me before you get home," Miriam says, already turning around, ready to leave. "See ya!" she shouts, fading into the crowd.

I look back at the bar, right at Philip. He hasn't moved and is still looking in my direction, patiently waiting with the ice wrapped around his hands. Taking a deep breath, I gather some courage and walk towards him.

"Come with me," I whisper in his ear once I am close enough. He doesn't move, so I leave my head where it is, inhaling his scent. "Let's have fun," I insist.

"Your definition of fun and mine are different," he says, standing up and towering over me.

"Shall we test that theory?" I tease him.

Philip doesn't say anything, so I take matters into my own hands. I surprise him by placing my fingers around his neck, and slowly getting on my tiptoes until my face is so close to his neck that I can feel the warmth radiating off him. My intrusive thoughts win the battle, and I scrape my teeth over the soft skin.

"Stop playing," he warns when I get impossibly closer to him, feeling some friction from his jeans against my bare skin.

"I am not doing anything," I tease.

His reaction surprises me, and there is nothing I can do to avoid what is about to come. Strike that, I don't want to avoid it. I have been craving this for the longest time. He wraps his hand around my neck, grabbing by my nape hard enough that I wouldn't be able to move it if he tried to kiss me. I bite my lip, anticipation filling me. But the kiss never comes.

"Tell me what you want, Selene," he says, his lips close to my ear, sending shivers of pleasure down my spine.

"You know what I want."

"Use your words, Sparks."

"I'd rather show you."

Philip's eyes grow wider, and I'm sure he thinks I'm bluffing, but I prove him wrong before he can say anything. I run my hand over his shoulder, resting it on his neck and pulling him towards me. Our lips finally meet for the second time. I give him a soft peck at first, an innocent kiss that doesn't last long before turning into pure passion. Philip holds onto my waist, digging his fingers into my flesh. He is devouring me just the way I need him to.

At some point, I feel one of his hands moving onto my back, tracing my spine until he finds my hair, and tugs on it so he can get better access to my mouth.

I let him do that. I let him order me around and enjoy the sensation of his body pressed to mine while our mouths are at war. We are so close that we are practically one, and I feel his growing erection in his jeans pressing against my center. My head feels dizzy from everything I am feeling right now. It's too much, but it's not nearly enough.

I try to breathe, feeling my legs shake from the excitement. Then, I stand on my tiptoes and pull him towards me to kiss him harder.

"Let me take you home," he whispers, leaving a trail of kisses on my neck.

"No."

"I don't mean it like that."

I raise my brows at him. "How do you mean it, then?"

"I just want to be with you in a place where everyone isn't looking at us." I pull my gaze from him to see everybody around us staring at us.

How could I be this dumb?

"It's fine, remember? Cameras aren't allowed in here." I breathe a little bit more evenly, still feeling anxious and ashamed of my behavior. "Do you already regret this?" he says, running a hand through my hair.

"No, I don't," I admit.

"Let's get out of here. I will take you to your place if you prefer that." One part of me wants to go home and get tucked in bed, but the other is dying to know more about Philip and spend some time with him, meet the real him.

"Take me to your place."

"You are allowed to change your mind at any second," he says, and I give him a peck on his soft lips.

"I always forget that you actually live in Monaco," Selene says while I observe her from where I stand in the kitchen. She's already made herself at home, gracefully removing her high heels as I fetch some drinks.

I relish the sight of her perched on the sofa, her eyes wandering around the house. "I forget I even have a house here," I quip, handing her a glass of wine.

"First-world problems." She sighs.

I settle down beside her on the couch and run my hand over her shoulders, savoring the feel of my fingertips tracing her naked shoulder. This woman is intoxicating, and I know that she will be the end of me. When did it go from hate, to friendship, to whatever this is?

"Careful, I might start thinking there's a heart in there," she says, pointing with her finger at my chest where my heart beats.

"You'd be right to believe it's hollow," I say, grabbing her hand and pressing a soft kiss on her palm.

"You're quite the storyteller," she remarks, stifling a yawn as she rests her head on my shoulder, her wine glass temporarily forgotten in her hands. The image is heartwarming, and I don't even mind the possibility of her spilling her drink all over my pristine white sofa. Material possessions hold little value when I can have her like this.

"Let's get you to bed before you drift off," I whisper, planting my lips on the crown of her head.

"I can't go to bed like this," she protests, looking down at her blue dress that has now started riding up her legs, leaving little to the imagination.

"Definitely not if I want to be a gentleman," I tease.

I would never do anything she wasn't comfortable with, but damn, if my mind isn't picturing some of the most inappropriate visuals I could ever come up with.

"I think we already established that you are not one."

"Perhaps, but you are not the only one who values consent, Sparks." I stand up and take the wine glass from her hand, letting it sit on the coffee table in front of the couch. "Come on, I will give you something to sleep in."

I lead us up towards the white marble stairs that lead to the upper floor where there are more rooms, and when I am about to go up the first step, Selene stops herself to admire one of the paintings I have collected.

"One day I will have a house like this," she says her eyes shiny. "With hundreds of art pieces like that," she says pointing with her chin towards my precious Klimt hanging in the wall.

Sometimes, I forget how young she is. I can see her appreciating and touching the pieces of art decorating the walls of the corridor before we make it to my room.

"Do you like art?"

"I love history, that's why I know about art."

RHAE AEDEN

I can't contain myself and wrap my arms around her waist, her back pressed to my front. It's nearly impossible to keep my dick under control. It has a mind of its own when it comes to Selene.

"Come here, you can snoop tomorrow. It's bedtime."

I spin her around carefully, trying to not make her dizzy. Noticing how tired she is, I carry her in my arms, as I lead us upstairs. When we make it there, I notice Selene's gaze fixated at the far end of the corridor, where a shelve filled with helmets from a lifetime of racing adorning the walls stands proudly.

"My dad would kill to see this," she says, and a laugh escapes me. Behind every girl obsessed with Formula One is a proud father who showed her the sport when she was a child, and Selene is no different. "You smell too good. It's not fair," she mumbles and then bites my neck.

"Behave, Selene." I groan. I'm already struggling enough to keep my dick inside my pants. The last thing I need is for her to start playing games that neither one of us is ready to play yet.

"If that is what you want." She huffs when we make it inside the bedroom, and I drop her on top of my queen-sized bed, only to turn around and search for something she can wear.

"That's not what I want," I say through gritted teeth. "But for now, it will have to be enough." Finally, I find a black shirt and throw it directly in her face.

"Hey! That's rude."

"I will give you some space so you can get changed. The shirt should be longer than your dress but let me know if you want some shorts or something."

I leave the room and go to the guest bathroom to get ready for bed too. When I check myself out in the mirror, I notice a smile there. My face looks relaxed, a different sight than usual.

I like this feeling, but I'm also terrified.

CHAPTER TWENTY-NINE

Selene

The morning sunshine grazes my face. I let out a sleepy yawn, not feeling quite ready to wake up yet. In my slumber, I reach for the blanket, intending to wrap myself in its warmth, when an unfamiliar and oddly comfortable weight slides over my waist. I open my eyes and am met with a realization: I'm not in my own bed.

The white silk sheets don't belong to me, and the cozy pressure against my waist isn't the bulk of a comforter; it's a man's hand. A man who is awfully close to me. I can even feel his breath on my hair. I turn into rigid stone, unwilling to even breathe for fear of waking him up. My thoughts are racing, trying to remember last night: the party with Miriam, dancing with Philip, and... oh – *we kissed.* More memories flood my mind: Philip bringing me home, our conversation on the sofa, and me ultimately falling asleep.

Panic sets in and all I can think of is how to get out of here. I raise my head just slightly, squinting to find my dress in the room.

"The dress is in the bathroom," Philip mutters with a sleepy voice. "If you're planning to escape, at least do it in silence."

For a moment, I don't dare to speak. He removes his hand from my waist, and I get out of bed, my tiptoes propelling me toward the bathroom. Inside, my dress lies in a crumpled mess. I startle at the sight of myself when I see my reflection in the mirror – my hair is a tangled mess, and my mascara has somehow managed to end up all over my face.

"Why?" I mutter to myself as I attempt to scrub away the inky mascara with toilet paper soaked in hand soap. I take my time putting myself back together.

When I make it out from the bathroom, a shirtless Philip is waiting for me. I can't help but steal a quick glance at his chiseled muscles and the enticing V shape just above his waistline. He's a living dream. But the dream turns into a nightmare when I notice he is holding my things, and his expression is less than friendly. He wears the same icy mask I've seen him put on when he deals with the press. *When did I become the enemy?*

RHAE AEDEN

"Put this on before you leave the building," he says, handing me an oversized black hoodie, followed by my purse. "I don't need any scandal about an escort leaving my apartment," he comments, his words cutting through the air like a razor.

"Don't treat me like that," I mutter, accepting the hoodie.

"This is a quid pro quo. I can be rude, and you can." He pauses before he can make a mistake, but it's too late.

"Finish that sentence, Philip," I challenge.

"I thought you, of all people, would be above trying to sneak out in the morning," he says, a wounded tone lurking beneath his normally cool demeanor. *I hurt Philip Burton.*

"I wasn't trying to sneak out," I defend, trying to make amends, but we both know it's a lie. "Maybe I was," I confess with a sigh.

"Why?"

"No lo sé..." *I don't know.* My throat tightens, a lump forming, and I don't dare meet his gaze for fear that my eyes might betray me and start shedding tears.

"Then figure it out, Selene," he demands, leaning against the door frame, his presence casting a spell over me. "I'm not known for my patience, and I'm not interested in playing games." His voice resonates with an intensity that leaves me feeling cornered beneath his imposing frame.

HAMMER TIME

I should feel vulnerable, but with Philip, I never feel like that, no matter how well he plays the bad guy. Right then, I realize that he makes me feel safe. It's the world he lives in that I don't want. I have zero interest in becoming the new target of the press. They hate Philip, and I am sure they won't show me any mercy. I'm ready to give him an explanation, but Philip is faster than me.

"Listen for once, Sparks," he commands, his thumb grasping my chin, coaxing my head to tilt it upward and look him straight into his precious eyes. "I've got three races in the coming weeks. I'd appreciate a decision before Silverstone's chequered flag drops."

"Are you giving me an ultimatum?" I ask.

"Yes," he replies.

"Why?"

"You can't kiss me one day and sneak out the next."

"But—"

"I've already called an Uber for you. It's waiting at the entrance. I'll see you in two months," he announces, dismissing me, and before I can muster a protest, he strolls out of the room, leaving me with a hangover and a complex decision to make.

RHAE AEDEN

The Uber drops me off right at the doorstep of my apartment complex. I can't help but realize that Philip must have memorized it when he drove me home before the season started. I walk up the stairs and ring my own doorbell two or three times, trying to give Miriam time to get decent in case she needs it. I have the key jangling in my fingers when she swings the door open, and the volume of her voice nearly splits my aching head in two.

"Where were you? I've been calling you all morning!"

"Sorry, my phone died," I mutter, struggling with my hangover.

Her eyes dart past me, scanning my body. "You're wearing a man's hoodie," she points out and then her eyes widen in recognition. "No way."

"Shhh," I hiss, pushing her into our apartment.

"Tell me what happened," Miriam demands.

Just then, a two-meter-tall blonde girl, emerges from Miriam's room. I am surprised by her sudden presence and utterly mesmerized by her beauty.

"Dobryy ranok!" *Good morning*, she greets in Ukrainian. "Sorry for the intrusion, but I have to get going." Anastasia giggles and moves closer, planting a parting kiss on Miriam's lips.

"I'll call you later," Miriam promises.

"I hope so," the blonde says, and then they exchange one more kiss before Anastasia leave.

"Wow," I cheer in excitement for my friend, causing my headache to get even worse. I go to the kitchen counter and make myself some coffee, hoping it will ease my pain.

"Her looks are just the tip of the iceberg." Miriam sighs. "She's smart, kind, and her personality is even wilder than mine."

"That's a high bar."

"I know. I'm just not ready to commit," she confesses.

"Does she know?"

"We haven't had that chat yet."

"Have you considered an open relationship?" I ask.

"I don't think so. If I decide to settle down, I want it to be exclusive, you know? But never say never."

"Talk to her, you will figure it out."

Miriam seizes the moment, staring me down with a loaded look. "Speaking of talking, spill the tea, Selene."

I lay it all out for her, from the night at the club, the way to his house, the talk on the couch ,and my morning escape plan.

"Why in the world would you do that?" Miriam asks.

"I don't know," I admit. "I'm just not in the mood for complications right now."

"What do you mean?" She raises an eyebrow.

"I'm carving out my own career here, and I'm not about to add a complex relationship with a guy who's the poster child of a problematic driver, with a god complex."

"Don't forget his delightful mood swings," Miriam adds.

"Exactly!"

"That's part of his charm." She smirks.

"Well, his princely charm came with an ultimatum." I sigh. "I've got until Silverstone to figure out what I want."

"Then use the next two months wisely," Miriam advises, her words laced with a hint of mischief.

CHAPTER THIRTY

TWO WEEKS BEFORE SILVERSTONE

Philip

Whoever thought it was a brilliant idea to book me for a press conference right before a race clearly has a unique sense of humor. But it comes as no surprise when I find out Jessica is the one behind it. I can't expect anything more from someone like her.

The past month has been crazy, relentless press tours, events, and a disastrous last race that has everyone doubting me, again. No matter how many races and titles I secure, they always circle back to the same topics.

You're only as good as your last race, and if mine in Azerbaijan is any indication, I'm far from being the best. It was an absolute dumpster fire with a DNF right before the last lap. I'm trying to call in my good luck from Monaco, for tomorrow's race in Canada. But let's face it, the prospects aren't looking too bright for the team. I only managed to qualify in sixth position yesterday, though Munguia managed to get up to fourth.

Jessica's annoyingly sharp voice interrupts my train of thought as we march towards another improvised set in the middle of the paddock. She reaches for my bicep, and that's when I snap.

"Don't touch me. Respect my personal space."

"I—I—" she stutters.

"Who's the interviewer, anyway?" I cut her off.

"Sasha, Sasha Valine." *Isn't she Selene's friend?* "You need some good press and given her connection with Selene, she's willing to help." That's a surprise.

I haven't heard anything from Selene since her attempt to escape my house while I was still asleep. It was a clear message: 'I don't need or want you.' But now, things seem different. She doesn't usually deal with press stuff, so why did she recommend Sasha?

"I wouldn't have picked her myself, but—" Jessica's sentence is cut short by Sasha, who stands a few paces ahead of us.

"You wouldn't have picked me because you don't know how to do your job." Sasha gains my respect with just one sentence.

It's clear why they call her the 'Blonde Dread.' She's got quite a reputation. Sasha is known to be ruthless, but in the best way possible, always delivering top-class interviews and insights. We all respect her, though some might be a bit scared. On top of that, she looks like she could kill you with that platinum blonde hair cut in a short bob just below her ears, a straight nose, and big, piercing black eyes that seem just the colour of the pits of hell. There's an air of mystery about her, and despite her petite, innocent appearance, there's something that says she could annihilate you if she wanted to.

"Nice to meet you," I say as our hands meet in a firm shake. "Shall we get started?"

"Sure." She gestures for the cameraman to start rolling. "Do you have a lot of accidents?" she kicks off with her first question after a brief introduction.

I stifle a scoff. "Well, that depends on who you ask."

"I'm asking you." She smiles.

"No, I wouldn't say that, even though I've had my fair share over the years." I've had some pretty bad accidents, but I don't think I've had more than the average driver. This is an extreme sport; accidents are just part of it.

"Would you say that those accidents are a result of your aggressive driving style?"

"When there are twenty of us fighting for first place, if you're not driving aggressively, you're just not cut out for this. You need a certain kind of hunger to compete at this level, and if you don't have it, you're in the wrong place. You always need to go for the gap, and sometimes that means you need to be aggressive."

Sasha smiles in approval and then looks down at her cards, ready to ask her next question. "Do you think there are drivers who don't belong in F1?"

I'm enjoying this. "I thought you wanted to talk about me." We both chuckle at the joke. "Not everyone's on the same level, hence the underdogs. But not every team has the same car, and that affects their performance too."

"Do you think there are bad drivers winning just because they're in good cars?" She is good, I could tell that already, but she has just proven that she isn't scared of asking the right questions.

"Yes," I answer simply.

"Do you have a good car?"

I catch the double-edged question and give her a wide smile. "I have good hands to drive a good car."

"Then why wasn't yesterday's result as good as you claim to be?" I see why they call her the Blonde Dread.

"The car is designed for a different type of race. The Canadian track demands a unique set of car modifications, and we haven't cracked the code for optimizing it on this circuit," I explain.

"Munguia seems to have found the best set up."

"He's an outstanding driver; occasionally, he'll be the one securing the top spot."

She examines the cards she's holding, then reads a question out loud. "It's still early in the season, but do you see him as this year's world champion?"

"I only envision myself as the champion this year. The competition is fierce; João and I are neck and neck in points, with Oliver closing the distance between us in the standings. Any one of us could become the winner, but if I want to win, I've got to visualize it happening. So, I'm not picturing Oliver or anyone else who isn't me with that trophy in their hand."

"That's a winning mindset," she remarks.

Is that a compliment?

"What are your thoughts on previous claims that you've received preferential treatment from the team in past races and allegations of cheating?"

"Firstly, getting team priority isn't cheating. People need to start understanding that," I emphasize. "There's always a first and a second driver, chosen based on who's performing best and who has the better chances. Oliver outperformed me yesterday, so he's the team's priority today."

"Isn't that frustrating?"

"It was a tough qualifier; now, all I can do is push hard and hope to drive better than him," I explain.

"Well then, we wish you the best of luck." She shifts her focus back to the camera to wrap up the interview. "Stay tuned to watch the race in a couple of hours. Thanks, Philip, for this fantastic insight, and we hope to see you win today."

"Cut," the cameraman calls.

I stand, ready to go back to the garage and away from the cameras, even if I have to admit that this interview has probably been the best of my career.

"Thanks for everything. I hope to see you again soon." I offer Sasha a smile.

"Wait!" she calls out, forcing me to stop. "I've got something for you." She hurries away and comes back practically running, holding something in her hand. "Selene gave me this," she says, handing me a white envelope.

Did Selene write me a letter or something?

"Thanks," I say, my gaze locked on the envelope.

"No problem. She's a friend of mine. Good luck today." She grins, a genuine smile rather than the one she usually flashes the cameras.

I'm gone in seconds, racing back to my motorhome, the envelope heavy in my grip. Once inside, I tear it open, and two stickers tumble out of it. I instantly recognize the design—a modern twist on the Michelangelo hands printed on a sticker paper in black. Behind it, a note:

> *I might not be there to touch the helmet, but hopefully this brings you a bit of luck too.*
>
> *Selene*

Overseas races are a godsend, mainly because they happen in the afternoon, not in the middle of the day, when I can enjoy some *siesta* time.

This time, Anastasia's joining us at home. She's been hanging around more often with Miriam whenever she's in town. I secretly envy how adorable they are together. I know I said I didn't want a complicated relationship, but I can't stop thinking about Philip. I even miss him—not enough to send a text, but just enough to send him a gift.

"So, they had a race yesterday to determine today's starting positions?" Miriam's been attempting to explain to Anastasia how races work, but the poor girl's looking more confused by the minute with all the information we've been dumping on her.

"Kind of," Miriam says. "Yesterday, they had three qualifying sessions: Q1, Q2, and Q3. By the end of each session, the five slowest cars get eliminated, and so on, until they reach Q3."

"Oh, I see. So, it's all about the timings?"

"Yes," my friend says enthusiastically.

"Isn't that your boyfriend?" Anastasia calls out, pointing at the screen where Philip's chatting with Michael next to the track.

"He's not my boyfriend," I clarify.

I can't tear my eyes away from the screen, trying to spot if he decided to use the stickers I sent him, but he hasn't put them on his helmet yet.

"*Kvitochka,* why won't your friend admit that she wants him?" Anastasia tells Miriam as if I wasn't in the room, sitting next to her.

"Because she's as stubborn as a mule," Miriam replies.

"I am not stubborn."

RHAE AEDEN

The cameraman moves closer to Philip, who takes a cellphone from Michael. He quickly types something and hands it back to him. Right then, my phone buzzes between my legs, and I grab it in a hurry.

Unknown number: Nothing compares to your hands, but this will have to do.

Unknown number: See you in Silverstone.

"Put your phone down and watch," Miriam urges.

"Yes, I'm telling you, he's into you," Anastasia shouts in giddy excitement.

I fix my gaze on the screen where Philip is now showing off his helmet to the camera, proudly displaying the new design with the hands touching both sides of his helmet.

CHAPTER THIRTY-ONE

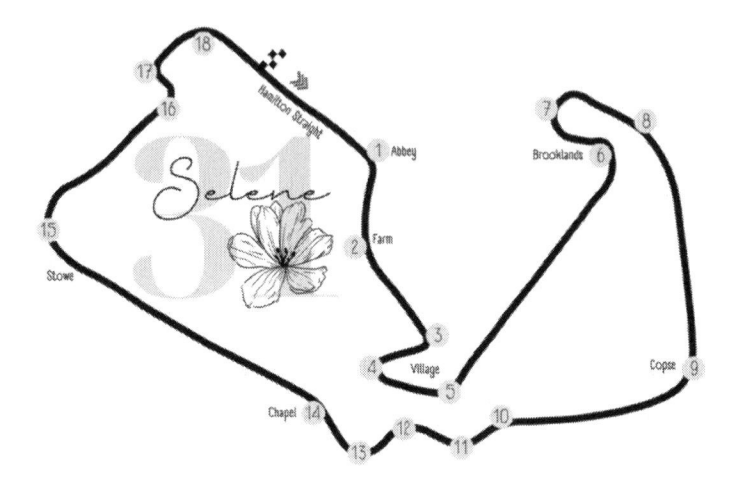

Philip and I have barely talked since the he messaged me before the Canadian GP. There have been some texts here and there, but whenever things got remotely interesting or deeper, he would make sure to remind me about his ultimatum. I wasn't sure how I'd even make it to Silverstone, but last week, Philip sent me the tickets and booked everything in my name for another racing weekend on the track.

And now, just like last year, I'm in the VIP area, sipping on a glass of champagne and trying to calm my nerves. There are a few other VIPs in the room, including Munguia's wife and kids. I could try and start a conversation, but my concentration is pinned to the TV that shows Philip in his car. His helmet is peeking out of the cockpit, and I realize he's sporting a new design. It's the same concept as always, the

Cavaglio horse, the quote, two flags, and the Michelangelo hands outlined in white. I don't bother hiding my grin. I absolutely love that he's made me part of his design.

The countdown for Q1 begins. Philip and Munguia exit the garage almost simultaneously. We're all waiting to see how today unfolds, hoping to see both drivers in the top positions. Q1 and Q2 go by quickly, and Munguia and Philip make it into Q3. João, Oliver, and Philip have been trading the top three positions for the last half-hour.

Philip's driving style is aggressive as usual, but it's obvious that he knows what he is doing at every corner, except for turn six. For whatever reason, he's struggling and losing precious time there. It should be easy for him, but he taps the brakes when he approaches it.

"Vamos, tú puedes." *Come on, you can do it.* I genuinely believe in him. He's got this; he just needs to shake off whatever's bothering him.

Philip goes for another attempt, and time is running out. Two minutes to go.

He starts his last fast lap, practically flying. Munguia is having a bit of trouble in the second sector. Raindrops start falling on the track, but it's not enough for any of the teams to switch to wet tires.

He keeps pushing , getting faster and faster towards turn six. He barrels through the straight, refusing to let up or falter as he approaches that corner.

HAMMER TIME

"Vamos!" I scream.

Philip finishes the lap without any errors, the rain intensifying as he paints the final sector purple, clocking the best time of the session and crowning himself the provisional polesitter. Nobody celebrates until Munguia and João cross the finish line, both slower than Philip.

Nobody can top him.

The cars start their cool-down lap, with some heading back to their garages. With the session finished, the drivers try to drive back, but it proves an almost impossible task when the rain starts pouring harder. Philip's tires aren't made for these conditions, and he's struggling to keep control of his car, even at a slower pace. It slides onto the wet part of the track, and he loses control around turn six. The gravel in that corner saves him from crashing right into the safety barriers at the track's edge.

Suddenly, it all comes together in my mind.

That's where João had his accident last year. Philip is scared.

Thankfully, he climbs out of the car with minimal effort, and his voice comes through the radio, assuring us he's okay.

I don't think he really is, though.

RHAE AEDEN

The track is deserted in the late afternoon, the rain has finally cleared, and all the support races have wrapped up. Only one person remains at the track.

Philip is sitting on the gravel at turn six, lost in contemplation. His racing suit is slung low on his hips, revealing his torso covered by the snug-fitting black fireproof undershirt that is slightly wet from the rain. My heart breaks a little when I see him like this, and my mind can't stop thinking about ways to help him.

"Hey." I approach him from behind. He's so deep in his thoughts that he didn't even hear the gravel crunching under my feet.

Philip turns his head toward me, surprise flickering over his face for a brief second. "What are you doing here?"

"Nice to see you too," I say and take a seat next to him on the chilly ground. "Are you okay?" I ask, even if I know the answer already.

"What do you think?" he grumbles, his gaze still fixed on the corner of the track in front of us.

"I don't have a psychology degree, remember?" I joke, and, from the corner of my eye, I catch a faint smile on his face. "But in my amateur opinion, I'd say you've got a case of PTSD."

"Why would I have that?"

"It's normal to be scared, you know that, right?" I want to comfort him, but I'm aware that pushing too hard might make him retreat and shut me out, like he always does.

"I can't afford to be scared. If I'm scared, I'll lose focus, and if I lose that, I risk a crash at three hundred kilometers per hour," he replies, finally looking at me. For the first time in almost two months, I'm met with that intense stare of his, and only now do I realize how much I've missed him. "Being scared could cost me my life. So, no, I can't afford to be scared, Selene."

"You're right; you can't. That's why you've got to confront your fear before the race starts." I stand up, and he raises his head to follow my movement. "*Vamos.*"

"Where?"

"I've got a surprise for you." I extend my hand, and he takes it, rising to his feet. He tries to let go, but I keep a firm grip.

"What do you want from me, Selene?"

"I'll explain later, okay?"

Philip doesn't answer, instead he follows me without a word. I smile at him, even if he doesn't see it. I don't mind not being the center of attention; all I want is for him to make peace with whatever's going on in his head.

RHAE AEDEN

We walk alongside each other in silence around the track and back into the garages. Michael is waiting there for us with one of Cavaglio's street cars, a sleek black beast that may not be as fast as Formula 1 cars, but it roars just the same.

"She's a beauty!" I say to Michael, who throws the car key over the roof for me. "Thanks for this."

"You've got her for half an hour; please be careful,"

"Give me that." Philip tries to snatch the key from my hand, but I'm quicker.

"Ah, ah. I'm driving first."

"No, you're not."

"I drove your Lamborghini, remember?"

"This is a racetrack. And that"—he points at the car—"is not a toy, Selene."

"I promise to hold your hand if you get scared. Now, get in the car." He doesn't move. "Are you scared?"

"No, I'm not."

"Then get in."

He looks at me defiantly but decides against saying whatever is on his mind, opening the passenger door and sliding into the car. He buckles the seatbelt as tightly as possible.

"Why are you doing this?" He sighs.

"You need help, and you're too stubborn to ask for it."

HAMMER TIME

I drive us out of the garage, intentionally drifting. Philip's knuckles turn white as he clutches the door handle.

"Come on, have a little faith." I exit the pit lane just before the first corner in the Abbey. We zoom through the first sector, heading into Brooklands just before turn six.

"Slow down, loca!" Him calling me *crazy* in Spanish makes me burst into laughter.

"Are you going to throw up?" I tease, pressing the throttle even harder. The car drifts slightly, but we make it through. And, suddenly, Philip starts laughing too. It's the most precious sound I have heard in my life. "Not bad for someone who isn't a pro, huh?" I say, feeling a bit lightheaded from the adrenaline.

"An economist, a psychologist, and now a driver too..."

"Whoever said you can't do it all clearly never met me." I stop the car at the starting line after finishing my lap and step out.

"What are you doing?" Philip calls out from inside the car. I rush to his side, open his door, and lean in to undo his seatbelts. I sense how he stops breathing for a second when I am close to him, and the feeling it gives me is better than any rush of adrenaline a car could give me. "Your turn."

"Why would you want to drive with someone who's damaged?" he says when he steps out of the car. His words hit me right in the heart.

"You're not damaged." I tell him, lifting my hand to his jaw, and he instinctively leans into my touch.

"You sure act like I am. We kissed, and all you did was try to escape me."

"That wasn't about you," I reply.

"Then what was it about?" I hesitate for a moment, struggling to explain the thoughts that have been swirling around in my head for months. "Whatever," he says, gently pushing me aside as he starts to walk away.

"Wait!" I call out. "Please, just one lap. Do this for me, and then we can talk about what happened." He looks at me, mistrust in his eyes. "Just one," I insist.

"Get in the car," he orders, and I jump into the passenger side before he can change his mind.

Philip starts the car, accelerating faster than I ever could. My pulse races more than when I was behind the wheel, the adrenaline rush taking over.

"Let's see if you're really not afraid."

I clutch the door handle, laughing nervously, a mix of fear and excitement washing through me as we race past Abbey. We're racing at over two hundred and fifty kilometers per hour as we approach the cursed turn. I'm terrified, but I don't flinch, fearing that Philip will see it. I'm determined to give him his confidence back, not make him doubt himself more.

If he doesn't believe in himself, then I will.

Finally, he takes the corner so fast, I fear we'll end up in the gravel and spin, but we miraculously stay on the track. I scream in happiness and Philip chuckles a little.

"Again!" I urge him.

"What do you want, Selene?" he asks as we near the end of the lap.

"I told you, another lap!" He momentarily takes his eyes off the road, making my heart race even faster.

"What do you really want?" he repeats, still looking at me.

A deep fear of crashing floods me, and I can't help but wonder if I'm crazy for doing this. But then I remember Philip is behind the wheel. He knows this track like the palm of his hand, and I know he would never put my life at risk, no matter how mad he is at me.

"I don't know," I admit, realizing I can't keep playing games. "I've never regretted the kiss or any moment with you." Philip's eyes return to the track, and I finally take a breath. "It's just—the people—" I start, cutting off when I can't find the right words.

"You're afraid of people seeing you with me?" He pushes down on the throttle as we continue, and I can't help but feel exhilarated by the danger. That must say something about my sense of self-preservation.

"Yes. Well, no! Not like that!" I scream confused. "You're Philip Burton! Eres una eminencia en el mundo del deporte y yo... yo soy solo yo." I switch to my mother tongue unable to keep up with the adrenaline and fear as we approach turn six. *You are Philip Burton. You are a legend and I am... I am just me.*

"Being just you is more than enough, Sparks," he says, taking his foot off the gas pedal for the first time. His hand makes it to my thigh, which he caresses with extreme care.

"I don't want to be the next girl seen with Philip Burton, not when I'm trying to find my own path in this industry," I confess for the first time.

"So, what? You don't want to be seen with me?"

"I want to be with you."

"But?" We finally make it back to the pits, and Philip guides the car into the garage.

"I don't want the world to know. I don't want the press to know. I just don't want my private life to become public. You've seen the tabloids. I'm *lucky* the press hasn't figured out who I am. They'll devour me! They'll say I'm only working for Cavaglio because of you. They'll say you're a predator for being seen with someone over ten years younger, and—"

"Shhhh." Philip unbuckles his seatbelt and leans into my seat, cradling my head between his large hands. "Don't get ahead of yourself," he whispers.

"Did I scare you?" I ask.

"I'm the predator here, so you should be the one scared of me, not the other way around." He gives me a teasing smile. "Whatever happens can be kept quiet."

"This world isn't known for keeping things quiet. People literally move across the world to try and see you in person," I argue.

"Selene, don't get ahead of yourself, okay?" It's incredible how Philip can switch from his brooding self to this caring person sitting in front of me, consoling me.

"I'm a Virgo. All I do is plan ahead."

"Come on, you can plan my race tomorrow." He gives me a soft kiss on the lips, then exits the car. "Let's get through the weekend, and we'll figure everything out when we're back in Monaco."

That sounds like a great plan, and it's enough to calm my nerves. This situation is far from ideal, but it's one that might just work out. Maybe I'm a fool for being willing to risk my future to spend the present with Philip.

But I've pushed him away often enough to know the pull he has on me will always bring me right back to him.

CHAPTER THIRTY-TWO

Philip

There's nothing like coming back home after months of traveling between countries, especially when I'm bringing the Silverstone trophy back with me after a complicated race. The original plan was to stay in the UK for a couple of days, but as soon as I got released from my team duties, I jumped on a plane back to Monaco, following a certain redhead.

Life as a racer is as rewarding as it is exhausting. Today, I'd much rather relax on the couch, but I need to hit the gym and work on the plan that Michael sent me this morning. So, I make my way to my home gym. The view of the stunning Monegasque coastline keeps me going as I warm up on the treadmill.

I'm in the middle of my workout when the doorbell rings.

I'm not expecting anyone, and Michael is only supposed to be here later, not now. The doorbell rings again, so I quickly climb the stairs to the entrance. Without bothering to look through the peephole after the third ring, I open the door.

"Who the h—"

"Surprise!" A woman under a cap, dressed in all black with shades covering her face, says to me.

My heart races, fearing that a stalker has made it into the building, but I quickly realize it's Selene.

Before I can say anything, she pops a bottle, probably champagne, and the cork shoots into the air, bouncing off the doorframe and landing square on top of my head.

Selene's mouth forms an O-shape. "Sorry," she mumbles. She forgets the champagne entirely, making a mess all over the foyer, distracted by the sight of me.

"See anything you like?" I tease as her eyes roam down my body.

"You wish! Are you going to let me in, or do you want me to stand here all day long?"

I step aside in response. "Who are you hiding from?"

"What do you mean?"

I give her a look, raising my brow as I shut the door.

"Oh, that... I was afraid there would be paparazzi."

"Come here," I put my arms around her waist, pulling her close before planting a kiss on the top of her head. She smells incredible.

We stay like that for a while, and I want to believe that whatever is happening between us might actually work, that it won't blow up in our faces. But part of me knows that happiness like this can't last too long in my world.

"You're sweating." Her words vibrate against my chest.

"Hmmm."

"Let go of me!" she squeals and wiggles, trying to break free from my embrace.

"I'm happy to see you," I whisper and, against my will, release her waist and cup her chin with one hand, leaning in to kiss her on the lips.

"You saw me yesterday," she whispers and then gives me a soft peck. "What's your plan for today?" Selene asks, creating some space between us.

"I was midway through my training session, and after that, I wanted to have a session in the simulator."

Her eyes gleam with excitement. "You have a simulator here?"

"Yeah?"

Before the word has even left my mouth, she bolts towards me and jumps into my arms. "Can I use it?" she squeals, her legs wrapped around my waist.

"No," I tease her, wanting to see what she'll do even as I lead us to the room where I've set up the simulator.

"Please?" She pouts.

"You look so pretty when you beg." She rolls her eyes, and I can feel the tension building in my pants. She doesn't say a word, but I know she's noticed, judging by the way her body has gone rigid in my hands.

"I can be very convincing," she teases and nips at my neck.

"No pongas el horno a calentar si no vas a usarlo." I can't help but blurt out the Spanish phrase, my mind muddled by her closeness. *Don't start the oven if you're not going to use it.*

Selene gives me a look, attempting to keep her composure, but she fails, bursting into laughter. "You did not just say that!" *Did I break the tension? Did I say it right?* "I love it!" She laughs again.

"Okay, time to go down, monkey."

"No," she protests but still unwraps her legs like a good girl.

I open the door to my simulator room, noticing Selene's mouth opening as if she wants to say something. It falls shut again when she sees the room. Two red simulators are placed next to each other.

"Why do you have two?" she asks.

"Michael likes to play, and I'm guessing you might enjoy it too." I turn on the ceiling lights and lower the blinds to create a dark room effect. "Sit in this one," I instruct her, pointing to the simulator close to the window. "You can come here whenever you want, but there's one rule, always use the one close to the window. The other one is configured for me, so please don't touch it. It's a pain to set up."

"Copy."

"I'm serious."

"I'll never touch that one and will always stick to the one next to the window," she promises, trying stay serious, but the smile on her face gives her away.

"Good girl. Now sit inside." Selene doesn't need any further encouragement. She slips into the seat, and I lean down, helping her set up.

"We can race against each other," she suggests.

"I'll just win over and over again." But I set it up so we can race each other anyway.

"Maybe, but you don't know how good I might be," she says. "Let's make it a game."

"Isn't racing already a game for you?"

"Well, then let's sweeten the pot. Whoever wins gets to ask a question, and the other *has to* answer." There is a glint of excitement in her eyes, like a kid who is about to open their Christmas presents.

"Just questions?"

"We can make it three rounds and the one who has more wins at the end gets something in return?" she suggests, the mischief in her eyes intriguing me.

"Define '*something*.'"

"What do you want?" Her tone sounds wary, but she isn't scared.

I give her a half smile, savoring the anticipation. "I'll tell you when I win," I reply, determined to win now.

I set both simulators to game mode, selecting Monza for the first race. Three laps. Selene has a better start in the simulator, her car surging ahead, allowing her to lead the first lap. I push myself to pass her before the second lap, but she overtakes me again. Fortunately, luck is on my side when she makes a mistake midway through the third lap. She spins but manages to avoid a crash and regain control of the simulator, but she isn't quick enough to overtake me before the lap is over.

"First question is mine," I announce.

"You better make it a good one…" A strand of her hair hangs in her face, so I lean over to tuck it behind her ear.

"Was I your first crush?"

"Are you serious?" She huffs.

"No, I'm just teasing you. What's something that you value?" I ask.

Selene takes a moment to think about her answer.

"My family. They're the most important thing to me. I have my goals, my life, my passions, but those are worth little without them."

"Miriam counts as family too, I assume?"

"Of course. She's like the sister I never had." She pauses for a second to smile to herself. "Next round," she instructs, snapping her fingers at the screen, urging me to hurry up.

I choose the streets of Monaco for the next race. It's one of the most challenging courses in the simulator – a small misstep and you'll find yourself hitting a wall. This time, I have a better start than Selene. She struggles in the first lap, trying to familiarize herself with the street race, but she quickly gains speed in the second lap. As the third lap begins, I'm still in the lead, but she's closing in. My focus wavers, distracted by her, and I graze a wall. Forced to slow down, she takes the opportunity to overtake me, and there's nothing I can do to regain my position.

"Yes!" she cheers in excitement.

"Not bad for—" I begin, but she cuts me off by pressing her index finger to my lips.

"If you say, 'not bad for a girl,' I'll kick you in the balls," she threatens.

"—for someone who is driving in a simulator for the first time," I finish, removing her finger from my lips.

"Why don't you set the record straight with the press?" she asks, switching topic.

"What do you mean?" I feign ignorance.

"Don't act dumb."

"I didn't care what they said about me after my mom died. I had no family and nothing to work hard for. I hit a whole new low back then. I wouldn't say I had an alcohol problem, but I definitely tested my limits before I joined F1. Every night I went to a party, hoping to feel something besides the pain of mourning. But nothing helped, and all I could think about is how much I missed my mom. My mental health problems started back then too. Eventually, I became ruthless and aggressive, and the press saw an opportunity to make money from it. People used me more and more for my connections, money, and spotlight. But then, I got paired with Michael as my trainer, and he helped me regain control of my life. I got into therapy, worked on my anxiety, my depression and my grief, and then I got my seat in F1."

"I'm so sorry, Philip," she says, trying to hold back her emotions.

"Don't worry about it. Honestly, I never cared about them, so I didn't bother to set the record straight, it just became part of my life."

"You say you don't care, but that's not true."

"It doesn't matter what I say or do. It's been ten years since I joined the sport, and they still see me like the broken man who managed to beat their golden British boy. They made a villain out of me, and when they saw how much money it made them, they continued the storyline. Now, I'd rather keep my real personality for my inner circle."

"Your inner circle consists of you and Michael."

"It's an exclusive circle."

"Am I in it?" she asks.

"Yes, you are." I lean in to give her a soft kiss. "What track do you want to race now?"

"Hmm, I need to win this one." She takes her time scrolling through the options even though she knows the calendar by heart. "Mexico!"

"Mexico it is, then." I would've preferred Brazil, but the Hermanos Rodríguez track is one of my favorites on the current calendar.

Selene takes the lead after a fantastic start, but I race through the first set of turns perfectly. She overtakes me on the straight but loses the advantage in the next tight turn. We drive side by side for a few meters, but I play a little dirty. She falls behind before I cross the finish line, securing the win.

"No!" she screams, letting go of the steering wheel. "No, no, no."

"Now, onto my prize," I say, giving her a wicked smile.

"This is so not right!"

"Sparks, it's called a motorsport race. Don't play if you're not confident you can win."

CHAPTER THIRTY-THREE

Selene

"Just tell me what you want," I urge him, bracing myself for what I expect will be a sexual innuendo. The tension between my legs suggests I wouldn't mind it, but I'm not ready for anything like that yet.

"You, in a long, green dress," he replies.

I roll my eyes at his response. "I'm not sure I like where this fantasy is going."

"It's not a fantasy," he says, "You'll know what those look like when the time comes." I have to bite my lip at his words.

"Don't tease me with a good time, Philip,"

"What I want from you is a night out in Paris for an annual gala. I'm receiving an award."

"No," I blurt out before he can even finish the sentence.

"You have to say yes. After all, you made the rules."

"Philip, they're going to see me. I told you I want to keep things between us," I respond, my irritation starting to come through.

"I respect that; but this gala is a masquerade."

My eyes widen. He's been planning this for a while, hasn't he?

"When is it?"

"A week before the French GP. Will you come?"

"I'll think about it."

"I'll take that," he says, a smile covering his face. I smile back at him, noticing how much he's been smiling recently, especially compared to when I first met him. It warms my heart to see him so happy and less like his usual grumpy self.

"You know, I came here with an actual purpose in mind," I say, standing up and extending my hand for him to take.

"What purpose?" he asks, tilting his head with curiosity in his gaze.

"I thought we could have our first date." The words tumble past my lips with a tremor.

"I'm not an expert in dating, but shouldn't I be the one planning something for us?" His tone is playful. "At least that's how it worked back in my day," he jokes.

As much as it pains me to admit it, I've done my fair share of snooping into Philip's personal life. The fact that he's a celebrity makes it all too easy. There's a long trail of supermodels and movie stars in his past. His dating adventures are all over the internet—movie premieres, fashion events, casino parties, and yacht trips—all well-documented by the paparazzi.

I want to stay as far away from that scene as possible.

"I thought an intimate meal at home might be better since we're still trying to avoid being seen together…"

"You must be the first woman to say that." I shoot him a lethal look.

"I was thinking, maybe we could order some food and have lunch here?" I suggest, and when he doesn't respond, I start babbling nervously. "It was just a thought; we don't need to do that. I can go now. I'm sorry; I don't know what I was thinking, coming here unannounced. I—" I'm about to go on when Philip interrupts me.

"If you say you're sorry one more time, I'll spank you," he teases. My heart skips a beat at the realization that I'm not opposed to that idea. "You can come here whenever you want. My silence wasn't because you overstepped, which you didn't. I just would've liked to be the one to come up with a plan for both of us."

"Well, you can plan our next date."

"Deal. What do you think about ordering some Thai? I know a place that has the best takeout." I love his enthusiasm and his willingness to play along.

"I'd love that," I answer.

RHAE AEDEN

After ordering an excessive amount of Thai food, Philip leaves me to take a shower. The restraint I exercise to avoid snooping through every room in his house is remarkable, even to me. I decide to stay in the living room, taking in the art piece displayed there.

It's a modern and minimalist space with a full-sized replica of 'El Bosco' dominating the room. It's like Philip himself, cold on the outside but full of vibrant layers underneath.

I busy myself by setting the table, searching for glasses, utensils, and plates. Juggling them with care, I carry them to the table, positioned in front of a glass window that provides a breathtaking view of the coastline. It almost feels like we're having a beachfront picnic. It's a bit melancholic that I get to date someone like him without actually dating him in the traditional sense. But I do have my reasons, and whatever's going on between us, it's just a situationship.

The doorbell rings, dragging me away from my thoughts, and I rush to answer it.

"Delivery for Philip Burton." The delivery guy's enthusiasm wanes when he sees me instead of Philip. "You're not Philip Burton."

"Obviously not."

"Are you a new girlfriend?"

"No," I answer, panicking. "I'm the cleaning lady."

"Ah, okay. Here's the food. Hope he enjoys it," he says as he hands me the bag and heads back to the elevator.

"I never knew my cleaning lady was that hot." I'm about to reply with a snarky comment, but my words freeze as I turn to see Philip standing there, shirtless, water droplets glistening on his bare chest as they trickle from his wet, black hair.

"Please put on some clothes," I mutter, praying that I don't start drooling.

"Why? Seeing you so flustered might become my new favourite thing, Sparks." He smirks that damn smirk that could melt any woman's heart. I'm in deep trouble.

"Put them on," I beg. "I'll get the food sorted out."

"You're so boring."

"I'm trying to show restraint," I retort.

"You've already shown plenty of that," he quips.

"Go get dressed," I insist, hoping he'll listen this time.

"I like a bossy woman," he says, his footsteps fading as he heads upstairs.

When Philip returns, we have lunch together. It feels like the first time we can truly be ourselves. Within these four walls, it's just him and me, enjoying each other's company.

Despite never making public appearances, his *abuela* – he never calls her anything else – is still very much a part of his life, and he adores her. He visits her in Spain as often as he can so he can spend some time with her. All the different sides he's showing me of himself are only making me fall harder for him. I only wish that he would let the world have at least a little glimpse of those sides of him. I understand why he doesn't want to show anyone, but I'm still convinced the world would show him some appreciation if they knew everything he's had to go through.

"What's one thing you'd love to do?" Philip asks, taking a bite of his dumpling.

"That's a deep question," I say, thinking I'll need a long time to come up with an answer when a vivid image immediately comes to mind. "I want to see the Rosetta Stone in the British Museum. It's on my bucket list," I confess.

"That makes sense, You mentioned you like history," he says, showing off his impressive memory.

"How about you?"

"I'd like to visit Egypt. I've never had the chance. I've traveled the world, but I've never truly enjoyed it. I'd like to visit places as a tourist, and you're not the only one with a passion for history." He chuckles.

I don't think he realizes how much of himself he's revealing to me, and I can't help but wonder if he has shared this much with other women... or if I'm a lucky one.

The front door abruptly swings open, causing us to startle and for our moment to be ruined.

"Well, if it isn't my favorite couple." Michael struts inside, making his grand entrance. Philip shoots him a death glare, but that doesn't stop Michael from joining us at the table. "Can I have some of that?" Michael asks Philip, eyeing the containers of Thai food.

"Go away," Philip barks at him, gesturing for him to leave.

"No, Michael, stay," I chime in. "Be nice," I say to Philip. "Please, take some." I motion to the containers, most of them still full. "We ordered more than enough."

"You're a real one, S."

"No problem. I was leaving anyway."

"No, you weren't," Philip says, looking at me, puzzled.

"Yes, I was," I reply calmly, standing up from my seat. Philip grabs my arm, and I walk closer to him, lacing my hands around his neck. He holds my waist, making sure I don't leave. "It's getting late, and I need to get home to do some work."

"Can't you work from here?" Philip persists.

"I don't have any of my stuff," I explain. Out of the corner of my eye, I see Michael helping himself to a plate of food. It doesn't feel like the right moment to act this intimately with Philip, not with Michael around.

"We can do something before I leave for the next Grand Prix," Philip suggests, and I slide my fingers through his unruly dark hair. "I fly to Austria on Wednesday morning, but I'll text you."

"Do that," I say. I want to kiss him, but I can't bring myself to do it with Michael present.

"Let me walk you to the door," he says, noticing my discomfort, and accompanies me to the entrance. "Text me when you make it home."

"I will," I promise. The added privacy of a few meters between us and Michael gives me the courage to step onto my tiptoes and plant a kiss on his lips. It starts as a gentle peck but quickly intensifies. I loop my arms around Philip's neck, my fingers finding his hair as he nips at my lip. A soft whimper escapes me, and I can sense its effect on him.

"I'll see you soon," I whisper breathlessly, finding it difficult to pull away from this amazing man.

CHAPTER THIRTY-FOUR

Selene

I decide to walk from Philip's house to mine, a stroll that should take less than an hour. Plugging in my earphones, I play some music and head home, enjoying the warmth of the sun on my skin.

I am not too far from Philip's place when I get a weird feeling, as if I'm being followed. I look around for anything out of the ordinary. I even remove my earphones to heighten my awareness of my surroundings, but I can't find anything strange around me. I walk a few more steps, but my heart is already racing, paranoia and anxiety creeping in. The air feels thin, and breathing becomes almost impossible. Once again, I turn, and the world blurs as I crash into someone. Gasping for air, I murmur an apology.

"Sorry," I say, my eyes struggling to focus.

"Selene?" I hear a man's voice. "Selene, are you okay?" he repeats. After blinking a few times, I finally recognize the person in front of me.

Mark.

Seeing him isn't exactly a relief, but it's better than being pursued by paparazzi.

"Do you want me to call someone?" Mark sounds genuinely concerned, but my headspace is far from ideal to have him this close to me.

"No, no. I just need a minute," I assure him, closing my eyes and taking deep breaths.

And then it hits me.

"Are you following me?"

"What? Why would I be following you?"" Mark appears offended and surprised by my accusation, as if he hadn't harassed me after our breakup.

I raise an eyebrow at him.

"Okay, I understand where that's coming from. I've received some help since then. I'm sorry for what I said and did. I'll leave you alone now if you think you can make it on your own."

"Good for you," I retort sarcastically. "I think I can manage it from here. I'll call an Uber now."

"Sure. Good seeing you, Selene."

"Bye," I say, focused on ordering an Uber.

HAMMER TIME

Mark walks away, and the Uber arrives, bringing me home in mere minutes. I only allow my guard to drop when I'm inside the apartment, feeling safe and shielded from the outside world. I must deal with my fear of being seen as Philip's... what? Plus one? Latest conquest? Girlfriend?

I'm not even sure what we are.

"Don't go there," I hum to myself, refusing to entertain these thoughts. Our relationship is unconventional, but it's working, and I need to maintain my positive attitude.

I put on some music that blasts through the house speakers and start working to distract myself. As I check my inbox, a couple of emails from Cavaglio are at the top of the list. One from Sarah catches my attention, but before I can delve into it, my phone buzzes, demanding my attention.

Philip: Are you home yet?

My face lights up with a smile upon seeing his name.

Me: Yes

I scan Sarah's email, but an incoming call interrupts me.

"I told you to call me when you made it home." Philip's voice is full of concern.

"Sorry, I got a bit distracted," I confess.

"Are you okay?"

"Yeah, thanks for checking in," I reply, opting not to share the details of my encounter with Mark and my spiraling paranoia. It's likely all in my head, and I need to figure out how to overcome it.

"Okay." Philip doesn't seem entirely convinced but drops the subject. "Can you have dinner tomorrow?" he asks, shifting the conversation.

"I could, if we're having it in London."

"What do you mean?" he asks.

"I received an email from Sarah. She wants me to attend an in-person meeting at the British headquarters."

"Then we're going to London, darling," Philip says, his enthusiasm catching me off guard. I've quickly realized that dating him comes with countless unexpected twists and turns. "Do you want to stay the night there or come after my meeting?" he asks.

"Are you coming with me?" I'm taken aback by his offer, what kind of person plans a date in another country?

"If you want me to, yes." I can't help but smile like a schoolgirl with a crush. "I have to be in Monaco in the morning, but I can join you in the afternoon."

"I would like that," I admit, already daydreaming about the two of us in London, enjoying our first proper date.

"I'll get us reservations."

"Nothing fancy, please," I beg, my fear of being recognized creeping back in.

"Don't stress about it, okay?"

"Okay, I'll see you tomorrow."

London is my favorite city in the world. The charming people, the stunning city, and the rich history at every corner make it impossible not to fall in love with the place. I thrive in the midst of the Brits, and being here for work adds an extra layer of excitement to the experience.

I'm just a bit blindsided since I'm not entirely sure why I've been asked here. I haven't been involved in any projects since my time in Italy.

The Cavaglio Nero London Headquarters is precisely as depicted in pictures: a towering glass building reflecting the gray sky. I walk in through the revolving doors just as two women exit. Sarah is already waiting for me at the entrance, speaking on the phone but hanging up as soon as she spots me.

"Selene, darling. It's so wonderful to see you again."

"It's great to see you too, Sarah," I reply, choosing to hug her instead of offering a handshake.

"Come, I'm quite short on time."

"Sure, what's on the agenda?" I ask, attempting to find out what exactly I am getting myself into.

"We have something for you," she says as we head towards the elevator. "I apologize for doing this very last minute, but there have been some internal developments, and we needed you here today."

"Any specifics?"

"You'll see," she says, her smile sending my mind spiraling through various possibilities, but I refrain from getting my hopes up. I don't want to be disappointed again.

Walking side by side, we pass the familiar offices that are a replica of the ones in Milan with their decor, and even though it's all the same, I find myself examining the space as if seeing it for the first time. We navigate a hallway lined with offices, and Sarah halts in front of one of them.

"Please take a seat," she says once we're inside, and I follow her instructions, settling into one of the two chairs arranged in front of her office desk. She sits in the other one, taking her seat behind the desk. "I'll be straightforward. We're quite impressed with your work during the first half of the season. You may have ruffled the feathers of a few sharks, but you've also left many of them thoroughly impressed. The good news: the impressed sharks outnumber the others." She pauses, my heart racing in anticipation for what comes next. "There's a new opportunity, and I'd like to extend the offer to you. I have the paperwork here with me." She flips open a black folder, the key to my future.

"This is incredible," I manage to say, struggling not to stutter. "I wasn't expecting this when I came here."

"Well, I wanted it to be a surprise." Sarah pauses for a moment, clearing her throat. "We want to hire you as the head of marketing strategy."

"What?" I blurt out, surprised. I feel a lump in my throat that I quickly manage to swallow. This is my dream position, everything I've been working towards, a role I didn't think I'd secure without a few more years of experience under my belt.

"I don't get it. This is a senior position."

"It is. Normally, we wouldn't have considered you," Sarah begins, "but working with you these past few months has opened a lot of eyes. We want you on board with us."

CHAPTER THIRTY-FIVE

Philip

I park the car a few blocks away from Cavaglio's headquarters and wait for Selene. Naturally, she wouldn't let me pick her up right in front of her coworkers. I understand her desire to keep us private. She's worked incredibly hard this year, and we both know all that work would shatter if people saw her with me. They might question her, even though we all know she doesn't need me to shine.

It doesn't take long before I spot her copper hair floating in the wind. She's almost sprinting towards me in her high heels, the broadest of smiles on her face that warms the blood in my veins. I return her smile, taking off my shades.

Finally, she arrives at my side and squeals before leaping into the air, wrapping her arms around my neck. It catches me off guard, but I savor the warmth of her body pressed against mine, her legs dangling in the air.

"Missed me?" I tease her.

"You won't believe what just happened," she says, excited. "You're looking at Cavaglio's head of marketing strategy!"

"No way!" The news takes me by surprise. This is great. It's everything she has worked for her entire life, and she is finally getting it. I am so proud of her, knowing the dedication she's poured into the projects she's worked on for our team.

"Yes way!"

I scoop her up again and spin us around in the middle of the street, reveling in her happiness. "That's my girl." I kiss her and then set her back down. "I'm so proud of you."

"We have to celebrate this."

"I've got a surprise for you. Get into the car."

"Always so bossy," she mocks. "I'd like that." She gives me a peck and hops into the car, not allowing me to open the door for her.

I navigate the car through the London streets, which are a complete nightmare at this hour with everyone leaving work. Our destination isn't far, but it takes us nearly forty minutes to reach the British Museum.

"Where are we going?" Selene asks, her eyes glued to the colossal building.

"I just need to park the car," I say, sidestepping the question.

"Are you sure you've got the directions right? This is the British Museum, Philip," she points out as we drive past the grand structure.

I gently tilt her chin to divert her gaze from the building. I quiet her with a kiss. "Who's in charge of this date night?"

"You are."

"Good girl. Now get out of the car."

She obeys my command, and I watch her while I turn off the car and collect some of the things I brought.

"Turn around," I say, and she raises an uncertain eyebrow at me. I'm convinced she'll open her mouth in protest, but instead, she opts for obedience and twirls on her heels. I approach her from behind and cover her eyes with a blindfold.

"What are you doing!?" she squeaks.

"Give me your hand." I extend mine, allowing her to grab my fingers. "I promise you'll like this," I whisper into her ear.

"I trust you," she says, holding onto my hand as I guide us towards the museum.

We reach the entrance of the building where a security guard gives me an odd look. I press my finger to my lips, silently instructing him not to spoil the surprise.

"What's going on, Philip?" Selene asks, realizing we've been standing still for quite a while.

"Just give me a minute."

She doesn't reply, and I use that moment to show the guard the necessary documents for access. His eyes widen as he finally recognizes me. Selene fiddles with a ring on her finger, visibly vibrating with curiosity and impatience.

"Are we there yet?"

"Just a few more minutes." Without any warning, I place my hand on her back and the other behind her knees, cradling her in my arms to quicken our pace.

"Philip! Let me down," she says, giving my chest a gentle swat. "Anyone could see us!"

"I promise there's nobody here." She relaxes at that and falls silent.

It's right her and now that I realize I would move the world for her.

That I'd do anything for the woman in my arms.

Selene

Philip finally lowers me to the ground, my heels hitting the firm floor after what felt like an eternity. I can't even begin to fathom where he has brought us, but I'd be lying if I said I'm not intrigued.

"You can take the blindfold off." Philip's voice fills the room. I can't help but grin.

RHAE AEDEN

The light in the room is momentarily blinding when I remove the blindfold. But, after I blink a few times, my eyesight focuses, but my smile drops as the blindfold slips from my fingertips. Nothing could have prepared me for what's now standing before me.

The Rosetta Stone, its every side adorned with Egyptian hieroglyphics and their translations into other languages, is standing right in front of me in all its glory.

"How did you-" Tears of happiness gather in my eyes.

For a brief moment, I tear my gaze from the stone and survey the room, half-expecting to see tourists everywhere. But the place is quiet, there is nobody but the two of us sharing the space.

"You know, the usual. Name-dropping, a few season tickets, and a bit of cash can work wonders. We've got the whole British Museum to ourselves." I'm tempted to run into his arms and kiss him.

"Why? This must've cost a fortune," I protest in disbelief.

"It did," Philip concedes, "but I earn money to enjoy life, not to hoard it in a bank." He strides closer, now towering over me. "Let's enjoy it, Sparks." The way he says it is enough to make my knees weak.

So many times, I've fantasized about visiting London, seeing the mummies and enjoying history locked away within the walls of this grand structure. And now, I'm doing it with this man in the most intimate way, no tourists snapping pictures of the artifacts or kids screaming around.

It's just the two of us, surrounded by history.

"Thank you," I whisper, still in awe of what this man has done for me.

I love the gesture, but it also scares me. It's more proof of his devotion, how committed he is to whatever is growing between us. We could've visited like ordinary tourists, but here he stands, having reserved an entire museum just for us, allowing me to experience a date with a man who's seems to have walked right out of my dreams.

No one can ever compare to him. There will never be anyone else for me because no one can come close to who he is deep inside. If only more people could see that. No matter how they try to distort the narrative, he's not a villain; he's a knight in shining black armor. And now, he's mine.

"We've got the museum for two hours," he tells me.

"Then we better enjoy it," I say, stepping towards him, reaching for his hand. For the first time in a long while, I've stopped worrying about the future. The present is too perfect to focus on anything else. Sure, things may change eventually, but for now, this is exactly where I should be: savoring every moment.

We spend the night in the silent, grand halls of the British Museum, enjoying stolen kisses and running like carefree children. Our excitement is palpable as we visit the Egyptian mummies and Roman relics. From time to time, I catch Philip's eye, and there is a silent understanding between us that this is something extraordinary, something worth cherishing.

The night passes as we explore every hall, and by the end of it, I can't help but realize that something is blooming between us. Without realizing, without meaning to, I fall in love with him

"I'll go with you to the gala in France," I whisper when we're making our way outside after the best two hours of my life.

CHAPTER THIRTY-SIX

Philip

Austria turns out to be one epic disaster, thanks to a catastrophic engine explosion. This blow to my championship standings is like a kick in the balls. Munguia has snatched the top spot, with João hot on his tail, and I'm left a frustrating seven points behind them.

The French Grand Prix is next, and it better be damn perfect. I need almost ten points more than Munguia to have that first place back where it belongs. But before that, I have a night out with Selene, a much-needed break from the chaos. It's been two long weeks since our date in London, and I can't help but miss her. We have been keeping things even more secret by only meeting in private places since she got her new position, and I am craving having her next to me for everyone to see.

RHAE AEDEN

We decided to enjoy a day in Paris, a city I usually despise. The constant tourist paparazzi, trash littering the streets, dreadful traffic, and coffee that tastes like dirty water - nothing about this city usually amuses me, except, this time, I'm here with Selene. Experiencing the city through her eyes is a game changer. She stops at every building to snap a picture, appreciating every artistic detail and soaking up the culture.

Now, we're back at our hotel, preparing for the masquerade gala. Selene was in charge of booking the trip because I didn't want anyone to know I was in the city, and she had the *great* idea to get separate rooms. I struggle to understand why. If she wanted privacy from me, we could have had separate suites. But no, we've got rooms that are worlds apart.

So, here I am, pacing the hotel hallway, restless as ever, hoping for the redhead to finally come down so that we can get going. Left step, right step, and repeat.

"Hey." Her voice breaks through my restless mind.

I turn to face her, utterly unprepared. Her hair is cascading down her back in waves, framing her bare shoulders. She's wearing a green velvet dress that clings to her curves like it was custom-made, and those lips of hers shimmer in a glossy burgundy red that take my breath away.

I'm speechless.

My dick twitches in my pants, the possibility of her kneeling in front of me invading my thoughts. I want to take her back to her room and taste her, but we have a damn Gala to attend.

"Do you want a napkin?" I look at her with confusion. The blood isn't flowing to the right parts of my body right now, and I'm struggling to come up with any thoughts that don't include Selene in a bed with me on top of her. "For the drool." She gives me a smirk.

"Is stand-up comedy your plan B in life?"

"Nah, there's only plan A."

"We should get going if we want to make it on time." I say, looking at my watch, forcing myself to stop devouring her with my eyes.

The drive there is quite an adventure. The tiniest bump in the road, and Selene's nerves are sending tremors through the car. She's practically vibrating with anxiety and excitement. We arrive at the gala, and the driver stops at the entrance, awaiting our exit.

"Hey," I mutter, tucking a few errant strands of hair behind her ear. "Say the word, and we can head back to the hotel…"

"No," she says. "I wanted to come. I want to be here. I'm just a bit nervous."

"Do you want to know a secret?" I ask, and she nods eagerly. "I threw up before my first gala." I admit. Throwing up is nothing new to me, my body seems to get sick every time my mind gets too nervous. Some people faint, some scream, but I...I puke.

"You tend to do that a lot, Philip."

"I was trying to be supportive." I gently nudge her shoulder.

"You're doing a great job," she reassures me, patting my chest with her small hand, her pointy, red fingernails softly brushing against me. My mind wanders to dark places, imagining all the things those hands could do to me, and only me.

I clear my throat to regain some composure.

"I have something for you." Selene's eyes widen in anticipation as I grab two masks from the inner pocket of my jacket. Mine is completely black while hers is a shade of silver that complements her dress perfectly. "Turn around," I instruct, and she obeys, allowing me to tie the mask behind her head.

"How do I look?" she asks, turning back to me.

"Stunning." I leave a trail of kisses down the curve of her neck, a soft moan escaping her lips. She holds my chin with her hand, pulling me towards her, our lips touching.

"We should get going." she announces, trying to get control of her breathing. I can see her flushed cheeks under the mask, and I can't help but feel a sense of pride for being the cause of it.

Selene

The gala feels like a scene straight out of a movie. Every guest is adorned in stunning attire. Dresses and suits, all of them wearing jewels and elegant masks concealing their identities. For this one night, they can become anyone they wish, and they take full advantage of it.

"Care to dance?" Philip asks, catching me gazing at the couples gracefully waltzing.

I offer a gentle nod and take his hand, letting him lead me to the center of the dance floor. If someone had told me a year ago that I'd find myself here, with a man over ten years older than me—Philip Burton, no less—I'd have laughed.

But this is my reality now.

Philip twirls me around effortlessly, making it appear as though I have a clue as to what I'm doing. "When did you learn to dance like this?" I ask, intrigued.

"My mother insisted I learn," he explains. I wonder if he realizes just how much he misses her. "She didn't mind if I had my hands covered in grease during the day as long as I behaved like a little gentleman at night."

"That's adorable. I can't picture you ever behaving like that."

"Because I'm not a gentleman, Sparks." His voice takes on a low, husky tone as his hand glides down my lower back, leaving goosebumps in its wake.

"You make it easy to forget that sometimes." My eyes are nearly closed, my focus solely on the sensation of his hands traveling over my body.

"You might need a reminder," he murmurs, his breath grazing my earlobe. I intend to respond with a witty comeback, but he nibs at it, and all my thoughts disappear.

"Philip," I sigh, my vision hazy. It could be the glass or three of champagne I had in my room before we came, or the intoxicating moment, but all I know is that I want him.

"Selene," he repeats, his deep voice settling deep inside of me. How am I supposed to forget this man once everything inevitably goes to hell? How could I when he makes me feel like this?

"How long do we have to stay?" I ask after we have danced and mingled for a while. We probably haven't spent nearly enough time here, given that Philip was invited and had some duties to perform, but all I can think about right now are my own urges.

"Are you already bored?" He smirks, amused.

"I thought, considering your old age, you'd want to go to bed early," I tease, hoping he'll indulge me.

"Trust me, I do want to go to bed early. But not to sleep."

"Then let's go," I murmur in his ear.

Philip opens the door to his room, allowing me to step inside first. I can sense him behind me, his breath almost on my neck. Turning around, I grab him by his neck, applying the right amount of pressure so that his lips meet mine. There is nothing soft about this kiss.

It's everything.

He is everything.

I bite his lips and make him groan, my body aching with need. His hand holds my face, slowly moving towards my hair before spinning it around until he's fisting it. He pulls on it, the slight pain that it inflicts on me coated in pleasure.

We break apart for a moment, our foreheads touching and both our shoulders rising up and down as heavy breaths escape us. I use our little break to take him in. His hair is a mess from me running my hands through it. Some of the strands are falling over his dark eyebrows right into his eyes.

Philip lets me believe I'm in control for a minute, but then he breaks the spell. He grabs the back of my neck and presses me to his body again. I tilt my head up to give him better access to my mouth. I'm so close to him that I can feel his growing erection through our clothes and knowing that I am the cause for it turns on me even more. I can already feel wetness pooling in my panties.

As if I weighed less than a feather, Philip grabs my legs and lifts me up. I cross them around his waist, trying to get some more friction, tingles of delicious pleasure traveling through my body when I get what I want.

"Behave yourself." The command is low, but I keep trying to get more pleasure by rubbing against him.

He puts me on top of the desk right in front of the crystal window. The whole city could be watching what we're doing, but, right now, I'm more concerned with satisfying the need pooling between my legs. I kiss his neck and bite his skin softly, making him groan in pleasure. Philip sweeps his hand over my body, my breasts growing heavy and my eyes rolling to the back of my head.

"Are you wet for me?"

His eyes shine with wild desire while one of his hands trails up my leg and onto the most intimate part of my body. Goosebumps cover me when he pushes my underwear to the side. He looks at my slick slit at the same time he wets his lips, making me want to kiss him even more. I want those lips on every single part of my body.

"Don't play with your food," I complain, impatient when he doesn't move for too long.

He throws a seductive smile my way and, without any warning, he pushes two fingers inside of me. My mouth opens wide, a gasp of satisfaction leaving me while he pumps his fingers slowly in and out. I need more, so I place my hand on top of his, giving him silent instructions to go deeper and faster. With my free hand I grab the back of his neck bringing him towards me so I can kiss him. His face is as physically close to mine as possible, but not once do his lips touch mine, sending more desire through me.

"I want to look at you, Selene." The way my name sounds falling from his lips is sin incarnated. "And I am going to taste every single part of you." A glint of mischief crosses his eyes and before I can foresee what he is about to do, he withdraws his fingers. Before I can protest, he puts one of them in his mouth. Tasting me.

"Do you want a taste too?" I gulp, and part my lips halfway for him. Words have left me. He takes a second to pass his thumb through my slit, sending more sparks of pleasure through me. When he removes it, his thumb is glistening with my wetness, then the pressure stops, and his hand rises towards me, only for his thumb to end up in my mouth. I don't protest, licking it as if it were his dick.

"Such a pretty mouth. I am going to enjoy fucking it." I bite on his digit slightly before sucking it dry. He bites his lips and, all of a sudden, grabs my waist, turning me around. My back presses to his front, allowing me to see our reflection in the long mirror.

"Tell me what you want," he orders, stroking his hand down my dress, pulling until my breasts are free.

"I want you." I try to move my head to look at him, but with a firm hand, he keeps my head in place, forcing me to look at our reflection. "I want you to fuck me, Philip." My need for him takes over. I push my dress to the side while he takes my panties off.

"Do you want me to use a condom?" I can feel him zipping his pants down and freeing his length.

"I am on birth control. Are you negative?"

"I am. I got tested recently." For a minute, I feel insecure. "We have all types of tests done to know that we are healthy. And you're the only one," he whispers into my ear.

"What are you waiting for then?" I challenge, and he doesn't waste a second to meet my needs. In a single and fast thrust, he's inside of me.

"Hold on to the desk." I obey not only because he asks but because I am desperate to hold onto something.

If I were facing him, I would probably be biting his shoulder to muffle my moans, but we're in a different position, so my screams fill the room. Philip grabs me by my waist so hard I am convinced marks will be there tomorrow morning, and I can't help but smile at the thought of being marked by him. He spanks my ass, and I squeal but also smile enjoying the pleasure that the pain provides me. My eyes roll as I my orgasm builds inside of me.

Philip goes back to rubbing my clit and with a panting voice he says, "Pat my arm if it gets too much."

I nod, "Are you going to choke me?" I ask, eager for what is about to happen.

"I am going to make you remember this night forever, Sparks," he says confidently, and then chokes me with his other hand, taking the air of my lungs slightly. "Did you know that when the body has a lack of breath,"—he pants, his lips close to my spine—"it releases adrenaline and endorphins." Is that a question? I can't think. I feel lightheaded. The world is a fantastic blur of pleasure and enjoyment.

Philip whispers something in my ear, an instruction or maybe a command. All I know is that he's still choking me, putting the perfect amount of pressure on my clit.

"Don't stop," is all I am able to mutter with the little air I still have in my lungs. He picks up the pace and shortly after, I come undone.

"I don't ever want to stop," is the last thing I hear him say.

CHAPTER THIRTY-SEVEN

Selene

I stir in bed, snuggling under the blanket to evade the morning sunlight. Philip's strong arms are wrapped around my waist as vivid memories from last night flood my mind. It's all I can think of. That, and how much I want to repeat it again.

"Good morning." Philip's raspy morning voice fills my ears.

"Buenos días," I whisper, adjusting my position to look at him. My brain turns to putty when I'm met with his bare torso with his muscles on full display.

"Stop staring, or I might start to think you actually like me," he jokes, and I use the moment to climb on top of him, his hands resting on my thighs. I notice faint blue marks adorning my skin, traces of where his hands gripped me just hours ago. "Sorry about those," he says, his thumb gently tracing the marks as he notices where my attention has drifted to.

"I quite like them," I murmur into his neck. "I don't mind, as long as you don't leave them somewhere visible."

"Who do you take me for, a teenager?" He feigns offense.

"You're far too old for that, even if your stamina suggests otherwise."

"I could always give you another round if that's what you desire, Sparks." His voice drips with desire, and my core is already agreeing with it.

"As much as I'd love that, you've got to head to work," I remind him, glancing at the clock on the nightstand.

"I still have time before the free practice," he says with a mischievous glint in his eyes.

"Then I guess we can fit in one more round," I say, slipping under the covers to where his arousal strains against his boxers.

If only every morning could start like this.

"Darling, I'm home!" I shout when I walk through the door to our apartment in the early afternoon.

"Hello, my love." Miriam pops out of the kitchen, her curly dark hair up in bun. "Soo… How was it?"

"A-fucking-mazing."

"Spill all the dirty details. I want to hear it all." Her request is simple, and I don't waste a second filling her in.

I share every single little detail from our day in Paris. The beauty of city, the experience of being at a masquerade ball, the dancing, and the romanticism, because yes, I am a helpless romantic who is slowly falling in love. I skip the most private part of the night, wanting to treasure the memories and being greedy enough to keep them to myself. There is some possessiveness that comes with being with him.

"I am falling for him," I confess.

"Babes, you are not falling." Her hazel eyes shine. "You have already fallen and crashed." And I know her words carry the truth.

How could I not? It's hard to deny the truth. Falling for him was inevitable. Everything about him, even the clouds above his head are intoxicating. I tried to resist, but Miriam is right, I have fallen hard. "I guess I have," I admit. "What do I do now?" I ask Miriam.

"You tell him?"

I still don't understand the dynamics of our *situationship*. We are dating, but how can I date someone I don't want to be seen with? That isn't fair to him, nor is it to me.

"One step at a time," Miriam says as soon as she notices how overwhelmed I am. "For now, we enjoy the weekend."

HAMMER TIME

CHAPTER THIRTY-EIGHT

envy

Monaco was an excellent setting for romance stories to bloom with beautiful landscapes, amazing restaurants, and interesting people. But the city was small, so small that it made it difficult to keep things private because almost everyone knew everyone's whereabouts. Especially when those whereabouts involved people of public relevance.

She had been sitting inside one of those posh coffee places when they had met each other. People didn't really come to eat anything because it was more about sitting down and making connections, talking and plotting. That's exactly what she had done, talk and plot and plan the demise of the one who had wronged her. It had taken her time, too much time. Things had started to work against her but meeting that one person had put everything into perspective. Had she not met him, then she would be far from getting what she thought she deserved. No, she didn't think. She knew she deserved it.

HAMMER TIME

That other person was just a stone in the way, a stone that was about to be taken out of her path. She would crush that stone until only dust remained, nothing would be between them. The taste of imminent victory was a taste she relished, and she would savor it.

The bell at the door of the coffee place ringed, the sound of it taking her far away from her thoughts. The game was coming to an end. Soon, everything would be over. She just needed one last push.

The man walked over to where she was sitting, not bothering with greetings. Why would he? They had made clear that they did not like each other, but they did have a common goal. And, didn't the saying go, the enemy of my enemy is my friend… it certainly was something like that.

"Do you have them?" She went straight to the point.

The man in front of her didn't bother answering, he was too busy checking his surroundings, paranoia getting to his head. He scanned the room repeatedly and when he was sure nobody could see him or recognize him, he handed her the white envelope over the table. Slowly, so very slowly.

She snapped it out of his hands halfway, patience not something she had mastered yet. She wanted what she wanted, and she wanted it now. She took her time with the envelope, already knowing the contents of it. She could see how everything was going to play out, the end was near. Everything was going according to plan. The puzzle pieces were falling into place and in a matter of weeks, she would get exactly what she wanted.

Yes, spending the summer in Monaco was exactly what she needed, but autumn was rolling in fast and the second it arrived, he would be hers.

HAMMER TIME

CHAPTER THIRTY-NINE

Monza is the absolute peak of the season, my favorite track, and the first home of Cavaglio Nero Racing before they moved to the UK. The car is usually on full throttle over eighty percent of the time with those magnificent straights and speed traps. Six kilometers, fifty laps. I'm going to stand on the top of the podium by the end of the day.

But before that, I want to enjoy my time with the woman sleeping next to me. We had all summer long to ourselves, and somehow were successful at avoiding the press and the tabloids. Monaco was part of our playground, but we also visited other cities in our efforts to escape the paparazzi.

"Go back to bed," Selene yawns, half asleep.

"You go back to sleep," I babble, pressing a soft kiss to the top of her hair.

"Are you nervous?" she asks.

"It's an important race."

"And?" she presses.

"Cavaglio has not renewed my contract." I finally give in.

"What?" She almost shouts, now fully awake. "How? No, that's not right." I can see the wheels spinning inside her head as she sits up in bed.

"It's fine. They will make me an offer."

"Oh, trust me, they will," she says, snatching her phone off the nightstand. I take it from her, trying to avoid the bomb about to explode.

"Are you my agent?" She shakes her head reluctantly. "Then this is not your job."

"But—"

"Tscht." I also sit up so I can look into her eyes. "Don't go abusing your power." The realization strikes her. If she did whatever she wanted to do, people would start asking questions sooner or later.

"I'm mad at them." It's adorable how infuriated she is on my behalf. The world might be against me, but she has always proven to be on my side when I need her.

"Me too, but I'm going to give them another reason to renew my contract."

"What happens if they don't?"

"Volpella has been in contact with me." I have contemplated that possibility. I raced for them for one season in the past, right before I retired. We never achieved anything major together because they didn't have a winning car back then, not like they do now.

"You should tell me these things sooner."

"I'm telling you now."

"Talk to me when they happen, not who knows how many weeks after." She stands up from the bed, my t-shirt covering part of her naked legs in a beautiful way.

She starts picking up her clothes and belongings from the floor to get dressed, throwing one of my Cavaglio Nero jackets over her shoulders.

"Are you angry with me?" I ask, afraid.

"Of course not," she answers, her gaze focused on trying to find something on the floor.

"Then why are you leaving me?" Her attention shifts to me, and I move, sitting on the edge of the bed.

"I am not leaving you."

"Promise?" She nods at my question.

"But I would appreciate it if you would put me in the loop of things, okay?"

"I will do that, I just… I am used to being on my own. I didn't think it would matter to you."

"Philip, everything that concerns you matters to me." Her fingers stroke the left side of my face, and I lean into her touch, relishing every moment of it. "Get it through your thick skull; you matter to me. The only reason I was leaving is because it's getting late, and people will start leaving their rooms soon. I don't want to meet anyone in the hallway." She gives me a soft kiss, then goes back to looking for whatever item she has lost.

I'm starting to get a little tired of hiding. Not of her, but of the world and the constant 'what will they say.' I want to take her out and be able to kiss her whenever I want. I want to parade us around and show the world she's mine. But, for now, I'll take these stolen moments with her.

"I will see you at the race," she says.

"Okay." I walk her to the door and give her a kiss before she leaves the room, checking that nobody is in the hall.

My focus narrows to the red light above me. I may not have snagged pole position yesterday, but this race is mine for the taking.

The red lights vanish, and the race is on. Oliver gets a jump on me, but I speed up and pull alongside him mere meters into the start. Our cars touch as we head into the first corner. I'm forced to take the dirty side of the track, but luckily, I don't lose any position or sustain damage. There's plenty of racing time left. I can still win this.

HAMMER TIME

João remains a few seconds behind me after the first ten laps, slowly overtaking midfield cars, but not enough to make me fear losing my position yet. As we hit lap thirteen, the battle intensifies. Munguia loses control of his car at the chicane, and I seize the opportunity to make up some lost time.

Around the twentieth lap, João secures the third position, but we are all forced to slow down when a car crashes behind us, calling for a yellow flag.

"Is he okay?" I ask over the radio.

"Yes, he's out of the car," my engineer assures me.

I concentrate on driving during the slow laps while the marshals clear the track.

"Let's go for plan D." I sigh in frustration. A yellow flag was the last thing I needed.

"Copy." The response comes quickly.

I head to the pits where my pit crew is ready with a fresh set of tires. All I can do now is hope the soft compound lasts through the remaining laps. After the pit stop, I rejoin the race just behind João.

I've dropped one position, but my tires are fresher. The yellow flag clears the next lap, and my feet are on the throttle, ready to race. I make a move around the outside and overtake João. Through my mirror, I can see the driver in fourth place joining our battle.

RHAE AEDEN

Munguia holds onto the lead as I battle with the Brazilian driver. We make it a corner that almost results in a crash. The fourth driver slips past João, now challenging me.

Munguia loses control, his car spinning on the track in a 360, loosing so much time that he almost collides with me.

"Joder!" I scream, furious, adrenaline pumping through my veins.

We both lose our positions to João, who takes advantage of our mistake, snatching the lead right before the last corner. Now, I'm in third place, but I can still salvage this. I have to.

I hit the throttle, aligning myself with Munguia's car, spotting damage on it and noticing his rear tires are completely degraded. Hope remains. As we race and round the Parabolica corner, it becomes our playground for overtaking. Munguia passes João, and I use the momentum to do the same. I attempt to overtake Munguia right before the straight ends, but I miss my chance, his car slightly faster than mine.

Lap fifty rolls in, and I can't overtake him. My tires deteriorate further, and for the first time this season, I give up before the race ends.

CHAPTER FORTY

Selene

Philip finishes the race in third place. I can see him from where I stand beneath the Parabolica, where the podium is. He looks so disappointed. His lips form a thin line, and his gaze is lost in the crowd. It pains me to see him like this, now more than ever. He's still second in the drivers' championship, but I understand what winning here would have meant to him.

He cuts his celebration short, barely engaging with João and Munguia. He pops open a bottle of champagne, gives it a quick shake, and leaves the other two drivers to their celebrations. I can already envision the headlines calling him a sore loser.

But he's not that. He's just worried about losing his job, a job he's fought hard for. Nobody comprehends the extent of his dedication—the hours in the simulator, the efforts to grasp engineering and strategy. It's frustrating.

RHAE AEDEN

I leave the celebratory crowd with a single destination in mind. Walking through the crowds of people, I finally reach Philip's private room. I don't bother knocking on the door.

Philip is partly undressed when I make it inside. His racing suit is low on his hips, and the fireproof shirt is scattered on the floor.

"Hey," I whisper, closing the door behind me. Philip doesn't even look at me. "You're still second in the World Championship. There are plenty of races left." I try to console him, but I'm afraid my words aren't having the desired effect.

"I know, Selene. Trust me, I know," he says.

Before I can offer any further reassurances, someone knocks on the door, making me realize I shouldn't be here. I contemplate ducking into the bathroom to hide, but the person on the other side opens the door and enters without permission.

"Philip." Jessica's voice fills the room.

"What?" Philip snaps, grabbing his shirt to put it back on.

"Oh, Selene! I was looking for you, too!" Jessica claims, brushing off Philip's rudeness. "I can't do the press right now. Can you fill in for me?"

"I—I—" I stutter, caught off guard.

"Great! Here's the phone!" She tosses the device in my direction, and Philip has to catch it in the air before it hits me in the face. "Good luck!" she yells before slamming the door.

"Let's get this over with," Philip says, handing me the phone.

We walk side by side toward the press circle. Munguia is already deep into interviews, flashing a big smile, a stark contrast to Philip's expression. "It's okay," I say to him as we step into the circle. I attempt to offer reassurance with a smile, though my nerves betray me. I don't want to be here either.

The first reporter asks Philip some questions about the race, strategy, and the battle. He offers straightforward, concise answers, avoiding elaboration. I type responses on the phone, feeling extremely uneasy as I sense the cameras focused on me.

"Who's next?" Philip asks as we wait in line.

I check the phone to find the next interviewer.

"Cynthia Fox from—"

"Sphere Sports. She did an interview with me and Munguia," Philip says.

After a brief wait, the driver in front of us completes their interview. We take our positions on the blue carpet, facing Cynthia.

"Nice to see you again," she purrs. I spot some red lipstick on her front tooth but don't bother mentioning it. "How do you feel after the race?"

"Thrilled," Philip responds, his sarcasm flying over Cynthia's head. I can already tell that this won't end well.

"Do you think it has something to do with your new routines?" she asks, her question catching me off guard.

"Excuse me?" Philip replies, clearly as confused as I am.

"Your new routines? It's all over the press," she explains, handing him her phone. I try to see what's on the screen, but Philip blocks my view.

"Are you incapable of getting a job without dating a driver?" I need another moment to realize that Cynthia's question is directed at me.

"Selene has worked hard for her job," Philip intervenes on my behalf, composed but radiating anger in a way I've never seen before.

"The timing of these pictures would suggest otherwise," she says. My body tenses up, and cold sweat trickles down my spine. "It seems you already intervened in Silverstone last season on her behalf."

I snatch the phone from Philip's hand, finally snapping out of my shock. I'm greeted with pictures of us under many headlines: 'The mystery girl: New Cavaglio's Marketing Strategist,' 'Dating is All It Takes,' 'Burton Gets Girlfriend a Job in the Company,' and more. My worst fears have come to life. The comments are brutal. Multiple pictures of us appear, from the first time he drove me home, private parties after the Emilia Romagna and Monaco Grand Prix, and so much more.

"Philip, you always say that people who cannot contribute to the sport should step down," Cynthia quotes. "What is

Selene contributing to it besides instant gratification for yourself?"

"What are you contributing to it?" I retort, finally finding my voice. "Obviously nothing of journalistic relevance, or else you'd be asking questions about the race and not the drivers' personal lives."

Cynthia takes a moment to reassess the situation. "This is what happens when you take shortcuts."

"If you did your job well, you'd have discovered how her job is promoting inclusivity and supporting women in Formula One. Now, get lost," Philip says and grabs my hand, guiding us out of the press room.

I can feel judgmental eyes on me, critiquing my every move now that our secret is out in the open. My body feels entirely numb, and I'm not even sure how I'm walking.

"Just a few meters," Philip reassures me, sensing my trembling.

"I'm not feeling well," I murmur, my face growing paler.

"Hey, hey, hey," he says. "This is nothing, okay? We'll fix it."

I see red for a moment.

"How, Philip? How will we fix this?" I yell when we make it to the motorhome. "This is exactly why I didn't want to go public!"

"This isn't my fault, Selene!" he defends.

"Nor is it mine! But I'm the one paying for it," I say. "You always had to play the villain, and now all of it is falling on me, Philip." I regret the words the moment they escape my lips.

Philip gazes at me, and the anger that consumed him a moment ago seems to evaporate, leaving him with a stone-cold expression. "The door is open. Leave whenever you want," he says, devoid of emotion.

"Are you breaking up with me?" I ask in disbelief. "Is this really all it takes?"

"We were never together to begin with," he retorts.

"You don't mean that."

"I do." He doesn't even bother looking at me, maintaining a stiff posture in the middle of the corridor. "You never wanted this, or else you wouldn't be acting like this. You've always been ashamed and worried about the 'what-ifs.' Well, guess what? Everything has exploded right in our faces. You can walk out the door now."

"You are impossible, Philip," I say, frustrated and angry, holding back the tears in my eyes. I don't look at him; I just leave exactly as he suggested, slamming the door behind me.

HAMMER TIME

Sitting in front of my computer, I can't help but wonder how on Earth I still have a job. It's been three long days since everything happened. Three days during which I've remained holed up at home with paparazzi camped outside, eagerly waiting for any kind of information they can get. It feels like I've become the world's center of attention, and to some, I'm the number one public enemy

Miriam, in her wisdom, decided to take action and deleted all of my social media accounts. The harassment had become unbearable, and I couldn't stomach another hateful comment. As if this mess wasn't enough, Philip has gone radio silent on me, not a single word. If I had any lingering doubts about the state of our relationship, his silence would be answer enough.

A video call pops on my laptop screen. It's Sarah. Just when I thought things couldn't get any worse…

I muster a half-hearted smile as soon as the green dot on the camera turns on.

"Good morning, Sarah," I greet her, trying my best to appear cheerful.

"Hello, darling," Sarah responds with her usual tone—no anger, no rage, just kindness. "How are you holding up?"

"Everything's great. I sent a doc this morning for the quarterly update," I say, pulling up the same file on my computer.

"Darling, I know you're passionate about your work, but I want to know how you're really doing," she insists.

"I understand now why Philip hates the press," I admit.

"I don't want to say 'I told you so,' but I did," she says. I feel the urge to defend myself, but she continues without giving me a chance. "I'm not opposed to your relationship. There's nothing in the handbook that says drivers can't date team staff. However, I do encourage both of you to lay low for a while. Someone will talk to Philip today."

"Thanks," I mutter, not bothering to correct her about my no-longer-existing relationship.

"Teamwork makes the dream work," she concludes, flashing a reassuring smile.

"Sarah, I have one question. Did I get this position because of Philip?" I ask, my insecurity getting the best of me.

"He did ask Mancini to give you a job last year when we were in Silverstone." *Oh no.* "But Mancini ignored his request. You got this job based on your merits and hard work. I have to go now, but I'll stay in touch."

"Goodbye," I manage to say before she hangs up.

CHAPTER FORTY-ONE

Philip

I've practically relocated to Asia for the better part of September to compete in the three Grand Prix events hosted in that part of the world: Russia, Singapore, and Japan.

It's been a complete shit show.

I can't even fathom how I'm managing to cling to the second position in the championship. My motivation has been evading me, and my enthusiasm for driving is a mere shadow of what it was earlier in the season. The press harassment has reached new, unbearable heights these past few months.

And the worst part is that Selene has gone completely radio silent for the past month. No social media presence, no appearances at the track on weekends—nothing. *Nada.* The only sign I've received from her is a contract signed by her, just as she promised over a year ago.

RHAE AEDEN

This isn't how I envisioned this moment, her neat signature next to mine. We were supposed to celebrate this milestone or at least share some verbal sparring, but this silence is slowly killing me. Memories of Selene are a constant presence—the sound of her laughter, her passions, the countless long conversations we've shared, and all the experiences we've lived through together. I've never felt this way before, so alone, so utterly lost. I'd never met anyone who filled my life the way she does.

I miss Sparks.

Being without her is not an option anymore. She's become everything to me. I wasn't entirely oblivious to it before, but I didn't want to admit it, not like I do now. The truth is, I love her. It's the kind of love that consumes everything. The kind that makes me want to change to be a better man only for her.

The world can see me as a villain, but I'm willing to set the record straight for her. I need to fix things with the world before I can go back to her. She might hate me, but her hate is better than her indifference.

I stride into Sphere Sports' London office, determined to confront Cynthia Fox, the source of all my recent troubles. The grey weather outside mirrors my mood. I can barely contain my frustration and can't wait to give Cynthia what she deserves. The receptionist eyes me warily as I approach her.

"Good morning, sir. Do you have an appointment?"

"Tell Cynthia Fox that Philip Burton is here to see her," I announce, my tone curt and unapologetic. The receptionist's eyes widen as recognition dawns on her.

"Of course." I can see the fear in her eyes while she makes a call.

I stand there, unfazed by her nerves. Soon, she finishes and motions for me to follow her. We make our way up to the first floor, and I scan the room in search of Cynthia. However, she spots me first. With her usual disheveled hair and bright red lipstick.

"Well, well, look what the cat dragged in," she purrs, believing she has the upper hand. "What can I do for you, Philip?"

I decide to play her game.

"Is there a conference room in this building, or can't you people afford one?"

"Funny you should ask; we're cashing in more than ever with the news of your relationship," she informs me.

I take a step closer and lower my voice. "You don't want this to be a public execution."

"Please follow me," she says, her voice faltering for the first time. I can tell she's aware that I've come for her. We reach a door that leads to a private room.

"Take a seat," I instruct her, acting as if the office is mine, not hers. "We're going to play this game in reverse. I ask the questions, and you answer them. Understood?"

"Yes," she replies quickly.

"How did you get those pictures?"

"Someone sent them to me," she says.

"Who?" I ask, my voice firm, but she hesitates. "Tell me the truth," I demand, my patience waning.

"Jessica. She sent them to me."

"Jessica? My PR assistant?" I ask, stunned. The idea of someone so close orchestrating this betrayal is hard to swallow, but it's especially painful when the person behind this is as brainless as they get. "Who helped her?" I ask, aware that Jessica doesn't have enough brain cells to pull this off on her own.

"She used that Mark guy; they wanted some dirt on Selene," Cynthia reveals. "Honestly, I don't know the full extent of it. I saw an opportunity for a great story and went for it."

I shift the conversation, turning my attention to the bigger issue at hand. "How much money does your company make from Formula One?"

"I'm a journalist, not an accountant," she responds.

"Consider changing career paths," I threaten. "This company makes millions from us. Imagine what would happen if you don't renew your broadcasting rights. Imagine no drivers grant you interviews. Why would the company then retain the journalist who doomed them?"

"You can't do that!" Cynthia protests, her voice desperate.

"I am Philip Burton. Try me if you really think I can't." With that, I leave her, knowing I've crushed her confidence.

"Doesn't it bother you?" she screams, following me out of the room. "That people only ever talk about your scandals? About your shitty personality?" she keeps going, and, for whatever reason, I feel the need to confront her.

"No," I say, raising my voice to ensure everyone hears me. "The only reason you talk that nonsense is because it's the only way you can talk about me. I am Philip Burton; your headlines are just that, headlines that will be forgotten with time," I declare boldly. "I remain here, year after year. I work hard, and I win. If you can't handle my personality, that's your problem, not mine." I pause, looking around the room.

Everyone's eyes are fixed on us, and some are even taking notes, ready to write a story the moment I leave.

"Remember this: you made me a villain to sell more headlines, now face the consequences of your own actions because that villain is now coming for you. Time's up." I head for the elevator but stop before the doors close. "Don't ever mess with my girl again," I add.

"Is that a threat?" Cynthia dares to ask.

"It's a promise."

CHAPTER FORTY-TWO

Selene

With just three races left in the season, I find myself on a plane to Mexico, accompanying the team for a mysterious purpose I wasn't informed about. Miriam is sitting next to me, peacefully napping with a sleep mask covering her eyes and her lips slightly parted. Her sleep is only interrupted when the announcement about landing is made.

Throughout this time, I've managed to successfully stay away from any Philip related topics. Avoiding tabloids, steering clear of social media, and ignoring any rumors that may be circulating. This bubble of ignorance is the only place where I feel safe right now, and I am afraid that it's about to collapse.

Philip is obviously going to be in Mexico, and I can't help but wonder if we will cross paths again. How long can I continue dodging him?

I knew our relationship had an expiration date. Yet, I never thought about how things would work once that day came, and now after months have passed, all I can think about is him, only him. I know it will take a long time to forget, no matter how much it hurts.

Our plane finally lands, and we arrive at the hotel sometime past lunchtime. I covered the additional cost for Miriam this time. I needed my friend to give me some moral support this week, and she couldn't refuse a vacation in Mexico.

"Home sweet home," Miriam says, jumping onto the bed as soon as we enter our room.

"Hey!" I protest. "Don't fall asleep; we need to beat the jetlag."

"Ugh, it's going to be nearly impossible!" She yawns.

"How? You slept the entire flight."

"I don't make the rules," she says with a shrug, promptly jumping out of bed. "Come on, let's go to the beach."

After a quick shower to refresh ourselves from the long flight, we step onto the beach to find a breathtaking view of white sand and crystal-clear blue waters, surrounded by palm trees. It's exactly what I need.

HAMMER TIME

Miriam and I find a nice place near the water to sit down and sip some Mojitos that one of the pool boys offers us on our way there.

Eventually, Miriam asks the question that I have been hiding from.

"Will you talk to Philip?"

"Why are you bringing this up now?" I ask. I'm not sure if I'm ready to have this conversation, and I'm certainly not tipsy enough to dive into those emotions.

"You are going to see him sooner or later."

"I don't want to discuss him, Miriam."

"Selene, it's time to snap out of this sadness." Her words are both honest and sharp. "I know it hurts, but you can't stay sad forever. It's been almost two months."

"I know!" I reply with frustration. "I just can't deal with it right now."

"Why?" Miriam asks.

"Thinking about him hurts. It's as if a part of me got cut off. It's physically painful, and I can't breathe," I admit. "I feel like this is only the beginning, that I haven't really broken down yet, and when it finally happens, my heart will shatter into a million pieces. So, I'm avoiding it."

"Honey, your heart is already broken. Things can only go up from here," Miriam says with brutal honesty. "You should talk to him and get the closure you deserve," she suggests.

RHAE AEDEN

I recline on my chair, not being able to come up with an answer. My eyes close slowly, and I drift into a deep slumber filled with dark ocean eyes that follow me everywhere I go.

When I wake up, the sky has transformed into a canvas of orange and pink, and beachgoers are beginning to pack up and leave.

"How long have I been out?" I ask.

"About forty minutes, give or take," she answers, checking her watch. It hasn't been as long as I thought. "I'm heading back to the room; do you want to come along?"

"I think I'll stay and go for a walk," I reply.

"Alright, see you later." She waves before gathering her belongings.

I rise from my chair, feeling the sand between my toes, and stroll towards the water's edge. The ocean waves gently wash over me, and I soak in the beauty of the setting sun, pink clouds floating across the horizon. I attempt to keep my mind clear of my emotions and complications that have been plaguing me.

And then I hear it—a deep, familiar voice uttering my name.

"Selene."

"Philip?" I reply, my voice shaking. "What are you doing here?" I ask and blink, half-expecting for him to vanish before my eyes.

"I needed to see you," he says.

"You had two months to see me, to text me, to call me. You're out of time now," I say, all the pent-up frustration of the past weeks rising to the surface.

"Please, just listen." I begin to walk away, but he grabs my hand, much like he has countless times before. I can feel the tears welling up, but I refuse to let him see me cry over him.

"Why? You opened the door and told me to leave."

"That was the worst mistake of my life, and I'm trying to fix it, Selene." His voice is filled with determination but also sadness.

"No," I reply, shaking my head. "You can't just show up two months later and expect me to forgive you." I keep my voice steady, refusing to let it waver. I turn and attempt to leave him and all our problems behind for good.

"It was Mark," Philip blurts out before I get too far. "And Jessica. They leaked all those pictures of us."

"What?" I can't believe my ears.

"They were following us. Both of them concocted this whole thing and sold it to the press," he explains, trying to keep up with my pace.

"How do you know this?" I ask, still skeptical.

"I confronted Cynthia. Needless to say, she no longer has a job."

"Why? When?" I fire questions at him, trying to process his words.

"I went to her office a couple of weeks ago."

"And you're only telling me this now?" I blurt out, finally losing my composure. I feel like I'm on the verge of a breakdown, my rage coursing through every fiber of my being.

"I thought you might have seen it in the press."

"I haven't checked my phone in weeks, unless it's work. I don't even have Instagram anymore."

A tear of frustration slips down my cheek. Philip uses that moment to approach me, gently cupping my face with both hands to wipe the tear away. His touch is achingly familiar, and, for a brief moment, I let myself enjoy it.

"That's why Mark was following me that day," I murmur, more to myself.

"What do you mean?" he says, his eyes widening before his expression hardens into a look of anger.

"The day we played in the simulator, after I left your place, I felt like someone was following me. Then I ran into Mark and—"

"I'm going to kill him. Nobody touches my girl."

"I'm not your girl," I correct him coldly, finally stepping away from him.

"Selene..." He looks devastated.

"No, Philip. You told me so much bullshit, and at the first sign of trouble, you pushed me away," I say, my anger unrestrained. "I was the one with everything to lose, and I nearly lost it all. And the worst thing is that I would have taken the fall for you. You are worth it. But you tossed me aside. That's not how relationships work."

"I never meant to do that, Selene. I wanted you. I just needed some space and time…I've never done this, the whole relationship act, and I'm not good with feelings or words."

"Then you should've said so! You should've told me you needed distance and time, but you just shut me out." Miriam was right. I needed this closure, to unleash all the pent-up feelings I'd been carrying for weeks. "You don't just cast someone out. You talk to the other person and resolve things like adults."

"That's what I'm trying to do now."

"Too late," I say. "It's too late now, Philip. Let me go."

Finally, he lets go of my hand, and I turn around to walk away, back to my room, nearly sprinting. My head and heart are pounding as I slam the door behind me, and it's only then that I allow myself to start crying.

"Are you okay?" Miriam asks when she sees my state.

"I just saw Philip," I tell her, still shaken. "How did he even know we were here?"

"Don't be mad at me," Miriam says, dropping to her knees in front of me. "He texted me, and—"

"You didn't!" I'm on the verge of screaming at her, my emotions swirling. I'm overwhelmed, feeling too much all at once.

"You needed to talk it out. He needed a chance to explain himself," she explains. "Philip told me about Jessica and Mark. You should see the leaked videos of him giving Cynthia shit for what she did. If that's not a romantic gesture, I don't know what is."

"Show me." Miriam hands me her phone after searching for the video.

The screen shows Philip setting the record straight with Cynthia. If I weren't so upset with the world at this moment, I might have found Philip's actions quite charming. He has done numerous romantic gestures for me, but this one is probably the most significant.

"What should I do now, M?" I ask when the video is done playing, feeling absolutely confused and lost.

"Whatever your heart desires."

"You do realize this isn't a movie, right?" I tease.

"Well, it should be. You don't live out an epic romance story with a Formula One driver every day."

"No, you don't," I agree with a grin.

HAMMER TIME

CHAPTER FORTY-THREE

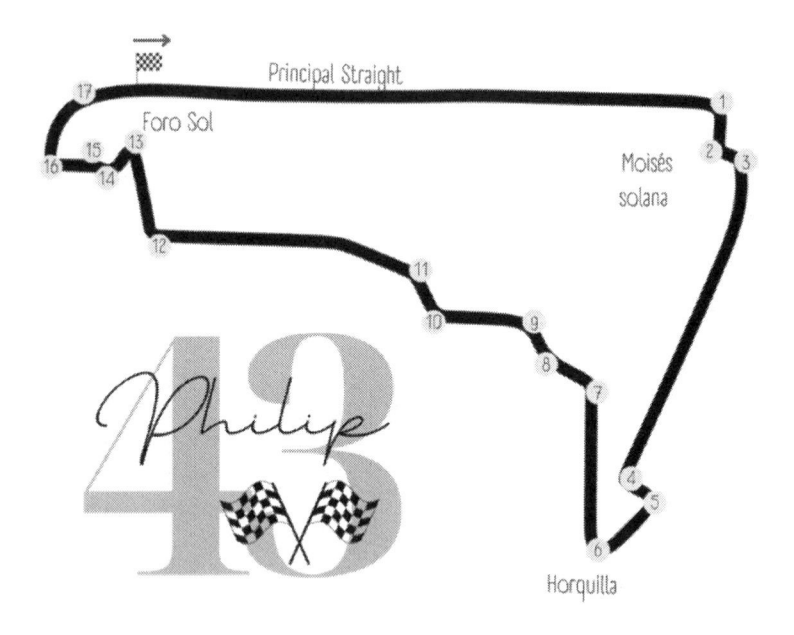

The race in Mexico is an experience every fan should have at least once. It's been on the calendar for a couple of years and sometimes it feels more like a grand party rather than a race.

João has been the king of South American tracks since he joined the sport, but this time, Munguia and I are ready to dethrone him. Yesterday, we had a fantastic qualifying session, with me taking the pole position and Munguia securing second place. I need those points to climb back to the top of the championship. I've been stuck in second place for far too long, and Munguia is itching to win his home race and surpass me in the standings. But I won't let that happen.

"¿Estás listo para perder?" *Are you ready to lose?* Oliver teases me as we both prepare in the garage.

"The only way you'll beat me today is if I have a DNF," I fire back.

"Don't say that," Mancini warns. "You are conjuring bad luck, Philip."

"I don't believe in that crap anymore," I answer, my bitterness showing.

Selene was one of the few good things that had happened to me in a long time, and she's gone now. We were never meant to be, but it still stings. Racing is all I have left, and the team hasn't offered me a new contract, so I need to enjoy these last few races. But it's difficult when my anxiety is all over the place. My vomiting sessions have become more persistent, and my nerves have a tighter grip on me. Winning and securing a new contract are my only motivations now, not fear or dreams.

"Okay, boys," Mancini says, addressing us. "Time to get out there. Philip, show them what you're made of."

"I will."

"Good," Mancini says, nodding in agreement.

"Prepare to enjoy the dirty air, Oliver." I smirk at him, then grab my helmet, one that still has Selene's touch on it.

Munguia heads to his car, leaving me alone with part of the crew for a few moments. I suit up, pulling on the balaclava before sliding the helmet onto my head. I'm ready to jump into the car when a voice starts yelling.

"Espera!" *Wait!* The voice calls out, and I turn around to see the most delightful shock of copper hair.

"What are you doing here?" I ask, surprised by Selene's unexpected appearance.

"I have to touch both sides of the helmet," she explains with a soft blush on her cheeks. "It's tradition," she says so quietly that I nearly have to remove my helmet to catch her words. Selene gets on her tip toes and touches my helmet, holding it in place and allowing me to inhale her perfume as she stands so close. She's intoxicating. "You have to win this," she says.

"I know."

"You *can* win this," she continues.

"Michael is my coach, you are my—" I stop before the words slip out.

"Michael is your coach. I'm Sparks, and I'm here when you need me." I can hear the unspoken words in her soft statement. *'I'm here even when you're not.'*

"Another chance," I mutter, unable to resist the pull of her presence.

"You told me not to talk about this before races."

"I've also said I'm a heartless asshole, but for some reason, my heart beats when you're around." Her forehead rests against my helmet, allowing me to peer directly into her eyes as I voice words I've never expressed before. "Another chance," I repeat.

"Win, and we can talk about it." Her motivation is all I need.

Selene

I head to one of the reserved rooms to watch the race with Miriam. The place is filled with familiar faces, including Munguia's wife and some influencers from a new program I've been working on, creating content for newcomers to the sport. I'm in a good mood, better than the last couple of days.

But then, I spot Jessica.

"Don't," Miriam warns before I can stomp over there and give her a piece of my mind. "We dress for revenge, and today is not the day."

"I will finish her," I whisper back, making sure only Miriam can hear me.

The race is about to begin, Philip, Munguia, and João lined up and ready to battle for the top spot. Philip needs this win, not only for the points but also for his morale.

The lights on top of the cars turn off, and Philip gets off to a great start, creating some distance between him and the others. Munguia also starts well, but João overtakes him after the first corner, though he soon loses his position when Munguia takes the clean line, leaving João no room to maneuver.

Philip is slightly ahead after a few laps, but he takes one of the turns too tightly, causing him to lose the car and briefly slip next to Oliver. But he quickly regains his confidence, and after a couple of corners, he's back in the lead, forcing the others to deal with his dirty air.

"Sí!" I scream in excitement, causing everyone to turn and look at me, especially Oliver's wife. She doesn't give me a dirty look, but she's clearly not pleased with my outburst. Honestly, I wouldn't be either if I were her.

The race flies by, and both Cavaglio Nero drivers have perfect pit stops, while João's isn't as smooth—one of the mechanics was missing his tire. Who forgets a tire in Formula One when the car has four wheels, right?

Somehow, he still manages to make up for the lost time on the track and even swaps positions with Oliver a couple of times as they battle for the second place.

"Vamos, Oliver!" his wife shouts, and I join her, clapping and cheering for our team.

Oliver ultimately manages to overtake João in the final stretch of the track after passing the Foro Sol, securing second place. Philip, on the other hand, is way ahead and has already secured first place.

RHAE AEDEN

He is on the way to crossing the finish line when everyone runs to the fence to welcome him. I go with the crew and start waving a Spanish flag, hoping he'll spot me. I'm still angry with him, but I can't help wanting to be there, to show him the support he deserves.

After the cool down lap, Philip finally arrives at the first-place sign, exits the car, and is met with loud cheers from all the mechanics. Jessica is also there, her ponytail bouncing, and I barely resist the urge to pull from it until it comes off. I restrain myself and focus on Philip, who runs towards his mechanics and jumps on top of them, letting everyone hug him and shake his head to celebrate his win.

"Another chance," he whispers, coming close to me in between the cheering crowd.

"We can talk later," I insist and give his helmet a playful shake, just like the other team members have done.

"Don't run, or I'll hunt you down," Philip warns.

"The hunt is the best part," I tease him before the press whisks him away for interviews.

"Selene!" Sarah calls from behind me. "Do you have a minute? I haven't seen you since—"

"Since way too long," I cut her off. "I thought it was best if I didn't attend any races for a while."

"Good strategy." She winks.

"I did get my job for a reason," I assure her. Any lingering self-doubt I might have had is washed away.

"Walk with me," she says, and I follow her, making our way through the team members to find a quieter spot to talk. "Philip told me about Jessica. I'm so sorry, Selene," she says.

"Don't be," I reply. "This was her fault, and hers alone."

"I know, but I should have seen it. She obviously has some sort of obsession with Philip. I'm not sure why he hasn't fired her yet."

"I have a feeling I do." Philip knows me well, and he knows this revenge is mine to take, not his. "And I might need your help to do it for him."

"I'm listening," she replies, intrigued.

The late afternoon sun casts a warm glow over the bustling track as I stroll alone, observing the team members packing up their gear. Philip's motorhome is one of the first in line, and I'm about to enter when I spot him outside, immersed in an ice-cold bath, with Michael standing in front of him.

"Hi, there," I greet them both.

"Well, hello, hello," Michael says, running a hand through his tousled brown hair, just as Philip opens his eyes.

"Leave us alone," Philip says.

"You need to do five more minutes," Michael insists, glancing at the stopwatch in his hand.

"Crazy asshole," Philip grumbles, but Michael simply tosses him the stopwatch and walks away.

"I can come back later," I offer.

"Don't you dare go now. We need to talk, and I am not a patient man, Selene." The way my name rolls off his tongue always catches me off guard.

"I think you are," I reply, kneeling to meet his eyes while he's submerged in the icy bath. "Why didn't you fire Jessica?"

"Because you can fight your own battles," Philip answers, and it's exactly what I needed to hear. "You're more than capable, and you've shown that time and time again. I'll fight anyone for you, but I'll also gladly stand next to you when you choose to fight your own battles," he says, knocking the air from my lungs. "I'm not a good man. If I were, I'd probably let you go, let you find happiness with someone better. But I'm not. I'm jaded and flawed, and I'd burn down every single man in the world if it meant you'd end up with me. I don't care. You're all I want now and all I'll ever want in the future. You're the only person I'll ever love. I'll respect your decision to walk away, but know that I'll never stop loving you, Selene."

"You love me?" I ask as if he hadn't already said those words with all his actions.

"I do," he confesses. "I promise I'll work on being more vocal about my feelings," he adds, taking my hand. His touch feels like pure ice, causing me to jump slightly in surprise.

"I promise to listen to your feelings through your actions," I respond. "I love you too," I confess, saying it out loud for the first time.

"This isn't how I pictured our first 'I love you,'" he jokes.

"You can still pull off a grand gesture if you want."

"Should I buy you a brand-new car or paint your name on a track by drifting the car?"

"The second option would be a very original grand gesture." I laugh. "But I only need you, nothing else," I say, offering him a smile for the first time in months.

"I missed you," he says, his lips so close to mine.

"I missed you too."

"Good, because I don't want to spend any more time away from you, starting now," he says. With a swift move of his hands, my head lands inside the basin, followed by the rest of my body

"Philip!" I scream at him with water in my mouth, while he wraps his arms around my waist not letting me escape from the cold water. "You did not just throw me in an ice bath," I yell.

"I told you; I don't want to be away from you."

"Look at me! I am all drenched," I say, starting to feel the cold penetrating my skin.

"I bet your clothes aren't the only thing that's drenched," he says, moving his hand slowly over my thigh and right under my skirt, stroking his finger over the most sensitive part of my body.

"Philip," I moan, parting my lips.

"Let's get out of here," he whispers in my ear, holding me in his arms as he stands up.

CHAPTER FORTY-FOUR

Philip

João and I find ourselves at the last race of the season, head-to-head in points, ready to put everything on the line for this ultimate showdown. Munguia is nipping at our heels in the standings, and any one of us can snatch the championship today. It's been a mentally exhausting season, but it's undoubtedly been the most memorable of my career.

"What's on your mind?" Selene asks, sitting on top of me as I lay in bed.

"I was just thinking about how stunning you look in the morning, especially after certain activities. You're glowing," I quip with a sassy grin.

"You're impossible, Philip."

"Probably, but you love me regardless," I reply, giving her a playful spank. She bites her lip and lets out a muffled moan.

"I guess it's too late to take that back now, huh?" Selene laughs softly, planting a trail of tender kisses from my abs up to my chest.

"One month and eight days too late, *amor*."

"Are you counting the days too?" she asks, her fingers tracing patterns across my skin.

"I can't forget our anniversary now, can I?"

"I guess you can't," she murmurs, giving my neck a soft, affectionate nuzzle.

"But as much as I'd love to stay here with you all morning," I start and sigh, "I have my last briefing with Cavaglio Nero."

"I can't believe they never extended your contract," she says.

"I have to tell you something." Her green eyes go wide "Don't be mad, but somethings happened over the weekend..."

Selene

I can't stop thinking about this morning's conversation with Philip. The man is a genius, a fucking strategic genius, and honestly, I can't stay mad at him for not telling me sooner. How could I?

But at this moment, I have other matters to focus on. I'm on a mission to get my revenge and clear my name. I didn't bust my ass the last few years to merely be recognized as Philip Burton's girlfriend. No way.

HAMMER TIME

I am Selene Soldado, Head of Marketing Strategy at Cavaglio Nero Racing.

Human Resources has received not one but two complaints, one from me and another from Philip, who clearly wants nothing to do with Jessica. She needs to be held accountable, but there's a hitch – she's Mancini's niece.

We needed her to expose her true colors. If she wants to play stalker, then she can show it to the world. I left her a note this morning, and now it's time to wait in the lounge for her reaction. Philip is sitting across the room with Michael, engrossed in their preparatory exercises before the day kicks off while I work on my laptop.

Fortunately, the wait isn't long.

Jessica strolls into the room, breezing right past me without a single glance.

"I always knew you loved me!" Jessica's eyes shimmer with hope, and for a brief moment, I almost feel bad.

"What are you talking about?" Philip replies, faking surprise.

"The note? 'Meet me at the workspace on the third floor. We need to talk,'" Jessica reads out loud.

"Oh, that," Philip says casually.

"I already know what you're going to say! I love you too. I've loved you since the first time I saw you. You're my soulmate," Jessica starts rambling. "It's written in the stars; our signs are a perfect match. You and I are meant for great things."

"You thought I was going to declare my love to you?" Philip arches an eyebrow at her. *This is even better than any scheme I could have devised.*

"Yes?" Jessica's face turns the brightest shade of red.

"Sit down," I order, rising from my seat.

She takes a moment to glance at me, then at Philip, then at Michael, and back to Philip. "Don't look at them, look at me," I demand, closing the distance between us.

"What's going on?" Fear flickers in her eyes, and I relish it.

"Thanks to you, I'm the most talked-about woman in Formula One." I maintain my composure. "Everyone has my name on their lips."

"I—I—" Her mouth opens and closes, like a fish gasping for air.

"Shhh," Philip hushes her on my behalf.

"I could have returned the favor and humiliated you ten times worse, but that would mean lowering myself to your level. Consider yourself lucky that I'm better than that." I pause to take a deep breath. "I'm not sure if you've got a high school crush on my boyfriend or if you're just a stalker. But whatever it is, get over it, because it's going to take more than that to break us."

"Please call security," Philip says, more of a general remark. "Your obsession with me is unhealthy."

"You are never going to see Philip again, Jessica."

"Philip is the love of my life!" Jessica finally blurts out, unable to stay silent any longer. "We're meant for each other," she says right as Mancini and Sarah make it into the room.

"No, you're not." I laugh.

"You think this is funny?" Jessica says, and then proceeds to scream, her face now impossibly red with anger.

"It is," Michael adds.

"You think you can take Philip away from me? He'll love me, he has to! You can't break us—"

"I'm not breaking you up because he was never yours to begin with."

"This is unacceptable," Sarah says and steps in. "We need to fire her. Selene, I don't know if you have time considering how busy you are with your team, but I'd like for you to take over Jessica's position for now."

"No, no, no, no!" Jessica pleads, looking at Mancini, whose face gives nothing away. "I'm your niece. He is the love of my life! You can't do this!"

"Jessica, gather your things. I'll pay for your therapy," Mancini says. "You are a disgrace to this family," he roars.

"No, please no. I love him!" she weeps, but it's too late. Security is already removing her from the premises.

"That was intense," Michael points out.

"My family has some… issues," Mancini says.

"Selene is the one who deserves an apology. So, apologize."

I raise an eyebrow, intrigued by the sudden turn of events. It's amusing how, theoretically, Mancini is Philip's boss, but it's always Philip who's in command.

"Excuse me?" Mancini's expression reflects his utter disbelief.

"Jessica is the one who leaked our pictures and concocted the false story about how Selene obtained her position. So, if I were you, I'd apologize to her."

"No need," I say to try and diffuse the situation, even though deep down, I'd love to hear Mancini say it.

"I—I—I—" he stammers. "I apologize. I wasn't aware that she had anything to do with that. Her obsession with Philip went too far, and I'll ensure she gets the help she needs. She won't be a problem again."

"Thank you," I say.

"If you'll excuse me, I must go now," Mancini says, excusing himself.

CHAPTER FORTY-FIVE

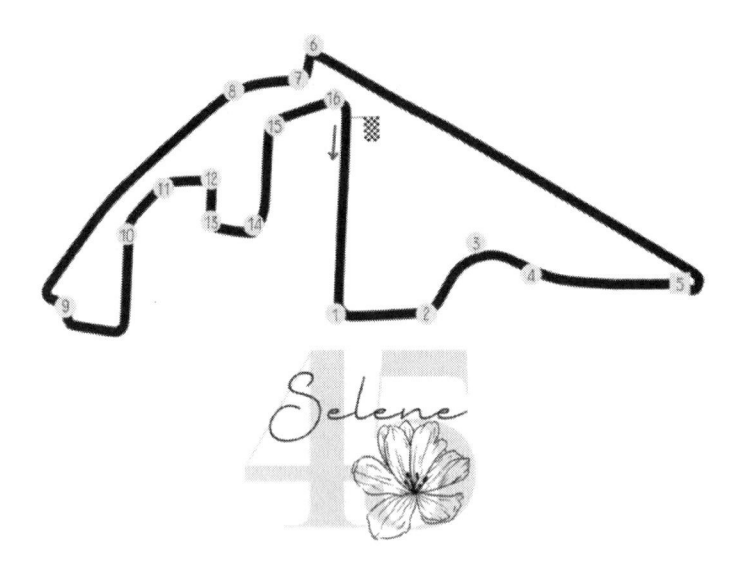

The lights go out, indicating the start of the race, and every driver races as if their lives depend on it, which is certainly how it feels at the moment. After all, three of them are competing for the title and only one can win it.

Philip secures the first position, and João tails him closely. He has a better start to the race and rockets ahead of Philip, leading in the first corner. Munguia takes a wide turn and drops back, but his recovery is swift, and he gains some time before the first lap wraps up.

A few laps tick by. Philip chases João, his driving bordering on reckless as he attempts to squeeze his car into every gap of the track. He's aching for that championship win.

Lap by lap, they inch closer, until finally, on the hairpin at turn nine, João makes a critical error, loses control, and brushes against Philip.

"Gilipollas de Mierda!" a furious Philip shouts over the radio. He miraculously avoids a full-blown collision, skidding off the track to avoid the collision, forcing him to gain an advantage over the Brazilian driver.

"Philip, you have to give your position back," his engineer warns.

"Bullshit! He's the one who shoved me out!" Philip roars.

"Five-second penalty if you don't," the engineer responds.

"Argh!" Philip yells in frustration, but we can see him relenting and giving back the position.

I can't believe all of this unfolded in just seven laps. The clock keeps ticking, Munguia galloping back into the race, narrowing the gap between the three of them. Philip stays glued to João's car, forcing him to take the dirty side of the track, trying to defend from his attacks, but Philip still can't quite reclaim the lead.

"Box box, Plan B," he says after nearly twenty laps.

"Copy," the engineer replies.

His car pulls in, and the mechanics rush to make the perfect pit stop. João mimics Philip's strategy, so he can maintain the first position.

Time rushes by, but not quickly enough. The Brazilian remains in first place, the gap between him and Philip slowly expanding.

"I think he's conserving his tires while João's going all out," Michael says, fidgeting with his beard.

"He has to win," I mutter, both hands pressed to my lips, eyes glued to the screen and fearing the consequences of any slipup. And fear was well-founded because suddenly, as everyone battles, a rookie from an underdog team crashes, prompting stewards to call for a yellow flag.

Everyone needs to regroup, slow down, and wait for the wreckage to be cleared. Most drivers choose to switch to fresh tires during this safety car period. Philip and João are no different.

The laps vanish, and before we know it, we're only ten laps away from the finish. The safety car exits, and the three of them look inseparable, their cars almost melding into one, racing in close formation.

The yellow flag turns green, and they're free to accelerate to top speed. Philip tails João, fighting for yet another championship. The crowd's roar fills the air while Philip tries to overtake João at the sixth corner, but he takes it too wide.

Both drivers are becoming aggressive, one defending himself from the attacks of the other.

In an attempt to defend himself from one of Philips attacks, João is forced onto the dirty side again, losing some speed, Philip notices it and takes his chance finally overtaking the younger driver.

"VAAAAMOS! SIII!" I scream my lungs out, jumping with Michael standing next to me.

Munguia is trailing them, and at turn five, he edges in from the inside, also passing João. Only three laps left. Munguia tries to challenge Philip, but Philip drives with such precision that Oliver can't keep up, while João clings to third place, trying to at least snatch back second.

Only one lap remains. Everyone in the garage falls silent, the tension unbearable until magic happens.

Philip crosses the finish line first.

He's a world champion!

I can hear the deafening roar of the crowd from my spot. Everyone in the garage erupts into madness. I embrace Michael, and he lifts me into the air while fireworks burst in the sky above the track.

"Philip, you are World Champion! World Champion!" Mancini says through the radio, and I can hear Philip' screams of joy.

"Pass me that," I say to Mancini, who's still shouting into the radio. I take the headphones from him and gesture for him to press the radio button. "Oh my god," I scream with excitement, my voice reaching a high pitch. "Eres el campeón del mundo! You are the World Champion, Philip!" On the other end, Philip's words are barely audible.

Michael and I dash to the fence to greet him. Fireworks still paint the sky. It takes Philip no time to reach us.

Finally, the car comes to a stop, everyone waiting for him to jump out of the car and run towards his mechanics. But instead, he performs a victory spin, tracing an S on the track with his tires, instead of the customary celebratory donuts. Tears stream down my cheeks when I realize what he has done.

All eyes are on him when he finally makes it out of the cockpit, his fists in the air as he jumps onto the ground and kneels next to the car. His helmet is still on, but I'm pretty sure he is crying underneath it. Mancini and some engineers run towards him, and lift him in the air, congratulating him, and then Michael tugs on my arm so we can do the same.

I rush towards Philip, who starts sprinting my way as soon as he notices me, and then scoops me up, twirling me in the air while I kiss his helmet. I'm so happy right now, I'm not even bothered by the swarm of press cameras snapping pictures.

"You did it, *amor*!" I tell him.

"Sei un grandee, Philip!" Mancini offers his praise as soon as he sets me down.

After everyone has offered their congratulations, Sasha approaches, ready to interview him, as we had planned earlier today.

"Philip, how do you feel after becoming the world champion at thirty-seven years old on your first year after retirement?" Sasha asks.

"Invincible," he responds, raking his fingers through his sweat-soaked hair. "This feels incredible. It was the plan all along. Becoming a world champion again after so many years of hard work."

"Do you think your age has made it harder to win this year?" Sasha probes.

"Honestly, I feel like I'm at the peak of my career. I've got a couple more good years in me." He winks in my direction, hinting at a secret only we share, for now.

"Is that a hint for those who haven't renewed your contract yet?" Sasha smirks, clearly aware of the answer.

"It's every racer's dream to compete for Cavaglio Nero Racing," Philip replies, "but it's a dream I've lived a few times. Winning with them has become second nature, and since I'm good enough to win in any car, I'll be racing for Volpella next season." The spectators go quiet, hanging onto his words. "I'll stick around to prove that it's the driver, not the car." He winks at the camera, his face radiant and joyful, a rare sight.

"How do you feel about all this?" Sasha asks, handing me the microphone.

"It's a shame to see him leave the team, but we're confident he'll achieve remarkable feats in his new endeavors," I reply.

"Care to introduce yourself?" Sasha winks at me.

"I'm the Head of Marketing Strategy at Cavaglio Nero," I answer confidently. "And Philip's girlfriend."

I want to say more, to make it known that I had earned my position, that it hadn't been handed to me. But this is Philip's moment, and I have no intention of stealing his spotlight. Plus, I've grown beyond caring about what faceless critics might say about me or my relationship.

I'm happy, in love, excelling at my job, and enjoying a perfectly public relationship. I don't need anyone else's validation.

THE END

FORMULA ONE VOCABULARY

YELLOW FLAG: warning to drivers that there is danger on the track ahead. Drivers must slow down and be prepared to stop if necessary. Drivers must not overtake other cars until they have passed the area indicated by the yellow flag.

RED FLAG: When a red flag is displayed, all cars must immediately return to the pit lane and stop, and the race will not be restarted until the red flag is withdrawn.

DIRTY AIR: The lead car's airflow is disturbed by its own aerodynamic devices, and this creates a wake of turbulent air behind the car that can affect the performance of the car following it.

DNF: It refers to a driver who did not complete the race for any reason, such as technical problems, accidents, or disqualification.

AKNOWLEDGEMENTS

Like Selene, I took a leap of faith, followed my dreams, and fast forward a few months, here I am, living my best life. So, I encourage you to do the same thing – don't be afraid to take a chance, even if it means failing. This book is proof that sometimes the best stories emerge from the messiest drafts. Chase your dreams, no matter how scary they are.

To all of you who've read my words and shared in the ups and downs, I can't thank you enough. You've been the most supportive bunch, and I couldn't have done it without you. I mean it. Your trust in the process and your enthusiasm means the world to me.

Mama, Papa, three books in, and you still don't know about my side hobby, but you have been my constant lighthouse whenever I needed you. You are the ones who have always had my back regardless how much I messed up, thanks for always believing in me even when I could not.

A big shoutout to Dr. Edi, who has not only survived one of my books but stuck around for a second one! She's the best reader any writer could ask for – eternally supportive, filled with brilliant ideas, a legend. Her reactions to my chapters are my secret motivation to keep writing.

Honorable mentions to my TikTok book besties, who have heard me talk about this story for months and have read the book just as many times as I have, thanks for always providing with the best advice. With them I also include my precious beta readers, Melisa, Marina, Selina, thanks for helping me shape this book from the very beginning.

Special thanks to Camille Dwight and Bridget L. Rose, whose counsel have made indie publishing possible for me, I am forever grateful to both of you for guiding me through this journey.

Printed by Amazon Italia Logistica S.r.l.
Torrazza Piemonte (TO), Italy